MURDER
in the Choir

A JAZZ PHILLIPS MYSTERY
Joel B. Reed

WHITE TURTLE BOOKS · CANBY, MN

Published by:

White Turtle Books
Canby, MN
www.whiteturtlebooks.com

Printed in the United States of America
First Edition

ISBN 1-933482-31-1

This is a work of fiction. The events reported and the characters who populate these incidents are figments of my imagination. Any resemblance between any of my characters and any actual persons, living or dead, is purely coincidental. As far as I know, there is no Oak Grove community near Nashville, Arkansas, although small settlements like it are scattered throughout the state.

Cover and interior design © TLC Graphics, *www.TLCGraphics.com*
Cover by Jim Zach, interior by Erin Stark

This one is for Noell, my partner and companion.

SMILEY JONES

The hit didn't fit. Not the normal way. There's usually a clear connection. It might be love. You know what I mean. It's normally the husband or the wife or maybe a jealous lover, someone now or from the past. Or it might be someone with a superheated crush—romance that's turned into obsession. Stalkers-turned-killer are pretty common these days. Then, at times, it's a crime of old-fashioned passion. She comes home from a visit to her sister or he comes home from a hunting trip and finds a nasty surprise.

That last one actually happened. I worked the case and the defense was very simple. It never made it to a jury. "No, your honor, it just happened. I would never have shot them if I didn't already have the gun in my hands. I guess I was so excited I forgot to unload my rifle. Yes, sir, the rack made it into Boone and Crockett. It was a record for the state." Of course, it didn't hurt that the case was tried in Dorado County, Arkansas, or that his honor's trophy bride had given him horns six months before with a county attorney. Or that this was well-known by the defense lawyer. The tricky part was the change of venue, and that cost a bundle. On the other hand, ten thousand dollars is cheap for a successful defense in a murder trial. Even on top of lawyer's fees.

So lust is one of the first things investigators look for. The other is money. Any of the seven deadly sins will do, but greed is a major player. You will never see it listed as the cause of death, but greed has probably killed more people than anything else. When it comes to murder, even a rookie knows to look for the insurance policy or the inheritance. The beneficiary goes right to the top of the list. It's the very first question: *Quo bono?* Who benefits from the death? Greed covers a multitude of other sins and it's something juries find easy to understand. So greed has a special place in the hearts of state's attorneys.

Of course, anyone who watches cop shows knows this. They also know that every once in a while the United States produces thrill-killers. Not all of them turn into serial murderers, but more do than you might expect. These crimes follow their own twisted logic, but within that logic, they do make sense. What we look for is the connection. There's a pattern, and following the pattern backward points to the killer. Doing that is just a matter of good police work—using your mind and asking questions. Perseverance pays off and a little luck doesn't hurt, either. Criminals are human and they make mistakes. Good police work is being alert enough to see it when they do and getting close enough to grab them.

Like I said, anyone who watches television knows this stuff. My knowledge comes from being a criminal investigator. Twenty years with the Arkansas Criminal Investigation Division—CID for short—taught me a lot, and I've spent the last several years as an independent consultant. Some of this was working as a consultant to the FBI in a couple of off-the-wall cases but never as an agent. Like many state and local officers, I have a love-hate relationship with the Bureau. I admire their dedication and, to give the devils their due, they normally do very thorough work. They also can be prime contenders for asshole of the year, riding roughshod over jurisdiction and treating local officers like peons. Nor are Fat Boys accountable the way most police departments are. So when they recruited me after attending their academy, I declined politely, though I appreciated the training. What I really wanted to do, after being patronized for six weeks, was to flip them the bird, but I am glad I didn't. They may be jerks, but they pay good, and I don't have to put up with their workaday bullshit. As a consultant, I can charge them extra for any *caca* rendered.

Maybe I ought to introduce myself. My name is Phillips: J.S. Phillips. I go by J.S. most of the time, and my friends call me Jazz. I picked that up from a high school coach with a south Arkansas rasp that could sharpen a hoe. It was imitating his way of saying "J.S." that became "Jazz" in the mouths of my teammates and the name stuck. I didn't mind at all. I could imagine what their fertile imaginations might do with my real name, so I hung with Jazz. The girls seemed to like it, and nobody learned my real name until it was published in the bulletin at graduation. That might have been bad enough, but there were lots of other class mates saddled with strange names I never knew before. We reached an unspoken agreement not to make it an issue. We all had too much to lose. Or so it seemed.

Don't get me wrong. My real name is not all that bad. It is unusual. Both my parents were band musicians and both my grandfathers were named John. They saw themselves as Bohemian by Arkansas standards, which means mildly eccentric, and they didn't want to call me Jack or Johnny. So what they came up with, given my dad's last name, was John Sousa Phillips. Fortunately for me, John Sousa is clumsy to say, and they understood how I might have to defend Sousa with my fists. Fertile young minds could turn it into Suzy or Sissy. So they went along when Grandpa Jack shortened it to J.S. and that's what the family calls me to this day. As an adult, I can admire my parents' creativity. As a child, I was terrified someone might find out who I really was, and I loved the sobriquet. J.S. sounded tough, like Robert Mitchum with a dead butt hanging out the corner of his mouth.

That's a nice word, isn't it, *sobriquet*? It sounds like something you might find in a boutique or an ice cream shop. There's nothing like French to take something that's as common as dirt, like *nickname,* and make it sound exotic. On the other hand, there's nothing like Latin to make something sound down and dirty. Translate "common as dirt" into Latin and you get one simple word: *vulgar.* I guess a rose by any other name is still a weed, but to Arkansas ears, *piscem natare doces* sounds like pissing on the ground twice.

This has nothing to do with murder. It has everything to do with how we Americans think about murder and other unpleasant things of life. We try to clean up killing in the way we talk about it. Consequently, police do not have departments of man-kill, but departments of homicide. Maybe we should take a cue from the good folks in the funeral business and call it the Department of Involuntary Passing. With the kinds of imaginations policemen have, that could lead to jokes about incontinence.

As Americans, we also split hairs in the way we think. With man-kill we call some things manslaughter and other things murder. Of course, when the state does the cold-blooded and premeditated man-killing, we call it execution which is another euphemism. I have to hand it to Oklahomans. When they kill a convict in a capital case, they're honest enough to list the cause of death as homicide.

With the case at hand, nothing made sense. There was no motive anyone could see behind the killing and that's why they called me. Not that they were all that interested in clearing the case of a black musician getting shot. The problem was that Smiley Jones was well-known in the jazz world and a national celebrity. He was also a deacon at his local country church and seemed clean as a whistle. Apparently, the man didn't drink, the man didn't gamble, and the man didn't use drugs or chase skirts. He was a quiet, gentle grandfather you would never notice until he picked up a horn or sat down at a piano or smiled. When he did, it was like the whole world went away. There were even those who claimed Smiley played a better horn than the great Sachmo, Louis Armstrong. I think that is stretching it, but with a guitar or piano, our man Smiley was one of the best.

Even the death of a celebrity can get swept under the rug after a brief scandal or under the right circumstances. This was not the case with Smiley Jones and I wasn't under any illusions the locals called me in because they wanted to solve the case. They were taking a lot of heat from the press and the state, and they called me in to show they were doing all they could to get it cleared. With me on the scene, it was a win-win situation for them. I would be their golden boy. They would get the credit if I solved the case, and if I didn't, I would take the blame.

Knowing this, I almost refused to take it. Outside consultants cannot afford to come up empty too many times. When they do, they stop being called. Nor did I have any lack of good excuses. I was in the

4

middle of another case at the moment, something that was shaping up to be a major serial killing. The press were not aware of it at this point, so there wasn't the intense pressure to get it resolved. Things were quiet and the killer had been inactive for several months, leading us to believe he was either dead or in jail. So we were doing the long, tedious job of looking at arrests leading to convictions after the last death we knew for sure was his. As it turned out much later, our work was useless. We were dealing with a she, not a he, a real black widow who preyed on adolescent boys. Her inactivity was due to a long stay in a mental hospital in a different part of the country.

The problem with Smiley Jones was the way he was killed. I made the mistake of asking for details because I knew the man. I had never met him, but I knew his music and I liked it, and the name caught my attention. When I heard what they had, I found myself intrigued. There was just enough evidence to promise a solution, but too little to suggest any obvious direction. It was a teaser and I was hooked.

Even then, I might have let it go. "Well, I'd really like to help you, Sheriff," I told the man on the other end of the line. "I just don't see how I can shake loose right now. You know—other commitments."

There was silence from the other end of the line and I thought he had hung up. While this was not very professional, I knew it wasn't personal. The man was under a lot of political pressure. I was just about to drop the phone in the cradle when I heard a familiar voice call my name. "Hey, Jazz, you ornery Coonass! How they hangin'?"

Steve DiRado and I go back a long way. "Hey, Dee, you worthless hound!" I shot back. "Haven't they fired you yet?"

"No such luck, good buddy," he laughed. "We got ourselves a real pisser here. I could use some help."

That got my attention. Steve DiRado is one of the smartest people I know and one of the most informed. He could have been a brilliant concert pianist or quantum physicist or just about anything else he wanted to be. The problem was that while all these things interested him, his consuming passion was crime. Or it might be more accurate to say his passion was justice. Long before forensic science became such a big part of police work, Dee was pushing the envelope putting the bad guys away. His ratio of cleared cases was phenomenal, and very few of his cases went south because of mistakes he made. Normally, the only help he needed was doing leg work.

"That good, huh?" I asked him. Dee chuckled but said nothing. He knows my hot buttons, when to press and when to give me time to think. I took my time. "What else have you got?" I asked.

"I take it you're in?" he shot back. He knew I was, but he needed to hear me to say it.

"What the hell," I told him. "You guys need someone to hold your hands. Usual rates, mileage, and per diem? My rates, not yours."

"You're on," he laughed. The natural state of Arkansas is notoriously cheap when it comes to paying expenses. The other side is that politicians don't value what they don't pay very much to get. I charge enough to make sure they pay attention. It's a matter of pride.

"All right. How soon do you need me?"

"How about the day before yesterday?" He laughed, but he was dead serious.

While Dee is one of the steadiest people I know, I could hear strain in his voice. I wondered what in the hell I was letting myself in for this time. "So the case is that hot already?"

"You have no idea, Jazz," he murmured. "I seem to be spending most of my time on the phone to Little Rock."

That wasn't good and I almost backed out. If it had been anyone but Dee, I would have. Life is too short for some things. "There are a couple of things I need to finish here, but I can drive down later this afternoon," I told him. "I can be there by three o'clock or so. Unless you want to send a chopper. Pea Vine would love that."

Dee laughed. Paul Vinson is the CID comptroller, sour and humorless, and not even the head of the division calls him Pea Vine to his face. "No, there are limits. I don't want to stroke him out!"

I called my wife to let her know I would be out of town for a few days. When Nellie heard where I was headed, she told me to be careful. There aren't many straight roads in western Arkansas, but US 71 between Ft. Smith and Mena is the worst there is for curves and poor drivers. It is one of the most dangerous federal highways in the entire nation.

On the other hand, it's also one of the most beautiful roads in Arkansas, and I didn't mind the drive at all. It was late enough in the fall for the trees to be turning, and the sweet gums were especially bright this year. The air was crisp and clear, the way it is after thunderstorms, and I drove south with the car heater on and the windows down. The only thing better would have been riding my Guzzi, but it was too cool for that and no room for my stuff. I don't carry much forensic equipment, but I find a laptop and a Kevlar vest useful. Nor do I like to go into a murder investigation unarmed. Part of my agreement as a consultant with the State of Arkansas is being carried on the books as a sworn peace officer who's allowed to carry a gun. Thank God I've never had to fire it at anything but paper targets.

The road straightened out a bit just before I got to Mena. I filled my travel mug with fresh coffee at a drive-in and headed south for DeQueen. I often wonder where some of these places get their names, but not enough to look it up. Some of them make sense, like Saratoga or Y City or Mineral Springs, but what about places like Needmore or Umpire? Nor can I seem to remember where places get their names when someone tells me. That's strange because I can tell you the most minute details of every major case I had. Nellie likes to remind me of this when I forget something she told me two days before.

There wasn't much color south of DeQueen, so I thought about what I knew about Smiley Jones. The Little Rock paper had run a human interest article on him several months back. I don't read the "Life and Leisure" section much and was doing the Sunday crossword when Nellie spotted it and passed it over. She knew I liked his music. I read it through twice, and I had it for good. Six months later, the details were right there, as fresh as the day I read them. Unlike the source of place names, my Memory Central must have decided the information was important.

The article was good and told me a lot I didn't know. One was that Smiley was born at home in a small black community not far from Nashville, the one in Arkansas. He retired there after a long career on the road. His legal name was Wilbur Orton Jones, Junior, which I didn't know, and he was much older than I thought. Like me, he got his sobriquet early in life and there was a reason. When he smiled, especially later in life, it was like seeing the pearly gates. He was all perfect white teeth, and the writer said Jones smiled with his eyes, not just his mouth. He wrote that when Smiley moved through a crowd, it felt like a warm, peaceful river reaching out to gather everyone in.

Like many other black musicians, Smiley began his career playing piano for local churches, but it didn't take him long to find out honky-tonks and bawdy houses paid better. So for a couple of years he did both, playing at road houses until the wee hours, then running home to change for church. That came to an end when he ran into a couple of elders in one of the places he played. The main attraction there was not the bar or the band, but the rooms on the second floor, and Smiley had spotted the elders coming down the stairs. Smiley told the reporter that, until they saw him, they looked like cats that had just swallowed a cage full of canaries.

The elders grabbed Smiley and took him outside. One of them showed him a pistol. The other offered him a one way ticket to New Orleans, and Smiley was happy to take it. He said that was the best thing that ever happened, because he got lucky right away. He switched to guitar, teaching himself to play in less than a month, and began working with a jazz band. Later, he put together his own band and did some singing as he played. He was good, even by New Orleans' high standards, so it was not long until he became well enough known to go on tour. The rest is an American success story. By the time he retired, Smiley had worked with every major jazz player in the country and with every major celebrity on the USO circuit in Korea and Vietnam. He was also a regular performer on national television.

While the writer mentioned there were some rough patches along the way, he didn't give details. I scribbled myself a note to check these out.

What I knew so far told me there were plenty of other places to look for the killer, but I wondered what might have happened during those rough times that might set murder in motion so many years later. While that had happened a long time back back and was low priority at the moment, it was something to bear in mind.

I stuck the note in my shirt pocket and began thinking through a list of things I needed to check. The information I got over the phone left me with a distinct impression the killer was not someone local, and I've learned to listen to first impressions. I didn't know anything for sure, of course. I didn't have enough facts even to write that impression in ink or to suggest a line of inquiry. Yet, I considered it a definite possibility.

I wrote myself another note and stuck that in my pocket, too. I would sort them later, but right now I needed to keep my mind open and let it roam. With written notes, I don't have to worry about forgetting things, and they help me clear the mental slate. One of the biggest mistakes an investigator can make is going too hard in the obvious direction and neglecting subtle, less promising leads. Going with the obvious works most of the time, and it clears a lot of cases. Yet, I've learned the hard way it can come back to bite you in the ass.

So I turned my mind to what I didn't know and made more notes. One thing I didn't know much about was Smiley's family life or what he had done since he retired. The article had been vague in this area and either of those might lead to motive and a killer. Everything I ever read about the man told me Smiley was one of the most popular men in show business. He was well-known as a gentle soul who never had an unkind word to say about anyone, and he was never demanding.

I assumed the same was true in his personal life, but one never knows. When things seem too good to be true, they often are, and a reputation like that normally makes me suspicious. Everyone has a dark side and when I hear too much praise, I normally wonder what the real story is. With Smiley, I had a hard time doing that. I didn't want to think ill of the man because I loved his music. That doesn't make sense because I know better. Some of the worst felons produce some of the finest prison art, and I knew I had to be very careful to be objective when looking at Smiley.

That also meant I might have a hard time getting accurate information. People invest a lot of hope in living saints, and coming across as a devil's advocate would not sit well. I was sure the information I needed to complete the investigation lay in some dark chapter of Smiley's history, but I would have to strike a careful balance to get it. Push too hard one way or another, and the sources dry up.

I pulled into Nashville about two o'clock with a shirt pocket stuffed with notes. Unlike it's counterpart in Tennessee, Nashville, Arkansas, is a sleepy little town of four thousand souls in the Ouchita Mountains in the southwestern part of the state. I'm not sure where Nashville gets its name, whether it's from the city in Tennessee or maybe in honor of the same person. Or someone else with the same surname. There's a Nash not far away, near Texarkana. Whatever the source, it's an old place, settled early in the 1800s and it has its charm. These days, Nashville describes itself as a "community of choice," which may sound odd for a town in the middle of the Bible Belt. Yet, I think what is being expressed is not a political stance, but the hope that people might choose to live there. I think those who like small, southern towns might find it pleasant. Certainly, the pace of life is much slower.

I pulled over and called the number Dee had given me when I talked to him earlier. I was looking forward to seeing him again. Even though we didn't see each other often, we always picked up wherever we left off last time, despite whatever might be going on around us.

Or maybe we grew close because of the stuff going on around us, the nature of our jobs. Even as partners in the Highway Patrol, we saw things every day that no one should have to witness. The only respite we had was each other and the trust that grew between us over the years, and I was surprised how much I missed that close connection when I moved to CID. While we didn't deal with as much awful stuff in CID, the things we did deal with were far worse. Like most police officers, I find it easier to deal with the immediate tragedy of a child killed in a car crash than with the ongoing tragedy of multi-generational incest.

So I was glad when Dee landed in the CID, too. I was senior enough by then to make sure I was assigned as his trainer and we became partners again. Not that Dee needed much in the way of training from me, other than being shown where we kept the pencils and hid the key to the john. I'm told the two of us became living legends in the CID, but I don't put much stock in that. We did close a lot of hard cases, and we put a lot of sick people away for a long time.

All this came to an end when I was promoted to head of the Division. I made Dee my chief supervisor and trainer, and he was my intended replacement when I retired. Yet, my retirement happened sooner than we expected. The politics involved got to be more than I could stomach and I took an early out. A political hack was promoted ahead of Dee, and Dee asked to go back to investigator, taking a cut in grade. This meant a cut in pay, too, but it was the kind of work he loved. When he stepped aside, the division went downhill despite the good work we had done to build it up. I hated to see that, but I didn't have cause to complain. After a while, it sent a lot of business my way.

The number Dee had given me was his cell phone and he picked up on the second ring. He gave me directions to the sheriff's office, and when I got there I found him waiting at the curb. Nor did he look happy. No one else might have seen it, but I did. He was torqued.

"Good to see you, Jazz!" He held out a hand that swallowed mine when I offered it. "Damn, I'm glad you're here." He looked me up and down carefully, noting my losing battle with gravity. Then he grinned. "I guess I shouldn't mention how good the pie is in the restaurant here. Nellie would nail my ass."

I laughed. "She tells me I block out too much sunlight."

He pointed to my shirt pocket bulging with notes. "I see you've been hard at work already. Let's grab a cup of coffee and talk about it." He nodded to a coffee shop across the street. "We can have some privacy there."

The shuck and jive didn't fool me for a minute. Meeting me at the curb was a bad sign. It told me something else was going on, most likely a turf fight over who got to run the show. That didn't make much sense since it was normally the county sheriff, desperate for a solution, who called in the state CID. Nor was Dee ever much concerned over turf or who had jurisdiction. His primary concern was preserving the chain of evidence and nailing the assholes who did it, and it was not uncommon for him to let the locals take most of the credit for a bust. His reputation made him welcome where a lot of investigators from Little Rock were not.

Sure enough, Dee confirmed that when we sat down and ordered. "I had to talk to you before the Fibbies did. They've taken over the sheriff's office."

I was surprised to hear the Bureau was involved in a local homicide. Dee nodded. "Yeah. I didn't know about it when I called you. They're trying to make this into a federal case. You know, the usual civil rights bullshit."

"Maybe you'd better tell me what's going on, Dee." I didn't bother to hide how I felt about this.

"The governor pushed the panic button. That's what's going on. He leaned on the Attorney General and Barton called in the feds. It was too late to head it off by the time it got to me." He shrugged. "Not that they consult me much these days."

Barton Smith was one of the hacks our current governor brought with him to Little Rock. He was as floppy as a flag when hot issues were on the wind, and his record as attorney general was less than brilliant. I detested the man.

"What are they claiming? Conspiracy to violate Smiley's rights?" I asked. This thing was beginning to sound more and more like a major disaster. I wondered if I should turn around and head back to Ft. Smith.

"Now, don't go backing out on me, Jazz. They saddled me with this thing and I need you to keep it from going south." I had to smile. Dee knows me almost as well as Nellie and can read me like a book.

"They can't have it both ways, Dee," I told him. "Their calling in the Bureau should take you off the hook."

"You would think so," he answered. "The thing is, I'm less than a year from full pension and the bastards are after me."

"You're the best man they have!" I protested. "They'd be crazy to let you go. Who'd get things done?"

"No one's arguing that Barton's sane," he answered dryly. "The word I have is that one of his nephews needs a job."

"You're civil service," I answered, but I knew that didn't matter. The attorney general was well-connected and most judges in the state were afraid of him. Nor did Dee choose to play the political game. There was no one more competent on a crime scene or on the witness stand, but he was out of his depth when it came to day-to-day politics. He simply couldn't see how politics mattered, and if things went bad on this thing, the hacks would hang him out to dry. It must have been pretty blatant because Dee doesn't normally pick up on this sort of thing.

"I need your help, Jazz," he said. "Once I get by this one I'll grab my pension and run, but I'm stuck with this one. They're pulling the rug out from under me every step of the way."

"You could always check into treatment," I said, and we both laughed. That's a common dodge of drug dealers who find they're on the brink of getting busted. They check into treatment in a facility in another state, and the law can't touch them until they're out. That buys time until their lawyers can buy judges.

"That might be a hard sell." Dee was known as the designated driver for the whole division. As far as I knew, he'd never taken a drink since coming into AA a dozen or more years before. Yet, very few were aware he had a problem with booze.

I thought about it a minute. This thing could really mess me up as an outside consultant and Dee knew it. He wouldn't have asked unless he was desperate. "How about I just shoot you in the leg?" I asked. "We could both say it was an accident. It might be less painful."

He laughed. "Don't tempt me. But you might hit an artery and I'd hate them to slip you the needle. Nellie would never forgive me."

"Well, let's hit it then," I answered, flagging the waitress for the bill. "No use putting it off."

"Maybe I should take up drinking again," he laughed as he followed me out. We both knew that was not an option. There is no problem in this world that drinking cannot make worse.

There was a distinct chill to my reception at the sheriff's office. The sheriff was all right with my being there and greeted me warmly. "Damned good to see you again, Jazz," he said. "I'm glad you came. The whole family is. Hope you don't mind the arm twisting."

The sheriff might have been glad to see me, but I could see the Fat Boys were not pleased at all. That alone damn-near made it worth the trouble of driving down, but I was polite. Not looking at Dee or the sheriff, I spoke directly to them. "I didn't know the Bureau was involved. When did this happen?"

Ken Spinks, the senior agent, answered me. "Well, we are, Phillips. So don't get in our way." Spinks and I go a long way back, too. I haven't figured out which rubs me wrong the worse—his arrogance or his stupidity. I do know he's well connected in national politics and I suspect that's how he got by entrance screening at the Bureau. It doesn't happen often, but it does happen.

"What's your basis for jurisdiction?" I asked. "This is a local murder."

"Civil rights," the other answered. He scowled. "Maybe conspiracy or a hate crime."

"A hate crime?" I asked. "Against Smiley Jones? What suggests that?"

Spinks jumped in. "We're the ones asking the questions here, Phillips. We're the ones with jurisdiction. You're here to answer our questions."

"I'm here as a consultant to the Arkansas CID and the sheriff," I shot back. Then I smiled. "Of course, if the Bureau is picking up the tab...?"

"The Bureau is not picking up your tab," Spinks snarled.

"Well, maybe I should call Lonnie and see if we can figure out how this is going to work. Maybe I need to bow out." Lonnie Schmidt is the FBI supervisor in Little Rock. He and I go back a long way, too.

I could see Spinks didn't like this, either. He had been around long enough to know I have a solid reputation among the senior staff in the Bureau. He also knew that included Lonnie, who likes the results I get and doesn't hesitate to say so. I didn't know his partner very well, but Spinks was not about to risk getting his tits in that wringer. The two of them might freeze me out with little or no cooperation, but they were not about to go up against Lonnie.

"That won't be necessary," Spinks said.

"All right, then," I told them. "But I expect full cooperation and full disclosure all the way. Any withholding on your part and I go right over your heads to Lonnie." They nodded, but I knew Spinks would cut me dead in a New York minute if he could get away with it. I hoped fear would keep him in line. "Fair enough," I said. "I'll do the same. Dee and I will work together and keep you up to date."

I turned to the sheriff. "We'll keep you in the loop, too, Sheriff. You know the drill. We'll keep what we find among ourselves until the case breaks. Just the five of us." He nodded. I knew there wouldn't be a leak through the sheriff, even though he was Smiley's cousin and would face a real grilling from the family. Then I decided it wouldn't hurt to put the Fibbies on defense. When I asked the sheriff the next question, it was all he could do to keep from smiling. "Tell me, do you have any sense this was racially motivated?"

Spinks' partner broke in and tried to answer, but I held up a hand. "Sorry for the confusion," I told him. "I was after the sheriff's gut feeling."

"Well," the sheriff drawled, taking his time and making the word a full three syllables. "I can't say I do, Jazz. 'Course, I can't rule race out, either. They is a lot of strange people out there nowadays. Seems they get stranger all the time."

Spinks rolled his eyes, but the sheriff ignored it. "It's not a family matter, is it, John?" I asked gently. Dee knows how I work and anticipated the question. Out of the corner of my eye I saw him watching the sheriff like a hawk.

The sheriff shook his head. "No, sir, it ain't," he said simply. "If it was, we wouldn't a had to call you, would we?" He smiled sweetly.

I nodded, satisfied for the moment. I could see Dee was, too. Nor did he miss the message. Sheriff Tanner was telling us that if the death were a family matter, neither Dee nor I would have ever heard about it. Nor would it have gotten to court. The alleged killer would have undoubtedly been shot trying to escape the county jail. Arkansas justice may be rough at times, but it can be damned effective.

I smiled back. We understood each other. "I'll want to see the crime scene and I'll need a desk to look over the file."

"Get real," Spinks interjected. "Crime scene is a mess. Dozens of people have been through there since it happened. There's nothing there."

"Yeah, and it's rained since then, too," his partner piped in. "Twice. Any trace evidence is probably long gone."

I didn't bother to answer. It doesn't matter how contaminated a crime scene may be. It always pays to look, even if all one gets is a sense of how things went down. There are some things neither time nor rain can wash away, and this was what I was after. Nor was it my job to train Bureau agents, even if they were open to it. Spinks and company were Lonnie's problem, not mine.

The sheriff nodded. "We'll set up an office for you over at the jail. We'll keep the file there so you can get to it anytime you need. Just ask the jailer."

"Thanks, Sheriff," I told him. "We're going to head out while there's still good light." Dee got to his feet, too, and we headed for the door. Then I stopped, turned back to Spinks. "Keep in touch, Ken," I said, pointing a finger at his chest. Spinks face turned red, but he didn't say a word.

Dee chuckled all the way to the car. "I forget what an asshole you can be," he said as we climbed into his cruiser. "You sounded just like Lonnie."

To give the devil his due, Spinks was right. The crime scene was a mess. The place where Smiley was shot was a small black settlement about a dozen miles out of Nashville. The houses were too spread out and too few to call a village, but there was a small complex of buildings more or less in the center of things and a paved state road wound its way north and south through the community, following the contours of the land. A hundred feet on either side of the road, the land fell off sharply, forming a long ridge that ran for miles.

This part of Arkansas has a lot of old stand pines left in places. Thinking they would probably be cheated by white loggers, the black people who had settled around Oak Grove used their pines for themselves. During the investigation, I learned the tractor-powered sawmill standing to the east end of the central complex provided most of the lumber for the buildings, and what little was not needed was sold to lumber yards as far away as Hope. That's where the money came from to buy hardware and glass for the community center which also served as a school before they started bussing. Now the pines that paid for this were giving way to kudzu, the Asian ground-cover imported to stop soil erosion after clear-cut logging. I guess it did just that, but what it also did was stop the natural replacement of the pines. Kudzu spreads like wildfire and in places it has wiped out entire groves.

The community center, where the shooting happened, faced north. It was a big white building in need of fresh paint but otherwise in good repair. Large windows were evenly spaced along the east and west sides, but there were none in the front or back. The entrance was a wide double door hung in the middle of the broad gallery porch which ran all the way across the front. Unpainted benches sat along the wall of the porch. To discourage casual borrowing, they were nailed to the floor.

The state road that ran through Oak Grove passed a wide parking area on the west side of the community center. Across the road from the center, a small general store with an old gas pump out front sat at right angles to the center, facing the parking lot. A crude sign on the solitary pump told us there was no gas this week.

Just north of the general store, I could see an abandoned blacksmith shop and another building that was boarded up. These all faced what looked like a dusty town square that lay across the road and directly in front of the community center. Scattered around the square were crude wooden benches set in the shade of a small grove of oak trees. It was these trees, planted by one of the first settlers, which gave Oak Grove its name. Later in the investigation, I would learn it was called Oak Ridge, too.

On the north side of the grove was a dirt parking lot, well-packed from years of use. Next to the parking lot, facing the community center across the square, sat a small white church fifty feet from the road.

There was no sign in front, but in this part of the world, it was safe to bet the church was Baptist. There was a bell in the steeple to call the faithful to worship, and over the lip of the narrow ridge, the tops of white crosses and gray headstones marked the cemetery.

Outsiders stand out like sore thumbs in settlements like Oak Grove, and I'm sure we did that day. Life in small towns is so unvaried that folks living there seem to sense when the smallest things out of the ordinary take place. That means anyone stopping for longer than a few minutes to enjoy the shade was sure to be seen, even if the watchers were not. Nor would the presence of a stranger fail to be discussed at length.

I knew the shooting would accelerate speculation. People would already be asking who might have done this, and I was sure names were being matched with unknown faces. The question was whether the family would choose to share this information with me or with anyone else from outside. Even though he was kin, the sheriff might not be in the loop on this one. He might hear about it weeks or months or years later, but not right away. No one likes a tattletale and, right or wrong, that's how talking to outsiders would be seen. Any information we got would have to be drawn out patiently, one piece at a time.

Knowing this, Dee and I were both dressed in khakis, open-neck print shirts, and hunting boots. That wouldn't fool anyone into thinking we were country folks, but it could help. We might still be pecker-woods from Little Rock, but not city-boys in suits, and in the eyes of rural folks, there is a difference. The way we dressed might give the Fat Boys reason to view us as hicks, but we stood a chance of getting information they never would.

I asked Dee to park his cruiser in the parking lot by the church, and we got out. From where we stood, it was less than a hundred feet to the porch of the community center, and I could see at least a dozen places where the shooter might hide. Given what I knew, one of the best spots would be right where we were standing.

The problem was that on the day Smiley was killed, a lot of people were in town. Some of them were strangers, but most were relatives of people living there or folks from similar little settlements within twen-

ty or thirty miles. They were there to help Smiley celebrate his birthday, which actually took place three days before. That meant the bush
telegraph was overwhelmed. There were simply too many different
faces there at once, and it would take the Oak Grove folks months to
sort them all out. Even then, some of these would certainly be overlooked.

"I imagine you checked out the parking lot," I asked Dee. "From
here it looks like the best angle."

"Yeah, but it was a mess," he told me. "It rained hard that afternoon
and there wasn't anything left by the time I got here."

"We might get lucky if he shot from a car," I said, mostly to myself.
"Assuming we know whose car to look at."

Dee nodded and we walked across the square toward the community center. As we did, I kept an eye out for anything that might have
been overlooked. That was force of habit. I didn't expect to find anything, and I didn't. Sloppy discipline breeds sloppy evidence, and I
smiled to myself when I saw Dee doing the same. I had taught him
well, and I had learned a lot from him, too.

When we got to the center, Dee walked to the east end of the
gallery porch and pointed to a faint chalk outline on the unpainted
boards. "This is where the body fell. Or maybe I should say, this is
where the deputy found it. Smiley was moved around a lot when they
tried to revive him." He pointed to dark brown smudges on the
unpainted wood. I could see at least three places where the body might
have been.

"Tell me how you see it going down," I asked him.

"As far as I can tell, Smiley was out here when it happened. It was
warm that afternoon and he had his coat off. It was draped over the
rail there, and there's no blood soak or bullet hole in it. There was
some blood splatter."

"You think the splatter was from the shot?" I interrupted.

"I don't think so, but it's hard to tell. Even if it was, the jacket had
been moved by the time we got here. It was in the deputy's cruiser."

I nodded. "All right, what about the body?"

"You can see where it was and how it was lying when the deputy found it. He had the sense to move everyone back, but it was too late by then. The people who found him moved him around a lot." He pointed to the grass in front of the porch. "There was a large stain out there, too, but the rain washed it away.""

"So he may have been shot out there?"

"I don't think so. One witness said that was where they laid him down when the EMS got here. They were carrying him to a car to take him to the hospital." He shrugged. "That's the only explanation that makes sense."

I nodded. The simplest explanation is normally the best, but this wasn't a normal case. "You're probably right, but we need to check that out with other witnesses. I take it the deputy took names and addresses?"

"Yeah, but why would the shooter stick around?" Before I could answer, he held up both hands. "I know. I have someone checking it out."

I nodded. I would've been surprised if he hadn't. "You're right on both counts. No one heard the shooting?"

"No, not a one, but they were all inside singing, and you know how it gets then."

"No kidding," I agreed. One of the great art forms in this part of the world is gospel singing, and even small communities like Oak Grove can field an impressive choir. When the choir hits its stride, a war could go on outside the building and no one would know. "I'm surprised Smiley was outside. Any idea why?"

Dee shook his head. "No. What makes it even more strange is that he was the guest of honor."

I thought a minute. Then the obvious explanation struck me. "Where's the outhouse?"

"Over the side of the ridge," Dee answered, pointing east. "You can see the top of it if over there."

I looked where he was pointing and saw the top half of an unpaint-ed privy with two doors. It was little more than weathered gray boards nailed together with a piece of rusty sheet iron to keep out the rain, but someone had cut a half moon into one of the doors and a star in the other one. What struck me was how well it blended into the wooded background. "Did the crime lab check that out?"

The sheepish look on Dee's face gave me my answer. "I don't know," he said. "It wasn't in the report."

"Well, let's have a look, then," I said. "There should still be enough light."

As we followed the well worn path to the privy, I noticed a row of tall shrubs. These were too well spaced to be wild, and it looked as if some thoughtful soul planted them to provide a measure of privacy for patrons of the privy. When we got to the outhouse, I looked back. Sure enough, I could see the porch and part of the east side of the center, but none of the windows was visible.

There wasn't much to see inside or around the privy, though the heavy shade and late angle of the afternoon sun made it dim. I took out a small flashlight I keep on my belt and looked around. That wasn't much better. There was just enough light to wash out contrast from my beam. "We better come back and look this over tomorrow," I told Dee. "I don't think this is where the shooter was, but we better check it out."

"Yeah," he agreed. "We never thought about looking down here."

"The way the body was found, you wouldn't," I told him. "It doesn't look likely from up there. It's a strange angle for a shooter to choose."

Dee looked around. "Jesus! There are all kinds of good places for a sniper to set up down here."

"That's only if the sniper knew Smiley would be standing at the end of the porch," I reminded him gently. Dee tends to be too hard on himself. "I only thought of it because I wondered if the reason Smiley came out was to use the privy."

"Or to meet someone at the end of the porch," he suggested.

"There is that," I agreed. "Let's get back up there. We can go over this place with a comb tomorrow morning."

We walked back up to the porch. The light was better on the path but neither of us saw anything out of the ordinary. When we reached the place where Dee had told me there were blood stains on the grass, I turned and looked back. From where I stood, only the very top of the outhouse was visible. Dee nodded. "No clear shot from there."

I walked onto the porch and looked around. From where I stood, I could see most of the buildings in the settlement. "Tell me about the body. What did the autopsy say?"

Dee shook his head in disgust. "By the time our lab got the body, it was as messed up as the crime scene." He nodded at my startled look. "I know. The EMS were supposed to notify our office immediately. Turns out they're volunteers and took him directly to the funeral home."

"That shouldn't have been a problem," I said.

"You're right, but the guy who owns the place was out sick. The guy on duty was just a kid who helped out part time. He washed the body and stitched up the wounds. By the time we got there, he was just about to pump in embalming fluid."

"Only a licensed funeral director is supposed to do that!" I protested.

"Yeah, but this ain't Little Rock," Dee told me. "Apparently the kid had done it before when things got busy. Several times. Our medical examiner said it was good professional work."

"You think the kid was just being helpful?"

"Yeah. Apparently he got pretty irate after he got done being scared. Claimed his boss taught him what to do. He said the owner was normally there to supervise." Dee shrugged. "I think he's telling the truth. From what I could see, the owner's going to need his own services before long. He's in his late seventies and not doing very good. Lung cancer."

I shook my head. "Too bad he didn't tell the kid to call the sheriff if someone was shot." He shrugged. "It didn't give me much leverage." He had a point. How do you lean on a guy who's dying, and probably full of morphine, too? "Like I say, he's not doing good. Wasn't playing with a full deck when I talked to him."

"Well, what do we have for sure?" I asked.

"There were three wounds, and the ME thinks he may have been shot three times. One wound was in the neck. The bullet went in here." He pointed at the right side of his larynx. "It came out the back of his neck and cut the jugular, but didn't sever the spinal cord. Another one went in through the right eye and came out the brain stem. That's the one that killed him. The third went in just under his sternum and came out through the hollow by his collar bone." He touched his left shoulder. "The strange thing is, there was no damage from bullet expansion, not even through the torso. The hole in his skull was a clean circle made by a .22 caliber round. So was the hole through his neck."

That surprised me. A lot of people get shot with the .22 long rifle rim fire, and it can be a lethal choice at close range. Muzzle energy from a hot load is greater than the larger .38 S&W pistol shell, but the higher energy means the bullet mushrooms to as much as twice its size and sometimes tumbles. The hollow point version breaks apart, sending a shower of tiny lead slivers to wreak havoc with soft tissue. That slows the slug down quickly, and most often there's not enough force left to punch through the skull a second time. The bullet normally stays in the body.

"Military issue?" I asked, talking to myself. The .223 the military uses is a wicked shell that doesn't make much of a bang, unlike some of the larger calibers. While the civilian version is a hunting shell designed to mushroom on impact and do maximum tissue damage, the military round carries a solid point that doesn't change shape. Nor does it lack the power to punch through a skull or all the way through the torso.

"That's what I wondered," Dee answered. "Who knows? Maybe we're looking at a pro. With a silencer and subsonic ammunition, he could have taken Smiley out in a crowd. The way it tunneled through the torso sounds like it might be from a hot load." His shrug was eloquent. "Or not. It didn't hit any bones."

"I don't want to go there just yet," I told him. "Unless there's evidence there's a professional involved. There are a lot of hand-loaders out there."

"That's the problem," Dee said. "We don't have any evidence, and what we have could go a dozen ways to Sunday. We're working blind."

Through all the rough times at the CID, I had never heard him so close to despair.

"Don't go there, either!" I said sharply. Dee is nothing short of brilliant in the field and can see things others miss, including me. Yet, there's a dark side to this gift. When he can't see his way through to at least one line of investigation, he takes it personally and gets despondent. The same thing happens when he makes his rare mistake. While the problem was much worse before he stopped drinking, Dee is like most alcoholics in recovery. He still suffers from what he calls *ocular rectitis*. Other folks call it a shitty outlook.

Dee looked up hurt, as if I had slapped him in the face. "There's plenty of evidence," I said gently. "We just have to find it. Focus on the investigation. Don't let the bastards get to you like that."

"Sorry," he said. "You're right. I got everybody and his dog on my back with this one. You're damned lucky to be out of it these days. It ain't much fun anymore." Then he grinned. "Maybe I ought to go to work for you. Retirement seems to be treating you good."

"It has its moments, believe me," I answered. "Now, tell me about that. Is it what I think it is?" I pointed to the wall. There was a reddish brown stain I had not seen before. It was in the shape of a human hand and looked liked blood.

"That's one of the jokers in this deck," Dee told me. "It is blood. Smiley's blood, and the print is the same size as his hand. Whether this is his hand print is not certain. There are no fingerprints or palm prints, and his hands were normal size."

I stood looking around. No obvious explanation how the handprint got where it did came to mind. "What do you think?"

"Well, if it is Smiley's hand print, then the neck shot would have had to come first. The eye shot would have taken him out immediately without much bleeding. Then, too, the angle is all wrong for the torso shot, unless the shooter was lying below him. There's no bullet hole in the ceiling of the porch, so that would mean it would have to happen down on the grass. I guess that's possible, but it doesn't seem very likely to me. It would explain the hand print, but there's no bloody trail showing that Smiley stumbled back onto the porch. No blood we could see on the roof, either."

I nodded. "It would put the shooter at a high risk of exposure, too."

"That's what I thought, but faking a heart attack would be one way of getting Smiley off the porch. But why bother? Why not just walk up to him and blow him away?"

"The amount of blood seems to say the throat shot came first."

Dee nodded. "Yeah, it probably would've killed him, but he might have survived if someone got the bleeding stopped. Still, the torso would have bled a lot, too. There was no way of telling. There was nothing in the hand print but blood—his blood—no fibers or other tissue."

I nodded and walked to one of the large smudges at the east end of the porch. "Let's say Smiley was standing here. He could've been shot from down by the privy."

"Yeah, if he was facing the outhouse."

"How sure is the medical examiner about the throat wounds? Which was entry and which was exit?"

Dee shrugged. "That's one of the main problems. Young Frankenstein at the mortuary really messed things up. The ME couldn't say for sure. He thought it went in the front, but he also said there was at least a forty-nine percent chance it came through from the back."

"Have you talked to the kid?"

Dee shook his head. "No. He's only fifteen and his dad's a lawyer. Refused to let us interview the kid at all. I'm working on getting him immunity, but the local prosecutor is being ornery. Apparently the kid's dad beat him up pretty bad in court a couple of times."

"Maybe we need to make the prosecutor an offer he can't refuse," I suggested lightly.

Dee laughed. "I'm not going to ask what you mean by that."

I looked around. Between the pines and the oaks, the light was going fast. "I think I have enough for today. I need to read the file. We'll come back in the morning."

As we walked across the square, an old man came out of the church and hobbled down the steps. He raised his cane and waved at us, trying to flag us down, and we turned and walked over to him. He stopped when he saw us turn and waited, breathing hard.

"You the police?" he gasped, leaning on his cane and squinting at us. He was short and slight, bent almost double over his cane. His hair had turned white, and I could see enough of his eyes to see they were rheumy.

"I am," Dee told him, holding up his identification. "What's the matter?"

"Luther done it!" the old man declared. "He ain't no damn good and he done it!" There were tears streaming down his face.

"Who is Luther?" Dee asked. "What did he do?"

"It was Luther shot that man!" His eyes were open now, wild.

I noticed another man appear in the doorway of the church. He looked around, then spotted us and walked toward us, limping.

"You mean Smiley Jones?" Dee asked.

The old man became even more agitated. "Who else done got shot?" he shouted, waving his free hand wildly. "Luther done it!"

The second man had reached us. He was tall and thin, with an air of quiet authority, and was dressed in a worn black suit. He took the older man by the arm. "Now Luther, you just calm down," he said. "You go sit up on one of those benches and let me talk to these gentlemen."

I thought the old man was going to argue. He glared at the tall man, as if trying to figure who he was, then nodded and hobbled off to the nearest bench.

"You've got to pardon Luther, gentlemen," he said quietly. "He hasn't been quite right in a long time." His voice was rich and well modulated, soft and gentle, but giving the sense of being able to shatter windows were it raised.

Dee extended his identification which he had not put away. "I'm Stephen DiRado, from the Arkansas CID. Who are you?"

"I'm Albert Jones, Officer. I pastor the church here." He looked at me. "Who is this?"

I introduced myself, extending a hand. The pastor took it. His grip was like his voice, firm and gentle with a hint of great strength held in check. "Dr. Phillips is our consultant on this case," Dee explained.

"Yes," the pastor murmured. "I've read a great deal about you in the papers, Dr. Phillips. You did very good things when you were with the CID." He turned to Dee. "I read the same about you, too, Mr. DiRado. It's a pleasure to meet you both, though I wish the circumstances were different. Poor Wilbur. Yet, with his condition, it may have been a blessing."

While his manner was open and welcoming, I saw wariness in the reverend's eyes. I also sensed there was also a lot more to this man than one would expect from a simple country pastor. It may have been the way he spoke, in his choice of words and the lack of any accent. Or it may have been the way he wore his once elegant suit, as if it were fitted to his body by a tailor. Despite his limp, he moved like a dancer, with purpose and no wasted motion.

"His condition?" Dee asked.

"Didn't your medical examiner tell you?" the pastor asked. "Wilbur had bone cancer. He was facing a world of pain."

"He told us, pastor," Dee replied. "I just needed to know if we were singing from the same page. Are you suggesting this might have been suicide? Or a mercy killing?"

"Not at all, Mr. DiRado. Just that he was spared a lot of suffering."

"How widely was his cancer known?" I asked. His eyes met mine directly, and I saw something there. I wasn't sure what it was, but I recognized it as something I would not care to meet in a dark alley.

"I would imagine only four or five people knew. He asked me to keep quiet about it, not even put him on the prayer list." The pastor shook his head. "He was a proud man. Said he didn't want to trouble his family or be a burden."

"Why did Luther tell us he did it?" Dee asked.

"He accidentally shot another cousin of ours," Albert Jones told us. "We were all very young and it wasn't his fault. It was someone else's gun, and Luther didn't know how to handle it properly. He hasn't been right ever since." He looked at the old man, now sitting quietly on the bench. "It might surprise you to know that Luther is actually younger than me. The accident aged him very fast."

It was hard to believe this strong man talking to us was Luther's senior. I had placed Albert Jones in his early sixties and Luther in his eighties. Now I realized I was at least a decade short. It also occurred to me the good pastor was someone who probably knew everything worth knowing about Oak Grove and its people. Whether he would choose to share this knowledge with us was another question. I decided to take the lead.

"I would like to know more about that accident, pastor," I told him. I saw shutters go down behind his eyes. "I wouldn't ask you to violate any professional confidence, but it would help to know anything you can tell us."

I could see the man was torn. Nor was it fear that troubled him. Looking back, I think he was considering the lesser of evils. Talking to us might open up areas of the past he would rather stay closed. Yet, not doing so might prompt us to probe into other areas even more unpleasant. I think he decided that in talking to us he could steer the conversation along the least unpleasant line.

He pulled out a pocket watch. Like the suit, it was very old and very elegant. "I have a prayer service in a half hour and I need to get ready for that. Perhaps some other time."

"We'll be here tomorrow morning," I told him. "Would that do?"

Albert Jones nodded. "Meet me here at the church at eleven." Not waiting confirmation, he turned and walked over to Luther. When he said something, the old man got up and followed. Together they disappeared into the church.

Dee sighed. "He knows something. I can smell it."

I nodded. "Finding out what it is may be a problem." Later, as we drove out of Oak Grove and the church caught my eye, something fluttered around the threshold of awareness in my mind. There was a critical question I needed to ask the pastor. Yet, for the life of me I couldn't figure what it was.

The Village Smithy

When Dee picked me up early the next morning, I had a better sense of the case. The motel was an easy walk from the jail and I spent a couple of hours going over the file. Then I went for a walk, something people don't seem to do very much in Nashville. I only saw one other soul out walking, a young woman in a sweat suit leading an old German shepherd that was having trouble keeping up with her pace. She passed me like I was standing still, and I had a moment of sympathy for the old dog. I walk at a good pace, clocking in at three miles in an hour, but she was going half again as fast.

As she passed, I wondered, as I always do, what her hurry was, how she might use the time she may have saved. For me, walking is not exercise so much as a time to get away, a time to set aside the concerns of the day and simply be still for awhile. So I don't wear headphones or listen to whatever it is people listen to as they walk or run. I listen to the sounds of the night, which is the time of day I prefer to be out, or to the music of the spheres. As I listen, I wait for whatever insights the universe may have to offer. The interesting thing is that answers to many of the hardest questions that develop in a case come to me while I walk. Moving my legs seems to get the gray matter going, too, and I read somewhere that this is true for most people.

Late October weather can go either way in this part of the world, but that night it was cool and clear, and there was a hint of winter ahead in the air. Like many small, rural towns, Nashville is one of those places where they roll up the sidewalks at dusk. The only night life I could see as I walked the town was at the drive-in burger barn.

Even there business was slow. Wednesday night is church night in rural Arkansas and I wondered why there were so few cars at the half dozen or so churches I passed. The tune from an old song drifted through my mind, but the times were not changing. They had changed a long time ago.

Other than that, no blinding insights into this minor mystery came to me on the walk. Nor were there any insights into the case. When I got back to the motel, I read for a while and went to bed relaxed. I slept well, feeling refreshed and ready for the day when I woke. By the time Dee arrived, I was dressed and hungry for breakfast. Dee, on the other hand, looked haggard. When I asked, he told me he had been on the phone half the night talking to Little Rock. However, he had found an AA meeting in town and seemed to be in pretty good spirits.

Among those he talked to the night before was the state medical examiner, and as we ate breakfast, Dee told me the results of tests that were just now coming in. Since it was such a politically sensitive case, the ME had asked the FBI lab to verify some of his findings, and that always takes a while. Nor were there any great surprises. The ME was simply covering his ass and did not expect anything new to be uncovered. What killed Smiley Jones was the bullet that passed though his eye, and the only real questions were who did it and why. Whether the fatal shot came second or third would only be important if there were a trial.

"What bugs me is where the bullets went," Dee said, taking a sip of coffee. "We looked in all the obvious places, and some that weren't so obvious. Nothing. It was like they evaporated." He chuckled. "I even wondered if someone had come up with a way to make them out of ice."

"Well, assuming it was a hand-loaded .223, that might not be surprising," I answered. "Suppose someone reloaded military shells and used the original solid nose bullets. If they didn't hit a building or one of the trees close by, they're probably lodged somewhere out under the kudzu. I doubt they'll ever be found. Not that we should stop looking."

Dee nodded. "Yeah, you're probably right. But you would think that out of three shots, we could find at least one."

I shook my head. "This isn't the city, Dee. There aren't many buildings to catch them. Then, too, our shooter may have chosen his vector with that in mind."

Dee smiled and I realized what I had just done. Calling the shooter as ours rather than his meant I had staked a claim. I was committed. They could fire me and send me packing, but other than that, I was in for the long haul. "Well, I hate to bring up the possibility of a pro again," he said, "but can you see your average killer being that careful...?" He left the thought unfinished.

I cleaned my plate and grabbed the bill. Dee tried to argue but I told him it was on the Natural State and I asked the waitress to bring us a couple of foam cups and to fill my thermos. From what I'd seen, there wasn't a place to get coffee in Oak Ridge. At least, there wasn't for peckerwoods like us.

It was foggy that morning as we headed out of Nashville and things did not improve. By the time we got to Oak Grove, the fog turned into a heavy mist and we were having to use the windshield wipers. When we got there about nine, there was no sign of life in town. Those who had jobs in other places were long gone and the weather was not good for being out. I was glad I had thought to bring along my rain gear. Even so, we were likely to get soaked if we had to go tramping around in the brush. I wished I had brought a change of clothes, too.

As gray as it was, there was little point in going over the outhouse right then. So Dee and I sat on the porch of the community center, sipping coffee and talking about the case. I knew our presence had not gone unmarked, and after about a half hour I saw someone slip out the door of the store across the road. It was a child, a boy of nine or ten, wearing a dark rain slicker. When he saw me looking, he disappeared behind the corner of the community center.

Dee had seen him, too. He looked at me, raised an eyebrow in question. I shook my head and we continued to talk quietly. At some point I became aware we were being watched and glanced around. I saw the door of the center move slightly, as if nudged by the movement of air, but I knew it wasn't that. There was no breeze that morning, and the door was held closed by a spring latch.

"Let's take a look inside," I suggested. Dee followed me into the center and we stood there for a moment, letting our eyes get adjusted to the dim light. Dee started to switch on the lights but I stopped him. Turning on the lights might draw more attention than I wanted at the moment.

As dark as it was, there was still plenty of light to show the layout of the center. One big room took up most of the space inside and this was divided into two equal sections. There was no ceiling in the room, only bare rafters with ceramic light fixtures strung down the center of each section. Wooden benches took up most of the space under the lights, but aside from those, that part of the room was bare.

At the end of the room opposite where we stood, there was a low platform with a wooden podium and four wooden chairs. To one side of the platform, in the corner nearest the outhouse, there was a door set at floor level, and an old piano stood facing the podium at the other side. There was a large blackboard directly behind the podium, but as far as I could see, there was no chalk nor any erasers. Except for the blackboard, we could have been in a traditional country church.

The sun must have been breaking through the clouds, for there seemed to be a little more light coming in through the windows. I walked to the center of the room and stood quietly. The light rain falling on the roof made a soft murmur, but I could hear nothing else. Nor was anyone there. I glanced at Dee, still standing by the door, and saw him nod toward the back corner.

The back door was open part way now. Against the light I could see the dark silhouette of someone's head craned around the door. I couldn't see the features or the eyes, but I was sure it was the boy I saw coming out of the store.

We stood like that for full minute, looking at each other and neither making a move. Then the door opened wider and the boy came into the room. He stopped a dozen feet away from me and looked at me gravely. I smiled but said nothing.

"Who you?" The words sounded like balloons popping in the still room.

"I'm J.S. Phillips," I told him gravely. "This is Officer DiRado. Who are you?"

He ignored my question. "He police?"

"Yes," I answered. "State Police. I'm just a guy who's helping him out."

The boy thought about this for a moment. "I got sumpin," he said. I nodded, but didn't reply. After a moment, he added, "Sumpin you wont."

"What is it?" I asked, taking a seat on one of the benches.

The youngster moved a bit closer. "How much you give?" he demanded.

"That depends on what it is," I answered. "If it's something good, I'll give you a dollar." I reached in my pocket and pulled out some change.

"Three dollar," he told me.

I put the change back in my pocket and shook my head. "No, if it's really good, I'll give you two dollars, one to look and one if I want it. But you got to show me first."

He considered this for another long moment. Then he nodded and held out his hand. I could see what looked like a spent rifle shell casing. What caught my attention was the color. Brass dulls with age, turning green as it weathers. Even if it's kept inside in its original box it changes color slightly, taking on a dull patina that grows darker over months and years. This casing the boy held out in his hand was still bright, which meant it was brand new. I felt a thrill of excitement, but tried to keep it off my face and out of my voice.

I took my time, as if I were giving the matter careful consideration. I reached for my wallet and took out two ones, holding them in my hand. I laid one of them on the bench in front of me and said, "All right I'm interested. Turn it around so I can see the open end. Again, he thought for a moment, then did what I asked.

The neck of the case was small and I nodded. "All right, I'll take it," I told him. I laid the other bill beside the first and leaned back. "What I really want to know is where you found that."

The boy approached carefully. Then, in a flash, he grabbed the two bills and jumped back where he started. I carefully picked up the empty shell casing, using a wire I keep in my pocket for just this purpose. I looked at the base. "It's a .223, all right," I told Dee. "Remington commercial casing. Civilian issue, not military."

Dee stayed where he was. I took out a self-sealing sandwich bag and put the shell in, tucking the whole works into a shirt pocket. Then I took a five out of my wallet and looked at the youngster. His eyes widened when he saw it was a five, but other than that, he showed no interest. "I was looking for that," I told him. "Now I'd like for you to show me where you found it."

The boy said nothing. He nodded toward the five I still held in my hand and pointed to the bench. "No," I said. "You have to show me first."

He looked at me gravely for a long moment, then shook his head. I put the five back into my wallet. After a moment, he walked back to the door, then stopped and looked at me. I sat for a moment, then took the five out again. His eyes grew even wider than before when I tore the bill and half. Then I laid one half onto the bench. "All right," I told him. "You take this half now, and I'll give you the other one when you show me where you found it."

"Ain't no good now," he told me. I wondered if it was just my ear or if he was losing some of his rural Arkansas accent.

I didn't think I would be able to convince him otherwise. So I picked up the torn bill and took two more ones out of my wallet and laid them on the bench. "All right. Two now and three more when you show me."

He considered this for a moment, then nodded. This time he walked up to me and did not run back after he picked up the bills. "I'm Jazz," I said, offering my hand. "What's your name?"

He looked at my hand for a moment, then shook it. "My name is Robert," he told me, his voice completely without accent now. His eyes were solemn.

"I bet your last name is Jones," I told him.

"How much you want to bet?"

"A quarter."

"You lose," he replied. "It's McNutt."

"All right, Robert," I laughed and tossed him a coin. "Why don't you show us where you found it."

Robert moved to the door and waved for us to follow. When we emerged, we found ourselves in a small clearing behind the community center. The tree line curved south from the corner nearest the road, making a hidden pocket in what looked like solid forest and brush. It was about fifty feet across at its widest and ran over the edge of the ridge. I looked around and saw we were not standing far from a line of photinias, the same one that gave the privy privacy. Yet, I could not see the outhouse from where I stood.

Robert stopped just outside the door and seemed to be lost in thought. Then he turned and walked to the west corner of the building. He stopped there a minute and looked out. Then he turned back to us and spoke in a quiet voice. "You wait until I'm across."

I heard Dee snort softly, the way he does when he is getting impatient. "What's the deal with him?" he asked so quietly I could barely hear.

I chuckled. "He doesn't want to be seen with us."

"So it's not cool talking to PO-lice around here," he murmured.

"Something like that." I saw Robert wave to us from the other side of the road. "Or it may be he's got a good deal going, and he doesn't want his mama to spoil. Let's move."

As we crossed the road, it occurred to me that anyone seeing us would probably think we were chasing Robert. Nor did I think this concept was lost on him. This was what he intended, and it struck me we were dealing with a very sophisticated ten-year-old. I must have chuckled because Dee answered me in the same quiet voice. "You spot it, you got it!"

"You got what?" Robert asked. His ears were much sharper than mine. I hope he didn't blast them away with loud music like so many of my generation did in the sixties.

"You got whatever you see," Dee answered him. He smiled.

Robert looked from one of us to the other, then shrugged. Without a word he turned and walked down a game path I could barely make out. We were walking through heavy brush at the edge of what must have been a steep drop-off, because all I could see to our left was brush and the top of tall pines. We were moving too fast to step carefully, and I hoped the copperheads and rattlesnakes were already tucked in for winter.

Robert stopped so quickly I almost bumped into him. Looking over his shoulder I saw what I thought was the back of the store. There was a door there and two windows, but the windows were tightly boarded up with unpainted plywood. To our left there was another privy, about twenty feet from the back corner of the store, and I could see what looked like the back corner of the blacksmith shop.

After a moment, Robert darted out of the brush and crossed behind the blacksmith shop. He disappeared into the space between the smithy and a third building that was boarded up. I looked around and then followed.

When we got to the spot where Robert disappeared, we found him standing about six feet into a space almost wide enough to be a walkway between the buildings. Except for weeds and a few rusty cans, there was nothing between the buildings. Beyond where Robert stood, the high weeds looked like they had not been disturbed for years. Some were from last year, slightly weathered, but still standing in the protected space. Others were lighter yellow, this year's crop, but only a few held any trace of green. Moisture from the soft day gathered on their leaves, dead and dying, turning some of them black and some deep gold.

"Right there," Robert told us, pointing between his feet. The weeds had been trampled there, but not much. The disarray could have come from him retrieving the spent shell.

"All right," I said. "I need you to stand over here behind us while we look around."

"What about my five dollars?" he responded. I heard Dee chuckle.

"Sorry," I said holding out three ones. I may have forgotten to pay him, but not the details of our deal. "This makes five."

Robert slipped behind us but made no move to leave. He watched as Dee and I carefully searched the space. "I already looked there," he told us.

"I know, but I have to be thorough," I answered. "How did you spot it with all these weeds?"

"Lucky, I guess," Robert said. I looked at Dee. He nodded. The kid wasn't telling us the truth but I decided not to push it right then.

"May be we'll get lucky, too," I told him. He answered with a snort, letting us know he wouldn't lay odds on it. I grinned at him, then noticed the privy behind him. It was very old, so old it looked like a good gust of wind could flatten it. I made a mental note to check it out when we were finished searching the space between the buildings.

"Yes!" Dee said. I glanced over at him just in time to see him frown.

"What do you have?"

"Looks like another casing, but this one's tarnished."

I moved to where he stood and looked over his shoulder. The shell was lying at an odd angle against the smithy. Weeds held its base up, but the light was too poor to see the marking stamped in the base. What I could see was that the primer was dented, telling me the shell was either empty or a misfire. "Let me get a picture," I said, reaching into the small rucksack I was carrying. Nellie calls this my purse. I use it to carry the things I may need on a crime scene, like paper and a pencil, water, extra film, vinyl gloves, and a small tool kit. I even carry a couple of high energy bars for those times I cannot take to eat.

I hung the camera around my neck and took out a plastic bag. Using a pair of tongs, I carefully picked up the shell. It seemed heavier than I would expect, and I was not surprised to find the bullet still seated in the neck of the casing. Holding it up to the gathering light, I saw that it was a .223, the same caliber as the shell I got from Robert.

"Looks like military issue," Dee said. "Could have cost someone his life."

I nodded. Misfires are the last thing a soldier needs facing hostile strangers trying to kill him. Then I noticed something else. "Maybe not. Look at the pin mark."

Dee leaned over my shoulder for a closer look. "I see what you mean. Looks like the pin barely touched the cap."

"What pin?" said Robert.

I had forgotten he was there. Normally, I wouldn't respond to questions like this. Cops keep what they find to themselves until the crime is solved, but Robert already knew about the shell, and I couldn't see any reason not to answer. Good will now might turn out to be bread cast on the waters later. "Can you keep a secret?" I asked.

Robert looked at me for a few seconds and nodded. I held the shell up so he could see the base. "See the dent in the center, there? The little round thing is the cap. When the firing pin hits it hard enough, fire shoots through a tiny hole under the cap. That makes the power explode and sends the bullet—the slug up front—down the barrel."

Robert nodded gravely and I continued. "See how shallow the dent is? That means the firing pin barely touched it, not hard enough to strike fire. So the bullet never left the gun."

Just then a voice sounded from the direction of the store, calling for Robert. "That's my mom," he said, and disappeared around the corner of the building.

Dee looked at me. "So what do you think? Dirty weapon?" One of the problems with the early Vietnam era M-14 was that it had to be cleaned often. Without constant care, the weapon would jam or misfire.

I shook my head. "I don't know. Could be. Or it could be brand new and someone missed some Cosmoline."

"Cosmoline?"

"Yeah, it's the greasy stuff the military used fifty years ago to coat weapons for long term storage. I'm not sure what they use now."

Dee raised an eyebrow. "We're not far from Red River," he said. Red River Army Depot was only a hundred miles away, just west of Texarkana. It employed several hundred civilians, any number of whom could have easily filched a military rifle from one of the older bunkers.

I shrugged. "I don't know if it matters. The shell Robert found was a commercial civilian casing, so this may not involve the same weapon. We can check the firing pin marks to see. At least, as much of the marks as we have. The one in the fired shell was deeper." I dropped the unspent shell into a plastic bag and marked it with the date and place we found it.

I looked around. There was no way of checking out the rest of the space between the buildings without disturbing the weeds. "Let's hold off on this for a bit," I said. "Let the crime scene team deal with it if we bring them back in."

We walked back to the area behind the buildings. "You want to stretch tape?" Dee asked. He meant yellow crime scene tape warning people to stay out.

"No," I said. "That'll only draw attention. Let's hold off for a while. We don't have anyone to enforce it."

"One phone call will take care of that," Dee reminded me, but I shook my head. I was looking at the outhouse directly behind the space between the buildings. It was old and looked as if it hadn't been used for years, but I noticed something and walked over to it. The door, now sagged so far it touched the ground at its outside corner, had been moved recently. Even though it had rained, I could see a faint scratch arced in the grass where it had been opened wide. The scratch looked fairly recent.

I walked to the privy and pointed to the scratch. Then I opened the door and stuck my head in. The tin roof was still intact and had done its job protecting the inside. A faded red seat was nailed to the cross boards, but the lid was up, showing a dark hole below. I backed out and carefully held the door open. "Take a look," I said to Dee. "Tell me what you see."

He stuck his head into the privy for a moment. "Doesn't look like the place has been used in a while." He grinned. "No paper...not even a Sears catalogue."

"What do you smell?" I asked.

39

He gave me a funny look. "I smell shit and piss. What else would I smell?"

"Nothing," I told him. "Did you see that old sack of lime by the door?"

"Yeah," he said. "So what?"

I sighed. One of Dee's shortcomings is that he was raised in town and grew up with all the comforts of civilization, including indoor plumbing. He had never had to lime the pit of an outhouse. "What you smell is fresh shit. Not from today, but from not too many days ago, either. The lime has killed the smell of the older stuff."

Dee was on it like a cat on a bug. "So our shooter could have used it?" he said. Then he saw the possibilities. "Well so could have a lot of people. The town was full of people that day. There aren't that many outhouses."

I pointed to the scratch marks. "Yes, but most of the people were gathered over by the church and the community center. They would have used the ones over there or maybe the one at the parsonage. I think it's unlikely that anyone came all the way over here to take a dump. The marks the door made in the ground would be much deeper if they had. It's only been opened once or twice."

Dee stuck his head back in the outhouse and shined his flashlight around the floor and the walls. "Well, I don't see anything obvious. Let's let the crime scene guys deal with this, too. Maybe we'll get lucky and they will find a print or a hair or something."

"Suits me," I said. "Why don't we check out these buildings while we're here?"

There was no easy access into the third building. The rear door was boarded over and nailed tight to the frame. The rust on the nail heads was dark brown, telling me they had been there for years. There were windows with broken glass for panes in the open side, but the weeds were grown high and completely undisturbed. The side next to the smithy was a solid wall without a door or any windows at all.

The door of the smithy seemed to be fastened shut, too, until Dee gave the handle a hard pull. Then it opened suddenly, almost throwing him off balance. Nor was there any protest from rusty hinges, and, when I looked, I saw dark stains on the old rust. Someone had oiled them recently. I pointed this out to Dee. "More stuff for Crime Scene."

What surprised me when we entered the smithy was how much light filtered through the planks that covered the windows from outside. There was very little left in the building, only an old wooden bucket that would fetch a premium at a flea market in Little Rock and a rusted-out iron washtub that held what looked like hemp feed sacks. There were two empty rooms at the back of the shop, both heavy with dust left undisturbed for years, but the dust covering the floor of the wide hallway between them was trampled down. I couldn't make out distinct tracks, so I moved carefully down the hall toward the open room at the front.

The wooden floor we were walking on stopped at the end of the hallway, giving way to packed dirt. A third of the width of the the shop front was taken up by a massive door that slid to one side on a heavy railing. On the other side, the one farthest from the store, there was a narrow door flanked by a wide window, and directly above the sliding door was another window—a large one. Both had been boarded up from the outside. However, most of the glass in the windows was intact and light trickled in through spaces between the boards, filtered by heavy dust stains on the glass that created a sepia glow.

The sun was above the tree line now, burning off the low clouds, and its light struck the building full-force. The effect in the still air of the shop was like a dozen spotlights throwing long beams of light across the interior and and highlighting dust motes in the air. I paused to take a couple of pictures with my flash switched off. At that point, I was not after evidence, just struck by the wonderful play of light and shadow and I hoped one of those shots turned out. If nothing else, it would make a marvelous addition to my collection of prints. While this might seem unprofessional, it was not. Over the years a number of these "unrelated" photos from crime scenes have pointed to lines of inquiry that turned into gold mines of information. So I have learned to trust these moments of imagination.

41

I was about to move on into the large room when Dee reached out to stop me. "Look there," he said, pointing. When I looked, I understood why he stopped me. On the right side of the sliding door, about a foot above the dirt floor, the sunlight streamed in a narrow opening about two inches by four. Casual inspection might have passed it over for a knothole, which is exactly what it was at one time. Yet in the direct sunlight, I could see the wood on all sides of the opening was much lighter than the surface inside, as if someone had carefully cut it away. From what I could see, whoever did this was careful to bevel the cuts so they could not be seen from the outside.

I brought my camera up and switched on the flash. I turned the lens out to full zoom and looked to make sure I had what I wanted. It couldn't have been better. I could see the cut marks around the hole clearly.

I pressed the shutter, then zoomed out for a wider angle. This time when I snapped the shutter, the flash revealed something I hadn't seen before. I zoomed in to be certain. Sure enough, I could see the outline of a long, rough rectangle made by a couple of feed sacks laid out behind the hole. The color of the fabric was about the same as the dirt, but from what I could see, there was no dust on the sacks at all. I pointed this out to Dee. He nodded. "It looks like someone was up to some serious sniping," he said. "I wonder if that's his."

I looked where he was pointing. Hidden in the shadows of the corner were the outlines of a soft drink can. I couldn't read the brand name, but the red and white striping were distinctive. I found myself getting excited. "We better call Crime Scene in, STAT," I told him.

Dee pulled out a cell phone. "Looks like a dead area here," he said, looking at his signal bars. "I'll have to use the radio in the car."

"I don't suppose there's a pay phone anywhere around here. Anyone with a scanner will know something's up."

"They'll know, anyway, as soon as the van gets here." While the crime scene van was a discrete silver, the bold lettering on the side doors and the back made it very clear what it was there to do.

"I was thinking about the press," I told him. "The last thing we need is a cable news van pulling in and messing things up. Where are they, by the way? I was surprised not to see any of them in Nashville."

He shrugged. "They're as lazy as anyone else. With the governor's office feeding them information, it's easier to stay in Little Rock."

"Why don't you check the store?" I said. "Or maybe, the parsonage. Surely there must be someone around here with a phone."

Dee gave me a look I remembered from when I was his boss. It told me I was being very unreasonable, at least in his eyes. The difference now was that I was no longer his boss and I could see him searching for a polite way to suggest this. "Never mind," I said. "I'm probably being too paranoid. I'll watch the place while you make the call."

Dee looked relieved. "I'll be discreet," he promised. "I'll ask for Casey by name." Kermit Charles Jones is the physician who heads up our state forensic team. Years ago he began signing his name using only his initials, and K.C., or Casey, quickly became his sobriquet among the other members of the CID. Yet, to the press, he was still Dr. Kermit Jones and we kept it that way in public situations, not only for him, but for the rest of us. It seemed to work. It gave us a degree of anonymity over the air.

I walked around to the front of the smithy while Dee was gone. Sure enough, I could see faint smudges on the weathered wood outside, but no sign of new cutting. We were dealing with a very careful killer, and it crossed my mind again that we might be dealing with a professional.

There was nothing else to see at the moment, so I walked around to the back to secure the building. When I did, I saw Robert coming out of the back of the store with a soda in his hand. He saw me and walked over. I closed the back door to the blacksmith shop and leaned against it. "Didn't know that door worked," he told me. "Whatcha find?"

"I'm not sure, Robert," I told him. I took a bottle of water out of my sack and took a sip. "It may be something or it may not. You ever see anyone hanging around back here?"

He gave me an appraising look. I pulled out the torn five and handed to him. "Why don't you see if they will take this at the store? Bring me a couple of diet cokes and a couple of bags of peanuts, and you can keep the change."

"This ain't no good," he protested, lapsing into his rural Arkansas accent. "I done tole you that already!"

"You're wrong, but never mind, then," I answered, reaching for the torn halves.

"We out of everything but Pepsi," he told me. "We do have diet that."

"Sure," I said. I've always thought diet Pepsi tastes like watered bleach smells, but it was caffeine I was after…and information.

Robert was back inside a minute. I saw his mother looking out the door to see who he was coming to see, and I waved. She stared at me for a long moment, then disappeared into the store without waving. After a moment, a tall, husky man came out of the store and walked in our direction. Determination was written all over his face and punctuated by his stride.

I decided to beat him to the punch. I handed him a card and introduced myself before he had a chance to speak. "I bet you're Robert's dad."

He acknowledged this with a curt nod, glancing at my card. "What you want with Robert?" he said in a tone that was just inside being civil. Thirty years ago such a tone with a white officer would have earned him thirty days and some hard knocks as a guest of the county.

"We were just talking," I answered gently. "Robert has been telling me a little about the town here."

"He ain't been here long enough to know anything worth telling," he answered.

"I don't think I got your name," I replied.

"I didn't give it," he told me.

"Is there some reason why?" I asked, raising an eyebrow and letting him hear just a hint of official tone. It was a warning, and one I could see he understood. But rather than answer, he took Robert by the arm and turned on his heel to go back to the store. Just then Dee came around the corner of the store and saw us.

I mimicked holding up a badge and Dee held up his identification folder. Robert and the tall man stopped and looked back at me. "You can talk to me or him," I said. "I'm easier."

"I ain't done nothing wrong!" the tall man said. The lapse into rural speak told he was frightened, more than one would expect. I wondered why.

"No, you haven't done anything wrong," I agreed. "Not yet. On the other hand, a police investigator has asked you to identify yourself and you have refused. It was a reasonable question."

The man looked back and forth at us, then shrugged. "McNutt," he said in a flat voice. "Robert McNutt. Senior," he added.

I nodded. "Thank you, Mr. McNutt. Do you own the store here?" He nodded, but said nothing. "Look, I'm not out to bother you, sir. We're here about the shooting two weeks ago and we need information. Have you owned the store awhile?"

"Twelve years," he answered, relaxing a bit. Then he shook his head. "No, it's been fourteen now."

I nodded. "That happens to me all the time. My kids call it galloping senility. Tell me, are you related to any of the people around here?"

He shook his head. For some reason he was unwilling to volunteer where he was from and again I wondered why. Some people are just like that, but I thought there was more to it. "That means you're still an outsider, doesn't it. I don't guess you'd hear much."

He shrugged, thawing just a little. "Well, sometimes. People talk in the store. I hadn't heard any talk about the shooting."

"That's strange, isn't it? I mean, something like that. You'd think they'd be rattling off a mile a minute. They must know something. Or think they do." I was careful to say that so he wouldn't take it as an accusation.

He almost smiled. "Well, I did hear a couple of them start talking about it the other day, but they shut up when I came out of the back room." Like his son, Robert senior lost his accent when he spoke in full sentences. "They were talking about Luther... something he said."

"I think we met him yesterday," I told him. "He was over at the church with the pastor. I got the impression he's not quite right somehow."

"I think you're right, but I don't know why." That was odd. From the easy way the pastor spoke the day before, the reason for Luther's condition was common knowledge here. Our grocer must be really out of the loop. Or, for some reason, he was reluctant to speak. Then it occurred to me he didn't want anyone knowing any information came from him. He had to live here, and it could be bad for business. I decided to let it go. Others would talk, gladly.

"Well, like I say, we're not here to trouble you, Mr. McNutt. That's all I really wanted. We may want to talk to you and Robert's mother later." I looked at Robert. "You've got a fine son. He seems to be interested in what we're doing and he's been helpful. He's welcome to watch, so long as he doesn't get underfoot."

Robert senior thought about that a moment before answering and I could see where the youngster got the habit. He looked at his son and I had the sense some understanding passed between them, though there were no nonverbals I could see. Then senior nodded, his head moving no more than an eighth inch. Allowing Robert to follow us around would let him keep tabs on us. To me it also told me he didn't have anything to hide, at least, not in regard to the shooting. There was something there, to be sure, something he was holding back. While it might be germane to the case, or might not, there was no use pressing him. We all have ghosts roaming the desolate regions of our souls. Nor do most of us really like police, not even cops themselves. Maybe it was that. I made a mental note to run his name through the computer.

Robert's dad walked back to the store. When he did, I noticed something about the way he walked, the way he placed his feet. While it seemed effortless, it was far from casual. It reminded me of a tiger I once watched in the wild: sure, powerful, and relentless. It wouldn't do to mess with Robert the elder. So why was he so afraid?

"Crime Scene is on the way," Dee told me once McNutt was gone. "So is a deputy from the sheriff's department. We might as well seal off this place now." He held up a roll of yellow plastic tape and a stapler. He handed Robert the roll of tape, keeping the tail end in his hand. "Walk this over to the corner, would you?"

Robert took the roll of yellow tape while Dee stapled one end to the corner of the store. "Your dad a boxer?" Dee asked. Robert didn't answer but dropped his eyes. "Well, he moves like one," Dee continued.

Then I remembered something. I couldn't recall the details, but there was a news story years ago about a young contender from Arkansas people thought might be the next Muhammad Ali. He was strong and fast and remained undefeated. Then, out of the blue, he quit just as his career was taking off. I couldn't remember his name, but it wasn't McNutt.

I became aware of Dee and Robert staring at me. Dee had apparently asked me something, but I had no idea what it was. "Senior moment," I said. "Be sure and do the outhouse, too."

I looked to Robert, who was staring at the outhouse and frowning. I could almost see the wheels spinning in his mind, trying to puzzle it out and not wanting to ask. I nearly laughed. Then I remembered what I wanted to know when his dad broke in. "What about it, Robert? Did you see anyone hanging around back here a day or two before the celebration."

He shook his head, still staring at the privy. "How about here? Did you see anyone here at the outhouse?"

This time he nodded. "Yeah, one man."

"Did you recognize him?" Robert's short answers were beginning to get to me and from the look Dee gave him, I could see he was losing patience, too. Yet, it would not help to push Robert faster than he wanted to go. He wasn't holding back or trying to balk. Growing up with his dad, he had learned to ponder before speaking.

"Did you recognize him?" Dee repeated the question.

Robert nodded. "Yeah, it was him. The guy that got shot."

"Smiley Jones?" I asked. "Are you sure?"

"Yeah, it was him. He waved at me."

"When was this?" Dee asked. He was done sealing the blacksmith shop.

"That day," Robert told us. "The day he got shot."

"Really," I asked. "How was he dressed?"

Robert shrugged. "Like everyone else. You know, Sunday go-to-meeting clothes."

"He was wearing a suit and a tie?" Dee asked and Robert nodded.

MURDER IN THE CHOIR

"Do you remember if he had his suit jacket on? Or was he in shirt sleeves?"

Robert thought a moment. "Shirt sleeves. He didn't have a jacket."

"Do you remember what color his coat and tie were?" I asked. The only reason I asked was habit. I didn't think it was significant, but the more details we had, the better.

Robert nodded, animated for the first time. "Yeah. I thought it was a cool tie. Sort of all different colors. Looked like a snake."

"A snake?" I asked. "You mean with its mouth open?" I held up my hand and cupped it like a cobra about to strike.

Robert shook his head. "No, like a regular snake, lying on a log. Sort of brown and shiny. Almost black." I tried to imagine what he meant, but couldn't. Maybe it was one of those fabrics that reflected light differently from different angle. I was about to ask what color pants and shoes he had on when Dee spoke up.

"What about his shirt?" Dee interjected. "What color was that?"

Robert pointed to me. "About like his, only no checks." I was wearing a tan and brown plaid.

"You mean tan colored?" Dee asked and Robert nodded.

I looked at Dee. This was a strange development. "Are you thinking what I am?" I asked. He nodded. "Why didn't the shooter take care of him back here?"

"Yeah," he said. "Why not take the easy shot? Why wait until he was out there and risk missing the shot? Or being seen?"

"There you are," a familiar voice said from the direction of the store. I looked abound and saw Spinks and his partner coming toward us. "What you got?" he asked when they got to us.

"We're not sure yet," I answered.

Spinks pointed to the tape on the blacksmith shop. "What about this?" he demanded. He pulled the yellow tape loose and grabbed the handle of the door.

I threw my weight against the door, jerking it out of his hand. Blood rushed to his face and he opened his mouth to say something. "Nobody goes in until Crime Scene gets done!" I cut in. "That may be the shooter's nest."

He glared at me. "You're supposed to keep us in the loop," he snarled.

"We just found it, not ten minutes ago," I told him. "That's why we're standing here. Waiting for Crime Scene."

"Who's that?" Spinks demanded, jabbing a finger at Robert. The youngster looked at Spinks with hooded eyes, his face a rigid mask.

"A local kid who was curious about what we are doing," I told him. I was about to tell him about the empty casing, but he cut me off.

"Well, get out of here," Spinks told Robert.

"No, wait a minute, Robert," I told him. I turned to Dee. "Get Lonnie on the horn. Tell him his cub scouts are screwing up our investigation. Ask him to get them the hell out of here." A smile tickled the corner of Robert's mouth.

Dee grinned and headed for his cruiser. "With pleasure."

"Wait a minute!" Spinks called after him and Dee stopped. "Look, maybe we got off on the wrong foot here," he added.

"No," I answered. "We didn't. You did. I'm not going to take any more of your bullshit. You either play ball or I'm gone, and if this case goes south I'll swear in court you are the one who screwed it up."

"So what are we supposed to do?" Spinks' partner asked. "Sit around with our thumbs up our butts?"

I looked at Dee. Kruger had a point. The FBI had been called in and they were a part of the investigation whether we liked it or not. "All right," I said. "We'll split it up. You stay with Dee and Spinks will go with me. Once Crime Scene gets here, we'll head back into Nashville and pool what we have." As much as I disliked Spinks, I preferred to have him where I could keep an eye on him. Then, too, he wouldn't try to lean on me the way he might on Dee. Apart from his asshole partner, I didn't think Kruger would be a problem.

"Why don't I stay here with DiRado?" Spinks said. "He can fill me in while we wait. Kruger can go with you."

I looked at Dee. His face was an unreadable mask, but I knew he would just as soon go through a proctological examination. Even so, it was a reasonable request. "All right," I told him. "But DiRado is in charge until Crime Scene gets here. No one goes into the smith shop or the privy."

"The shitter?" Spinks asked. "You found evidence in there?"

"Only a possibility," I told him. "Fresh shit. Stick your head in and take a look if you want to check it out. Just don't touch. You can smell all you want." Behind him I could see DiRado and Kruger grin.

"I'll leave that to the humps," Spinks said. Seeing the look on his face was priceless.

Kruger and I walked around to the front of the building. I told him how we had come to discover the nest and pointed out the opening in the front of the shop. He took out a small set of binoculars and looked at it closely. "Looks like fresh cuts," he said. "Maybe some flash burns, too. Any idea what he was using?"

I showed him the spent shell I bought from Robert and pointed out where it came from. I also showed him the misfire and told him our theory about that. I told him what we had seen in the smithy and about the scratches in the ground by the privy behind it. As we talked, I found the questions he asked were professional and on target. I decided he was sharp enough to have pegged Spinks' arrogance and bluster as a cover for incompetence. I wondered why Lonnie had paired him with Spinks, then concluded it was to make up for Spinks' mistakes.

I glanced at my watch. The morning was getting away from us but there was time to look over the outhouse by the community center before my interview with the reverend. I took Kruger across to the porch and showed him the bloodstains there and on the ground. Then, from the porch, I pointed out the privy behind the shrubbery.

"Why are we checking this out?" Kruger asked as we walked through the center and out the back door.

"Mostly to be thorough," I said. "As you will see, there are some prime spots for a sniper down here. Some of them offer a better shot than the shop, and we don't know it was the shop for sure. I'd say we're ninety-seven percent sure, but we could be wrong."

Kruger nodded. Being thorough is something the FBI understands and drills into all its agents. With most of them, it takes, but many of us remember their lab scandal from the nineties. "Look at that!" Kruger said, pointing to the traditional half moon cut into the outhouse door.

"Traditional country art," I told him.

"No, not that. On the outside of the moon." He pointed. The light was much better than the evening before, and I could see a faint smudge at the lower edge of the moon cut. "Looks like it might be gunpowder residue."

"Could be," I said, taking out a set of reading glasses. Trifocals are a fact of life for me these days, even though I have perfect vision beyond arms length. "Your eyes are a lot sharper than mine."

Kruger didn't say anything, but he seemed to appreciate even that faint praise. *Working with Spinks must be hell on earth*, I thought. I took out a pen knife and carefully opened the door with the blade, holding it wide enough we could both look in.

Unlike the privy behind the blacksmith shop, this one had seen plenty of use. There was a powdering of lime on the floor by the half-empty sack and two fresh rolls of toilet paper hung on nails on one wall. There was also a can of insecticide, probably for spiders. Privies attract flies, and flies attract black widows. Throughout the deep South, their stings are still the cause of too many deaths every year.

"Crime Scene is going to love us for this," I said, closing the door and taking out a roll of yellow tape.

"At least they're privy to what we have," Kruger said with only a hint of a smile.

"Better watch that," I grinned. "Play on words is a serious character defect."

"I know, but it's an art form, too. A pun is its own reword."

I looked at Kruger. "You know, Lonnie is the only other special agent I've come across with much of a sense of humor."

"And they banished him to Arkansas," Kruger said without thinking. Then he realized how that might sound. "No offense," he said. "That was not intended to put down your state. I love it here. Truly."

We walked a few steps in silence. Then Kruger said, "Look, I really mean it. I do love it down here."

I dropped into the patios of deep delta Arkansas. "Nah awfense takin', Mistuh Kroogah. Long ago we learnt to make allowances for the mental shortcomins' of owah Yankee visitors. Gene pool depletion, don't ya know. All the good uns move South."

Kruger laughed. Nor was he being unduly worried by my response. A single remark taken the wrong way can wipe out years of good work and can have a drastic effect on an agent's career. I suspect that's why they're so serious.

I told him about my appointment with the pastor and we crossed the park to the church. The door was locked and no one answered my knock, so we sat on the steps to wait. They were still damp, and after a moment I could feel moisture soaking through my pants. I looked at my watch and saw I was five minutes early.

I tried the door again a few minutes later, but there was still no response. I sat down again and Kruger and I continued talking. At a quarter past the hour, I decided I had misunderstood where the pastor wanted to meet and suggested we try the parsonage.

The parsonage sat about a hundred feet behind the church. As we walked there, I said to Kruger, "Remind me to ask you how a nice boy like you ended up in the FBI." He was still smiling when I knocked on the door.

A large, unsmiling woman answered my knock. I handed her one of my cards and introduced Kruger who showed her his identification card. I told her I had an appointment with the pastor at eleven. She told us to wait and disappeared into the house, closing the door behind her.

I looked at Kruger. He seemed to be listening intently, so I said nothing. We waited for two full minutes before the woman returned. "He is not available right now," she said. "Something came up." Her face was impassive, but there was no question we were being dismissed.

"I can wait," I told her. "Or we can come back a little later if that's convenient."

"He is not available at all today," she replied. Her face was still a mask, but I could tell she was lying and not liking it a bit.

"This is a murder investigation," I told her. "I need to talk to him very soon. I can get a warrant, if necessary."

She started to close the door, but Kruger blocked it open with his arm. "This is an FBI investigation, Ma'am. Is the pastor here?"

"No!" she said, throwing her weight behind the door and slamming it. We heard the dead bolt slide home.

We looked at each other, then turned and walked away. "What do you think," I asked Kruger.

"She's lying," he said. "I could hear her talking to someone in back. It was a man with a strong voice."

"You have sharp ears," I said. "All I could hear was a murmur. Could you tell what they were saying?"

"Yes. He told her what to say, but she didn't like it."

"So the pastor told his wife to lie," I said. "Any suggestions?"

Kruger shrugged. "Well, it is an FBI investigation and she lied to a federal agent. Some places that would get her arrested."

"That doesn't sound like your style," I told him.

"Spinks would," he said. "Think we ought to send him to see her?"

"You have a wicked mind," I told him. "But no, we'll take him at the water hole at dusk." Kruger looked at me in question. "He can't stay inside forever," I continued, nodding to the outhouse behind the parsonage. "I'll ask Dee to have someone bring him in when he comes out to use the john.

Kruger looked at me gravely. "Could stir up a hornet's nest. Think he knows something?"

"I think he knows a lot," I said. "I think he is trying to avoid lying."

"So he gets his wife to do it for him," Kruger murmured.

"As the Good Book says, he will have hell to pay for that," I grinned.

Just at that moment we heard a loud crash and the sound of broken glass coming from the parsonage. "Sounds like it's already started," I said.

"Hell hath no fury like a wife thwarted," he laughed.

A highway patrol car and the Crime scene van was parked by the road in front of the blacksmith shop when Kruger and I returned. Ben Weaver, the lead technician told me they were just about to head home from a case in Hope when Casey called to divert them here. "He told us to take shots of everything we could but hold off going into the shop until he got here," Weaver said. "He wants to see that for himself first. Anything else you want done?"

"Well, there's the space between buildings, but I want his take on that, too. I guess you could start with the outhouse there," I told him. "I don't think Casey would mind your going over it. There's not a lot there, but you might find some hair. Be sure to take some shots of the scratches in the ground there before you go inside."

"The outhouse?" he asked, looking to see if I was pulling his leg. "I'd rather dig up four graves than do one outhouse."

"Well, there are two, actually," I told him. "One here and the other over by the community center."

"Two?" Weaver screamed. "Well, joyful rapture!"

"It's a shitty world," I told him. "Think of it this way. It saves you a lot of digging." It was all Kruger could do to keep from laughing.

CHAPTER THREE

A Loose Canon on Deck

A deputy arrived not long after the crime scene van, and the highway patrol took off. Dee asked the deputy to keep watch on the community center privy and the space between the blacksmith shop and the other building until the technicians were done. Before going to the parsonage, Kruger and I had taped off a large area around the community center privy, so it would take them a while. The deputy nodded and found a bench in the park that allowed him to keep both in sight. I didn't like the fact he took a thermos and hunting catalogue with him. I would not have tolerated that at the CID, but I said nothing. After all, he was the sheriff's deputy, not mine, and we needed as much cooperation as he was willing to give.

There was not much more we could do in Oak Grove until the crime lab team was done. We arranged a meeting with Spinks and Kruger at the cafe in Nashville to go over the case and left. Spinks said he would be right behind us, but walked into the store. I didn't like it, but there was nothing I could do. I hoped all he was going after was a cold drink or a pack of gum.

I filled Dee in as we drove and he agreed with my assessment of Kruger. He also told me the scuttlebutt that Spinks had been transferred to Little Rock after he created a major mess in Boston. "Lonnie told me Spinks has enough political pull to keep from being sent to Butte, Montana," Dee said. "But he damn near got fired."

"I hope he doesn't take Kruger down with him," I said. "Kruger is pretty sharp."

Dee nodded. "I've run across him before. He does good work."

The lunch hour was over by the time we got to Nashville, but there were a couple of local businessmen lingering over their coffee. We took a table at the back of the dining room and, when the waitress came out of the kitchen, told her there two more joining us. She nodded and brought us water and coffee. Then she went back into the kitchen. I could see her through the pass-through. She lit a cigarette and stood smoking it under the stove hood, chatting with the cook.

We talked about the case for a while, but I was aware of time passing. The businessmen paid their tab and left, and I looked at my watch. We had been there for thirty minutes already and there was no sign of Spinks. "We did say to meet at the café and not at the sheriff's office, didn't we?" I asked Dee. He nodded. I could tell he was thinking the same thing I was. Despite our agreement, Spinks was going his own way.

"Well, there's not much we can do about it right now," I said. "I'll call Lonnie later. We might as well go ahead and order."

We were finished eating and working out a game plan for the next couple of days when the door to the café opened and Spinks came in with his partner. Kruger looked embarrassed, but not Spinks. Spinks walked with a swagger, and when I saw the snide smile on his face, I knew we were in for some bad news.

"We thought you were right behind us," Dee said. "Did you have car trouble?"

"No," said Spinks. "We were rounding up a prime suspect. Two of them. We've been over at the jail booking them."

"Oh, really?" Dee said in a dangerous tone. "Care to share who you brought in?"

Spinks laughed. "Sure. Albert Jones and Luther Adams." Kruger looked like he wanted to dig himself a hole and pull it in over his head. "Adams confessed."

"Jesus, Mary, and Joseph!" Dee swore. He looked like he wanted to tear off Spinks' leg and beat him to death with it.

"Sorry to steal your thunder," Spinks said. "We didn't have much choice once Adams told us he did it."

"Why did you arrest Pastor Jones?" I asked.

Spinks shrugged. "Take your pick. He lied to Kruger, and when we arrested Adams, he tried to interfere. So I busted his ass. Obstruction of justice."

"Just for the record," I said, "the pastor did not lie to Kruger. His wife did. And as for Luther's alleged confession, what he was confessing to was apparently a hunting accident that happened years ago. He confessed to us yesterday, but we haven't had a chance to check it out." I looked at Kruger. "I'm surprised you didn't straighten him out about the pastor."

Kruger shook his head. "I did."

Spinks broke in. "You're just sore you didn't make the bust," he sneered. "Jones told his wife to tell you and Kruger he wasn't there. Kruger heard him."

"Correct me if I am wrong," I said to Kruger. "The pastor told his wife to tell me he was not available. Period. He did not lie to Kruger. She did, but he did not."

Steve DiRado could stand no more. "You dumb shit!" he snarled at Spinks. For a moment I thought he was about to throw himself across the table at Spinks. So did Spinks, who shoved his chair back so fast his chair turned over, dumping him on the wooden floor.

"Hey!" yelled the waitress, coming into the room just in time to see Dee on his feet glaring down at Spinks. "No rough stuff or I'll call the police!"

"We are the police," I told her. Dee showed his badge. "Special Agent Spinks just tripped over his own feet getting up."

"We were just having an intense discussion," Kruger added, showing his identity folder. "The chair caught on the floor. He's all right."

"Oh," the waitress said. "Goodness. That's the second time that happened this week. I told Arly to fix it but his back went out." She tried to help Kruger get Spinks to his feet, but Spinks shook them off. He got up and stood there glaring back at Dee but not coming any closer.

"Well, I'm glad you're not hurt," the waitress told Spinks. "Are you gentlemen ready to order now?"

Spinks ignored her and stalked out of the café. Kruger turned to us and shrugged, holding his hands in supplication. "Don't worry about it," Dee told him. "I'm pissed at him, not you. Go cover your ass." I nodded and Kruger left the building.

I picked up the check, leaving more than a generous tip. The waitress was still a bit unsettled as I paid the bill, and I assured her things were fine. She nodded, mollified, but I knew the incident would be all over town before sunset. Life is tranquil in small towns, and the story of the fight between a state cop and an FBI agent would send ripples across conversations for weeks. No doubt it would grow as it passed from one fertile imagination to another.

Dee was waiting for me on the sidewalk. "I'm sorry about that," he said. "Stuff like that goes on with Spinks all the time and I've just about had it."

"Don't let him get your goat, Dee. The case isn't worth getting yourself in a jam."

"A worse jam," he reminded me. "This whole thing is turning into a real goat grope."

"Well, there is an upside," I replied. "It gives us some leverage with the pastor. We can lean on him and Spinks will get the blame."

"It can also get him off the case," Dee growled, still torqued.

"Yeah, but why don't you let me make the call to Lonnie? He may say 'no' and it's better if he says it to me." While Dee is a man who believes in plucking his own geese, there was a lot of sense in what I said. The name of the game these days is politics. Maybe it always was.

"All right," he said. "We may as well talk to Jones first. Hear his side of it."

We walked across the square and down the street to the dismal brick building that houses the county jail. Arkansas is one of the poorest areas of the nation in many of its rural areas, and Nashville was not a seat of prosperity. Nor is it in a progressive part of the state or one too concerned with the well being of prisoners. Such issues were considered a luxury, and the jail reflected that attitude.

The jail house was essentially a collection of iron cages inside a brick shell covered with a tar roof. Set at the center of a block without trees and surrounded by newly paved parking lots and a high chain link fence, the jail was a dismal place. With no shade or air conditioning, except for window units in the jailer's office, it acted like a solar collector in the summer and shed heat quickly in the winter.

The object was clearly punishment, whether the prisoners were guilty or not, and the interior was even more dismal than outside. The office suite was freshly painted in generic white with some attempts to soften the setting, but the cell block was decorated in the same dismal pea green as schools were throughout the South in the fifties. Only the floor was different, made of smooth, unpainted concrete, broken only by dark brown stains I thought must be blood. Combined with the blaze orange jump suits the inmates wore, the ambiance was anything but soothing. When in doubt, punish.

We stopped by the office the sheriff gave us to use. It had a desk and two chairs, and the glass partitions made it seem less cramped than it was. I asked the jailer to bring Jones there for an interview. For a moment, I thought the man was going to refuse, making us use the dismal interrogation room I'd seen near the cell block. Yet, a look at Dee's face convinced him it might be wiser to bend the rules.

When the pastor came in, he was shackled and cuffed, but I was glad to see he had not faced the indignity of being deloused and forced to wear an orange jumper. He was in a white dress shirt and faded black chinos, but his belt and shoe laces had been taken along with his tie. Even so, he carried himself with the same dignity I imagine he carried to the pulpit. Nor did he seem frightened. The only emotion I could see was a deep anger that burned in his eyes.

I decided to work the venom. "Good afternoon, Pastor," I said, offering him the best seat. "I regret the misunderstanding that precipitated this inconvenience."

"Inconvenience!" he spat back at me, holding up his cuffs. "You call these things inconvenient?"

"Let him loose," I told the jailer, who was watching from the hall.

The man started to refuse, but Dee looked at him with a raised eyebrow and held out a hand. The jailer gave him the keys and Dee unlocked Jones. Then he tossed the manacles and shackles to the jailer, who stepped down the hall to his desk near the front door.

"Please," Dee said to the pastor. "Have a chair. Can I get you water or something else to drink?"

"You can get me out of here," the pastor snapped, but he sat down. "Failing that, you can get me an attorney and one for Luther, too."

"We can do that," I answered. "On the other hand, this whole thing is not about you. All we're after from you is some information. We're not out to create problems for you or for Luther. If you insist on having an attorney present, it will delay getting you released…and Luther, too."

At the mention of Luther, the skin around his eyes tightened. "Don't you understand what this will do to Luther!" he said. "Keep me if you have to, but not him. He doesn't belong here. He's weak. Those animals back there will tear him apart."

"Yeah," said Dee. "It can get bad in here. I'll see what I can do about keeping him isolated from the others. But, if I'm going to stick my neck out, you're going to have to help us out, too. Up front."

The pastor thought for a moment. "I don't know," he said. "I'm not sure what they're holding me for. They think Luther is the killer."

"We all know he's not," I interjected. "Not if what you told us is true." The pastor nodded. "We also know Spinks is holding you on a thin bust. So help us out. I'll work things out with the Bureau."

The pastor thought for a long while. Then he shook his head. "I'm sorry, Dr. Phillips. I really do need an attorney present before I answer any questions. I would like to help you, but I don't trust the system. However, I will cooperate as fully as my attorney allows me."

I nodded. In his shoes, I would have done the same. Not only was he within his legal rights, but he was right in his assessment of the criminal justice system. One of the reasons for my retirement was losing confidence in the system I served. I had witnessed too many miscarriages of justice.

"All right," I said. "Would you be willing to talk to us about Luther's accident? Or to one of us, if not to both."

He thought for another long moment, then nodded. "Yes, I'd be willing to talk to you. You're no longer a police officer."

Dee smiled. "I'll see what the charge is." He headed up the hall to talk to the jailer, and I decided not to correct the pastor's misconception. While I'm not attached to any specific police department, I am still a sworn peace officer in the state of Arkansas. Not that it would matter that much in court, particularly in capital cases.

"Do you mind if I take notes?" I asked, and Jones shook his head.

I took a pen and a steno pad out of my rucksack and flipped to an empty page. I jotted down the date and time and the name of whom I was interviewing, and when I looked up, the pastor was smiling. "You're very organized," he said.

"Actually I'm not," I told him. "If I don't do this, I'm lost. My memory is not what it was."

"Whose is?" he murmured and, without prompting, began to speak. "There were six of us, all born and raised around here. There was Wilbur, Luther Adams, Luther Jones, Luther Goodman, and myself. We were the choir boys," he said, smiling at my frown. "Yes, with three Luthers in the choir it was very confusing, and there were times we took advantage of that. Among ourselves, Slide was what we called Luther Jones, because he first played trombone, and Luther Goodman was Goodie. Luther Adams was the only one we called by his given name."

He paused a moment to let me catch up. I read back what I had and he nodded. "Wilbur was about twenty years older than the rest of us, but it didn't seem to make much difference back then. He was like a kid himself, and he was who organized the choir. We did just about everything together, but what really made us close was music. We sang in the church choir together, but we also worked up our own music on our own. They call it blues now, and Wilbur used a lot of it to get himself started in New Orleans."

"You didn't perform as a group?" I asked.

"There wasn't much for us," the pastor told us. "We made the circuit of black churches here in southern Arkansas, but that was all gospel music. We pushed it as far as we could, messing with rhythm and syntax, but we couldn't sing our own music in church. The only place we could was in roadhouses and nightclubs, and we knew better than to ask the preacher about that." His smile was very sad. "You see, my dad was the preacher then: Albert Jones, Senior. He was a rather hard-shelled Baptist. No drinking or dancing was allowed, of course, but nothing that smacked of works of the devil, either. Since it took place where it did, he considered jazz and blues and ragtime the works of the devil."

"You still did it, though?" I asked.

"Of course," he said. "Since then I have come to understand that all music is sacred…at least real music. It's God's clearest way of speaking to us, but back then I was just being rebellious. I knew my dad was wrong to judge our music the way he did, but that didn't keep me from feeling guilty. Nor did it do much to bring my dad and me closer."

He paused for a long moment, then looked at me, assessing what he saw. "I see why you were so good as a policeman," he said. "I haven't talked about that in years."

I shrugged. "To tell you the truth, I just listen. People seem to talk to me."

"That's why," he said. "You listen and few do. The police I've known are either fools or trying to make themselves look good by finding a quick solution."

I smiled. "One thing my father taught me was that a person doesn't learn much when they're talking."

Albert Jones nodded. "Then I'm not learning much here, am I?"

I laughed. "No, I think you are. You listen with your eyes."

He looked at me intently for a long moment, then nodded but said nothing.

"We seem to be getting off the subject," I prodded gently.

"Yes," he said. "On the other hand, I'm always intrigued when I run into someone as intelligent as myself." The way he said it was not bragging. It was a simple statement of fact. "I expect you find yourself lonely on that accord," he added. "I do. One of the reasons I grieve Wilbur's passing so much is because he was one of the few people I knew who understood what I was saying, and what I was not saying, too. I suspect you listen for what is not said, too, don't you?"

He had me cold, so I smiled and nodded. "Silence can be eloquent," I said.

He nodded, then sighed. "You do understand that talking about all this is painful to me," he said. His eyes were soft now, and moist. "There was a time when I covered the pain with anger, but that was not good. Rage is a cancer that eats the soul."

I nodded. There was nothing to say. The pastor sighed. "Grasp the nettle firmly," he murmured softly, speaking to himself. "Remember the good." He was quiet for a moment longer and began speaking so softly I could barely hear. "We called ourselves the Soul Men Six. That way we could do what Wilbur did. Sing in church and at the roadhouses, too. Only we never made it to the roadhouses. Luther accidentally shot Goody, and we sort of fell apart after that."

He looked at me. "You wanted to know how it happened. It was stupid. We were out squirrel hunting. All we had was a single shot .22 rifle that belonged to Slide. He was the best shot, but we took turns and Luther was up. Goodie was out front being the dog. Whoever was dog would spot a squirrel and point where it went up a tree to whoever was shooter. The rest of us would stand real still and the dog would walk to the opposite side of the tree. Squirrels like to stay out of sight, so this would push the squirrel around to the shooter's side, so the shooter could pop him."

He looked at me and I nodded. We used the same strategy when I was a kid and we didn't have a good squirrel dog. The pastor went on. "We pretty much had filled our sack and that was the last one for the day. We would have let it go, but Luther missed all his shots and he wanted to get at least one, so we humored him. Problem is, Luther was always clumsy. He had the gun up and the safety off, but he didn't have a clear shot. There was a branch in the way. So he eased forward and he tripped. The rifle went off when he hit the ground, and the bullet hit Goody straight through the eye."

He stopped talking. When he turned to me, there were tears running down his cheeks unnoticed. "Luther has never been the same since. None of us have. Wilbur poured his grief into his music, and I suppose that was part of where it got its power. Slide was always a drinker, but after that he grew hard and sour and got in with a bad crowd. He got a job as roustabout for a carnival that came through a couple of years later, but I wasn't sure exactly whatever came of him until he showed up here again a couple of years ago, and we got reacquainted. I think Wilbur mentioned working with him on the carnival circuit for a while at some point."

Albert Jones lapsed into silence then looked up. "You're wondering about me, aren't you? What happened to me?"

I nodded and he continued. "I finished school and then went to Grambling, which is where my dad went. I did all right there. Played football and tried to leave faith behind. I stopped going to church and got involved in the civil rights movement. That became my God, freedom and self-will. I went up North raising money and recruiting Freedom Riders and sleeping with every white woman I could. There were a lot of them, too, and I've always wondered how many black kids I left behind."

He looked at me. "I'm not proud of that part, but back then..."

I nodded. "Everything was crazy back then," I said. "How did you ever make it back to being a pastor again?"

He laughed. "Ever read *The Hound of Heaven*?"

I nodded. "As I remember, it's a long poem, or maybe short prose set to poetic meter."

"Yes. Well, my own celestial hound just wouldn't let me be. Can you keep a secret?" He saw the look on my face and added, "It has nothing to do with your investigation, believe me. On the other hand, it would shock some of my good church folk around here."

I shrugged and he took that for assent. "I ended up in South Dakota at a Benedictine monastery. It was the only way I could get away from the women. I mean, it got so bad I was losing weight."

I chuckled. "God give me chastity, but not yet!" I said, quoting a famous Catholic bishop.

"Exactly." He was smiling. "Can you imagine what some of my folk might think about that! Yet, it was the most peaceful time of my life, and I almost stayed there. I loved the daily hours, the times for prayer, and I even came to really get into the Mass."

"Why didn't you stay?"

He smiled. "The abbot was a very wise man. He knew right off I didn't belong there, but he let me find that out on my own. This is where I am called, Doctor. This is where God wants me and where I belong. But, I still write to the brothers, and every once in a while I go there for retreat. I draw a great deal of nourishment from that well."

"My friends call me Jazz," I told him.

He thought about that for a moment. "Mine call me Albert," he answered and offered me his hand. I took it.

We were silent for a moment. "Is there anything else?" he asked.

I looked back over my notes and noticed something. "Did I miss someone?" I asked. "You said there were six of you and I only have five down. You, Wilbur, and the three Luthers."

"Yes, there were six of us. The other was Edward…Edward Posey. I forgot him, but people always do."

"I'm not sure I understand."

"Edward is one of those people who others don't seem to see," he told me. "We called him Eddie, and even though he was the youngest of us, he looked like Wilbur or Luther—Slide Luther. That was part of the problem, I guess. People always confused him with Smiley or Slide. Nor was he one to toot his own horn. He seemed to like being anonymous."

"Whatever happened to him?"

"No one seems to know." There was something in the way he said this that told me he was hiding something. I decided to come back to it later, if necessary.

"So he wasn't here for the birthday celebration?"

"No, I'm pretty sure he wasn't. I think I would have noticed. I did see Slide here, but I didn't get to visit with him much. Of course, I doubt he would have made much effort to talk to me just then."

"Why is that?" I asked. "Did you have a falling out?"

"No, nothing like that. He and I are friends and we visit from time to time. There were just a lot of people here, and at these things the pastor is always surrounded by people trying to get a word with him. Slide came here to talk to Wilbur and I had the impression he was keeping a low profile."

"Did he talk with Wilbur?" I asked.

"I'm not sure. I never noticed them together, but then there were a lot of people needing my attention." He shrugged.

I nodded. "I think that's all I need for right now. I really appreciate your cooperation. We will want to talk to you more when you have a lawyer."

He looked at me and nodded. "That's really not necessary now," he said. "I don't think you'll try to railroad me. Get your friend and I'll talk."

I shook my head. "As a friend, I wouldn't advise it. I'm not worried about me or Dee, but Spinks. No. You need to insist on a lawyer until we get the mess he made cleared up."

"A most unpleasant man," Jones agreed. "What's he afraid of? Or is it a racial issue with him?"

"I'm not sure, but he's scared and that makes him dangerous," I said. "Let me talk to his boss and see what I can do. In the meantime, insist on a lawyer."

I left to find a phone to call Lonnie. Dee saw me and headed my way. I told him Spinks was way out of line, and I was going to phone Little Rock. He looked at his watch and grinned. "Good luck. I just happen to know Lonnie is on the golf course this afternoon," he told me. "He hates to be interrupted."

"Maybe he got rained out," I said. "I need to talk to him right away."

"So insist on being put through. Seems to me you have good cause."

"Does he have a cell phone or pager?" I asked. "I'd rather go direct."

"Cell phone and state of the art." Dee took out a small address book and looked in it. He frowned. "No luck there." Then he stopped.

"Damn! What am I thinking?" He took out his cell phone and did something. He handed it to me. "Your tax dollars at work. I have the number stored here, and it's current. I talked to him on it two days ago."

The phone was connected when I put it to my ear. I listened to it ring a dozen times and was just about to hand it back to Dee when someone picked it up. "What!" snarled a surly voice.

"Hello, Lonnie. Jazz Phillips. Sorry to bother you. It's urgent."

"Just a minute." I heard him tell someone else he would catch up later. A few moments later he was back on the line. "All right, go ahead." There was no trace of anger in his voice.

"We may have a touchy situation here." I told him what had happened at the crime scene in Oak Grove, about our efforts to work with Spinks, and how the arrests were made. "There was no legal basis for the arrest," I said. "The sooner we get both men released, the less likely they are to raise a stink."

"Not possible," Lonnie told me. "At least, not with Jones."

"Why not?" I asked.

"Spinks sent us a set of prints right away when they were booked, and the system was not busy. We got an immediate hit. Jones has a federal warrant out for his arrest."

"What's the charge?" I asked.

"I don't know what the original charge was, but it must be something big. What we have on him now is a fugitive warrant that says he may be armed and dangerous. So there's no bail, either."

"What about Adams?" I explained what Luther was confessing. "He's an old man, Lonnie. Not well. We need to get him out right away."

"All right," Lonnie told me. "I'll call Spinks and tell him to get on it now."

"What about Spinks?" I asked.

"So what about him?" Lonnie's tone told me to step cautiously. I knew that in his mind, he thought he had already made a major concession.

"Don't you have something for him to do in Butte? I think his talents may be wasted around here."

Lonnie chuckled and evaded my question. "What about Kruger? How is he doing?"

"Kruger's a good agent. And a good man. If I were still with CID, I'd hire him away from you."

"He is good," Lonnie said. "I'm glad to have him." He fell silent.

"So, what about Spinks? You think you could put him on something else?"

There was a long silence. "Think about it, Jazz. Put yourself in my place. Right or wrong, the guy just made a major felony bust. Taking him off the case would be a slap in the face. The only way I could justify doing that is to put him in charge of something big. There's not a lot going on right now and, as you put it so well, I think his talents would be wasted."

It was my turn to be silent. It was Lonnie who spoke first. "Well, if there's nothing else, I need to get back to my game."

"All right, Lonnie. I'll write up what I have, and Dee will send you a copy. I think it may be time for me to go home. This is turning into a real disaster."

He spoke so softly I could barely hear him. "Well, if that's the way you feel about it. I never figured you for a quitter."

The words stung. "Then we're both surprised. I thought we were friends, but apparently not. Thanks for the heads up. I'll give you one in return. You might want to know is that my final report will contain everything I've told you along with your response. One copy will go to your headquarters in Washington and I wouldn't be surprised if one didn't end up with the *Washington Post*."

"You son of a bitch!" he snarled.

"As a matter of fact, I am," I told him calmly. "My mother was hell on wheels! I hope you enjoy Butte." I hung up. I looked at Dee. His face was grave. I grinned. "Forgive me, Father, for I have sinned. And I really enjoyed it."

"Are you really bailing out?" Dee asked me.

"Of course, not," I answered, looking at my watch. "Just wait. He'll call back. Three minutes, maybe five at the most."

Dee looked at me like I'd just told him the world is flat. "The *Washington Post*? For real?"

"No, at least, not yet. Having a nuke doesn't mean I want to use it."

Lonnie was more torqued than I imagined. It was a full seven minutes before Dee's phone rang. Dee answered it, and I could hear angry squawking from the receiver. After a minute he said, "Let me look around. He was here just a minute ago." He grinned and covered the microphone. "Guess who?" he asked. "Are you ready to talk?"

I nodded and he handed me the phone. "This is Phillips," I said, pretending I didn't know who was on the other end.

"Does this need to be a pissing contest?" Lonnie asked. It was the closest I would ever get to an apology.

"I hope not," I answered back. "I think I'm empty now."

"Would you let me see what I can do with Spinks?" he asked.

"I had an idea about that," I told him. There was stony silence from the other end, and I realized what I had just said. "Sorry. I wasn't being tacky. What I meant was, I have an idea what he could do to be useful to us both."

"I'm listening," he told me.

"There's a lot of stuff he can do with the computer in Little Rock," I said. I told him what I had in mind, which was mostly background checks on the people in Oak Grove the day of the shooting. "I know it sounds like scut work, but I need the information, and I don't have access."

"Kruger's actually much faster with the computer, and Spinks will want him to be assigned to that."

"Tell him that Kruger's going to be going through paper files," I suggested. "I know for sure Spinks would rather be on the computer than in the county file room. It's not air conditioned."

"I thought you liked Kruger," he said.

"I do. He and I will tackle any paper files together. I'm not sure exactly what we'll need there yet. I think I'll want to go over the computer-generated reports first. I could also use some good help on ground. Kruger seems to be good at interviews."

"He's one of the best. That's why..." Lonnie caught himself just in time. I was sure he was about to tell me that was why Kruger was assigned to Spinks, to clean up any messes. Such a remark would embarrass the Bureau. "That's why he won't be in Arkansas long. Someone else will grab him." Lonnie was almost civil now. "Tell you what. I can keep Spinks busy here on the case for a week, maybe ten days. How does that sound?"

"Like manna from heaven," I told him and he chuckled. I had no illusions that we were on good terms again. I don't hold grudges, but Lonnie does. I doubted I would ever be invited on a federal consultation again if Lonnie had anything to say about it. However, I doubted he would. I was still tight with the top agency brass, and I doubted he would object too strenuously. Some of us choose to live in Arkansas because we love it here, warts and all. Lonnie did not, and there was a reason he was assigned here—probably because of his temper. While Little Rock might be sufferance vile to him, Butte was worse and I doubted he would risk badmouthing me.

"I appreciate your letting Adams go," I told him. "At this point, I think he'll be glad to get out and won't raise a stink." I didn't think he had forgotten about it, but I wanted to make sure Luther didn't suffer from our falling out. "I'll give him a ride home. Maybe without Jones along, he'll tell me something."

"Good idea," Lonnie said. "I'll call Spinks."

I switched off the phone and grinned at Dee. "That was fun. You should have taken the bet."

He smiled back and nodded, but he looked worried. "Lonnie won't forget this," he murmured. "He holds grudges."

I nodded. "I know. I hope he doesn't forget. Maybe he'll stay out of our way. Or, maybe he won't. It really doesn't matter."

"What if Lonnie had not called back?" Dee asked. "Would you have quit?"

I shook my head. "No way. I would have still worked on it for you on the Q.T." I glanced down the hall to where the pastor sat waiting. "Why don't you sit in on the rest of this? I think it will be all right."

Albert Jones may have been surprised to see Dee come in with me, but he didn't show it. He looked at us calmly. "They're going to release Luther," I told him. "I'll give him a ride home."

The pastor nodded. "Good." When I said nothing more, he added, "I gather they are not going to release me."

"No," I told him. "There's a federal fugitive warrant out for your arrest. They're holding you on that."

"A fugitive warrant?" He was clearly surprised. "Well, I suppose I do have a common name."

"Actually, they picked it up from your prints." I watched him closely.

At first there was no reaction. Then I saw his eyes narrow and his jaw set. When he spoke, there was no question he was angry. "This is not right. I was given a presidential pardon. That warrant was voided. Years ago."

"Why don't you tell us about it, then?" Dee asked. "Maybe we can get it straightened out."

Jones looked at him coldly. "Don't play cop games with me, Mr. DiRado. I assure you it won't work."

"We're not playing games, Mr. Jones," I responded. "We're trying to figure out who killed your cousin, and I appreciate all your cooperation. The warrant is a side issue as far as I am concerned." I looked at Dee. "I'm done here."

He nodded and waved for the jailer to take the pastor back to the cellblock. "Have they let you have a phone call yet?" I asked. He nodded but said nothing. I handed him a card. "Have your lawyer call me if there's anything I can do."

"What do you think?" Dee asked me when the door to the cell block closed behind Jones and the jailer.

"I'm not sure," I responded. "The warrant is a surprise. I had him pegged as a straight arrow. I wonder what's behind it."

"Easy enough," said Dee, taking out his cell phone. "I'll have our guys run his name through the system. It shouldn't take long.

The call back from his office in Little Rock took longer than Dee expected. Thirty minutes went by, then forty-five. At some point, the jailer brought out Luther Adams for release, and I visited with him a bit while Dee waited. When it had been an hour without word, Dee called in and was told they were having trouble getting the information out of Washington.

We talked it over and decided to split up. It was getting to be late afternoon and someone needed to get back to Oak Grove to see what Crime Scene had found. Since it was a dead area for cell phone reception, I ended up driving Luther home while Dee waited for the call from Little Rock. We agreed to meet in Oak Grove an hour later unless something came up.

Then I ran into another snag. When I started to take him home, Luther wouldn't get into the car. He was docile enough when the jailer brought him out and while we visited. Yet, once we were outside of the jail by ourselves, he became anxious. "Where the pastor?" he asked. His eyes were wild.

When I explained the pastor was going to have to stay in jail a bit longer, the old man became agitated. There was no convincing him it was all right to leave Oak Grove until he talked to Albert Jones. Yet, when we went back into the jail, the shift was changing and the jailer was reluctant to let us see Jones until he got the sheriff on the phone. At some point, I remember Dee shaking his head, raising his hands to the heavens, and rolling back his eyes.

After talking to Albert Jones, the old man calmed down and agreed to let me drive him home. Once we were in the car, he asked to be taken to the drive-in for an ice-cream cone. I suggested a burger might taste good first, and he agreed. The carhop gave me an odd look when she came to take our order, but she greeted Luther by name. He told me she sometimes came to sing with the choir for special performances.

"You still sing in the choir, Luther?" I asked him.

"Oh, yes," he said, smiling for the first time. "I sing. I sing praise to the Lord!" He broke into a hymn, his baritone strong and resonant for someone who looked so old and frail. Several people sitting in cars next to us looked our way, smiling. One of them was our waitress, apparently on break. She turned and said something to the other people in the car. They all laughed.

Luther continued to sing while we waited, and I was struck by the changes I saw in his face as he did. The years rolled away, more with each passing verse, and with them went the deep lines of sorrow. When he finished singing, Luther looked like a young man in his thirties, a dusky angel, prematurely gray. Even as we ate, I could hear him humming softly.

When we left town, we rode in silence for a while. I took my time, driving well below the speed limit. There were some things I wanted to ask Luther, but I found myself reluctant to break the silence. It seemed to still resonate with faint echoes of Luther's hymn: calm, sweet, and deep as the sea.

As if reading my mind, the old man murmured, "It was Luther done it, Dr. Flips." I didn't try to correct his mistake. It's one I run into all the time in rural Arkansas, maybe because so many of the folk there have such poor health care and are hard of hearing. Or maybe their ears are not tuned to distinguish some sounds, the way the Japanese have trouble hearing spoken *r*'s.

I glanced at Luther. He was an old man again now, his eyes rheumy. "Pastor Jones explained to me all about that, Mr. Adams," I said. "It was not your fault."

The old man's sudden agitation took me off guard. "No! No! It was Luther done it. It was Luther! I know!"

"All right, Luther," I said. "All right. I believe you." He seemed to calm down a bit when I said this. I debated for a moment before asking the obvious question. "How do you know this, Luther?"

Once again he became agitated, but less than before. "I tole you. I seen! I seen Luther shoot him." He jabbed a finger at his left eye and raised his arms like he was firing a rifle. "Right there! Pow! Pow!Pow!" Then he burst into tears, racked by deep sobs. "Luther done it. I seen."

It was obvious to me he was confusing the recent death with the older one, and I could see why. Both were people he cared about and both died being shot in the eye. I handed him a handkerchief. "It's all right, Luther I believe you. Don't worry. I'll do something about it. Believe me, I will."

There was no sign he heard me, but after a while the sobs stopped. "Why don't you sing me another hymn, Luther?" I asked. "That last one was nice."

He didn't answer me, but after a long silence I heard him start to hum. At first I thought he was moaning, but then my ears picked up a faint tune. It was an old gospel hymn, slow and very sad, one you can still hear sung at funerals in country churches. When I looked over at him, Luther's eyes were shut tight, and he was rocking back and forth in time to the hymn. Nor did it seem strange at the moment that the rain started again just then, not mist, but big round drops falling like tears from heaven.

I parked by the church when we got to Oak Grove and asked Luther where I could drop him. "This fine," he told me and refused the umbrella I offered him. Ignoring the rain, he got out of the car and limped off down the steep hill behind the church. I wondered if that was where he lived.

I slipped on a poncho and headed across the road to the blacksmith shop. There was no sign of the crime scene team, but I did find the deputy waiting for me in the shop. He glanced at his watch. "I was just about to give up on you," he told me. "Shift ends in a half hour, and I was about to head for the house. Guy in the crime scene team wanted me to guard this until you got here. He's over at the community center."

I asked the deputy to give me ten minutes more. He was reluctant but agreed, and I headed for the center. As I stepped onto the porch, I saw why I did not see the crime scene van when we got to town. It was parked in the lot by the store, but I couldn't see anyone in it.

I found Ben Weaver and his technicians in the community center taking a break. When I walked in, Weaver said, "Hey, Jazz. I wondered what happened to you. Did you and Dee find a bawdy house?" The technicians laughed.

"Fat Boy blues," I said, then gave him a quick summary what happened with Spinks.

"I wondered what he was up to," Weaver told me. "I saw them busting the old man. Pushed him down on the ground and the whole bit. When the pastor jumped in, they busted him, too." He shook his head.

"Did either of them threaten Spinks or Kruger?" I asked.

"Not really. When they threw the old man down, the pastor tried to pull Spinks away, but he really didn't attack him."

"Where were you standing?"

"Down by the outhouse, maybe a hundred feet away."

"Would you be willing to testify?"

Weaver grinned. "Against Spinks? My pleasure. I've run into that piece of shit before. Damn near screwed up a chain of evidence."

"Thanks," I told him. "I appreciate it. You may not have to, unless things get sticky for Dee." I looked at the crew. "So, what do you have?"

Weaver reached into his pocket. "We found this lodged high up on the left side of the store front," he told me, showing me a small bullet in a plastic bag. It was long and pointed and looked undamaged, except for rifling marks on the side. "I didn't put calipers on it, but it's .22 caliber, probably from military ammo."

"In the store *front*?" I asked.

"Just under the eaves on the far right side as you face the store. What *is* very strange is that it was not that deeply embedded. About two inches at the most. We got lucky. It plowed into the end of a rafter. Four inches higher and we would never have found it."

"Any idea where it was from?"

Weaver had obviously been waiting for my question. "The shit house," he said, grinning. "The angle of penetration points in almost a direct line to the shit house. That smudge on the door is gunpowder residue, and when we get the lab tests back, I'd bet they'll point to military ball ammo."

"We're looking at maybe a hundred and twenty-five feet," I told him. "I'd say one fifty at most. Two inches is not much penetration for a military .223 at that distance."

"Unless something slowed it down," he said. "Like a body or a skull. That would account for the slight deviation in angle, too."

"Show me," I said, pointing to the back door, and the two of us headed out.

75

The rain had stopped but the grass was high and wet, and I could feel my shoes soaking through as we walked to the outhouse. When we got there, I went inside and shut the door, looking out through the crescent opening. Sure enough, I could see the upper right quarter of the storefront just over the side railing of the gallery porch.

"That's good work, Ben," I told him. "The angle is a little strange unless he was sitting down near the end of the porch. What about the other two shots? How would you account for them?"

"From what we found in the blacksmith shop, there must have been two shooters," he said. "We found gunpowder residue there, too, and I bet it matches what we found here."

"I can't make it work," I told him. "How do you see it?"

"I had some time to think about it while we were waiting for you," he said. "Say he was standing at the railing on this side of the porch looking toward the store. First shooter hits him in the neck, but it's not a fatal shot. Jones stumbles toward the wall and catches himself with his hand, making the bloody print. He falls back, catching himself on the railing but sliding down. Second shot nails him through the eye with the bullet we found. Then the first shooter nails him once more, just to make sure." He shrugged. "It would help if we knew where he was lying before he was moved."

We walked back to the front of the center, and I walked down the porch. Then I noticed something I had not seen before. "What's that?" I asked Weaver, pointing to some white spots on the porch floor below the side railing. There were dark brown spots there, too, which I assumed was blood.

He walked over to where I was standing. "Looks like bird crap to me." He took out a small scraper and ran it over one of the spots, collecting a bit of white material when the whole spot came up suddenly. "Too tough for that," he said, looking at it closely. "I would guess it's some kind of wax. You suppose they burn candles out here?"

"Maybe citronella," I said. "It looks too white for that."

"There's a yellowish tinge," he said, smelling the wax and frowning. "I can't tell for sure. My nose is still filled with outhouse." He scraped up a couple more samples and placed them all into an evidence bag.

I sensed a presence and looked up to find Robert watching us. I introduced him to Ben Weaver. "Ever seen anyone burning candles out here?" I asked.

Robert nodded. "Yeah, sometimes. When the mosquitoes are bad."

"Folks sit out here?" I asked, and he nodded.

"They smoke out here, too," Robert told me. "Ain't allowed inside."

"Was Smiley Jones a smoker?" I asked. "Did you ever see him come to the store for cigarettes?"

Again Robert shook his head. "He didn't smoke. Some of the other men did, but not him." He was studying Ben Weaver carefully. He seemed fascinated by the crew chief's vest with many pockets. "That's cool," he said and Weaver grinned. "You use all those pockets?"

"Most of them," Weaver laughed. "My girl friend says I wear my purse."

"Where did you get that?" Robert wanted to know.

"Mail order," Weaver answered, naming a major sporting goods outlet. "I had a hard time finding them anywhere else."

"What else did you find at the outhouse?" I asked Weaver, trying to get us back on track.

"The usual stuff. Hair, lots of different prints. Even a little blood. None of it much good for evidence. Looks like lots of folks used the privy, then and since. The only thing tied to the shooting was powder residue and a little gun oil on the outhouse door." I nodded, taking this in.

"He was wearing one of those," Robert said, pointing at Weaver's vest.

"Who?" I asked out of habit, distracted by what Weaver told me.

"The old guy who got shot," Robert answered.

"I thought you said he was wearing a shirt and tie," I told him. "The snake skin tie with lots of colors."

"Not that day," Robert said. "It was a long time before he got shot."

"How long before, Robert. Can you remember?"

He thought about it. "Five or six days. Maybe a week."

"You're sure it was him?"

Robert nodded.

"Where did you see him?"

"Same place. Behind that old store where you found the bullet."

"Tell me about it," I said. Robert looked at me and then at Weaver, but said nothing. At first I thought it was Weaver's presence that was putting him off, but then I remembered. I took out a couple of ones and offered them to him, but he didn't take them. Instead, he looked pointedly at Weaver's vest.

Suddenly, I understood. Robert was raising the ante. "Robert, that vest costs a lot more than what I've paid you." He said nothing, and Weaver wasn't helping. He was grinning. "I tell you what," I said. "You help us out for the rest of the case and I will personally order you one of those. But no more one or two dollar deals and not until we're done here. It may be a couple of months before you actually get it. Deal?"

True to form, Robert thought about it before nodding. We shook on it. "So what did you see?" I asked.

It turned out Robert was out in the woods behind the store several days before the shooting. The weather was nice and he was looking for any snakes that might still be out. I'm not sure exactly why he wanted them, but he saw a man out behind the store. The man was looking around a lot, like someone who didn't want to be seen, and that made Robert curious. When he saw the man go into the blacksmith shop, he crept closer to see what the man was doing.

The man was in the shop a long time, but Robert couldn't see much from where he was hiding. He did hear something—a soft scratching—but didn't know what it was. It went on a long time before the man came out. It was then that he saw who the man was and the vest he was wearing. When the man came out of the shop he looked around then slipped into the woods not ten feet from where Robert lay watching.

"That fits with what we found in the blacksmith shop," Weaver told me. "The edge of the hole you found looked like it was cut very recently, and there were shavings on the floor below it. I would guess he used a very sharp knife. It was cut clean with no splintering."

"What else did you find there?" I asked. Weaver didn't answer, but looked at Robert. I made an executive decision, one I hoped would not come back to haunt me. "It's all right, Ben. Robert knows how to keep his mouth shut. He's the one who found the first empty case. Anything classified you can put in your written report."

"I won't be sure until I get the lab results back," Weaver replied. "We found the usual debris. The good news is that no one was in there since the tracks were laid down. There is also a clear line of fire that covers the whole porch on the community center and the powder residue I told you about. The bad news is that the soda can was clean. No finger prints. We can check it for DNA."

"Good idea. What about the footprints?"

"They were all made by the same person. He wears a standard-width size ten, and these probably had crepe soles. There were no separate heel marks, and the edges were rounded. There were no sole pattern marks, either, but the guy walks on the outside edge of his feet. The side and back of the heel are worn down in a very distinctive way. I would guess they were old shoes."

"Any idea what size individual?"

"I'd say average, maybe on the small side. I would look for someone five nine to five eleven, between a hundred and forty to maybe one ninety. Or about half the men in the state."

"Nice of you to narrow it down so much," I said. "What would you guess from the debris?"

"I would guess African-American from the few hairs we found, and older, maybe, too. A couple of them were gray. They were cut short, about a quarter to a half inch."

"Any chance of a DNA profile from the hair?" I asked.

"I doubt it," he answered. "I didn't see any follicles. On the other hand, we do have enough to match general physical characteristics, and the lab may give us more."

"I don't suppose there were any empty casings." Weaver shook his head. "What about fibers?"

"We did find some. They look olive green, like this" he pointed to his vest, "but we need to wait for the lab to tell us what they are. My guess is that they are from the vest on the guy Robert saw."

I looked around. The gathering clouds were quickly dimming the afternoon light and I could hear distant thunder. "Are you pretty much done here?" I asked Weaver.

He grinned. "Unless you have another outhouse for my crew. They really appreciated that. Messy, but it doesn't take long. Not like the blacksmith shop."

I offered him a twenty. "Why don't you buy them a round on me when you find a dry county?"

He looked at the bill but didn't take it. "I appreciate the offer, but I can't do it, Jazz. These new rules won't let us."

"Even from someone on the team?" I asked.

"Especially from an outside consultant," he replied. "I can tell the guys you offered. They will appreciate that."

I nodded. Even Arkansas seems to be moving at flank speed toward the twentieth century. It's a pity the rest of the world is in the twenty-first. Or that major graft is overlooked or written into law while simple gestures of gratitude like mine are policed.

I decided to call it a day and check in with Dee. There was no sign of him yet, and I figured he got stuck back in Nashville. It was too dark now to see much in the blacksmith shop. I thought about going by to talk to the pastor's wife, then decided the wiser course might be to wait until I had someone with me tomorrow. I figured she was probably not too happy with her husband's arrest and would not hesitate to vent her wrath on anyone remotely official.

I was halfway back to the car when the lady herself came out from the church and waved for me to stop. There was no way I could pretend not to see her, so I turned and headed toward the building. She stepped back inside, out of the weather, and watched me approach through the open door.

I was prepared for outrage, but when I walked into the church, Mrs. Jones was quite calm. When I tried to explain the arrest was not my idea, she smiled. "Serves him right," she sniffed. "Asking me to lie for him like that!"

"Any idea why he did, Mrs. Jones?"

"Please, everyone calls me Emma, Dr. Phillips."

"Most everyone calls me Jazz, Emma," I answered and she smiled.

"He was trying to protect Luther. Did he explain about Luther at all?"

I told her about our conversation at the jail and Luther's release. "He headed down the ridge when we got here," I said. "Does he live down there?"

"No," she said softly. "He was probably going to visit Goodie's grave. He does that a lot...more since Wilbur was shot."

"I can understand why. That's two of their original group gone, both shot to death. I would find that very disturbing, even without being the one who was directly involved the first time."

"It *was* an accident, you know."

"Yes, Albert stressed that. Yet, I'm afraid knowing that wouldn't make much difference, at least not to me. I would say the same is true for Luther, too." She nodded her head. "What did you want to see me about, Mrs...Emma?"

Her face turned serious. "I don't know what they told you about Albert at the courthouse, but I wanted you to know the truth about it. There was a time he was wanted by the FBI, but he was pardoned. We have the paper in the safe deposit box. It was signed by President Carter...one of his last official acts."

"What was Albert wanted for?" I asked.

She gave me a long look. "I can't see how that matters, but it is a matter of public record. He was lumped together with a whole bunch of other people when the FBI was after the Black Panthers." Her face grew grim. "No, let me put that another way. It was when the FBI was trying to exterminate the Black Panthers. There was very little about it that was legal."

I had to agree. That whole chapter in FBI history is an embarrassment to the Bureau, and one I hope they never forget. Very few of even the most radical activists were prosecuted, even though they were guilty by their own admission. The reason they were never brought to trial was because the investigators broke so many laws so flagrantly in the course of the investigation that the government would have had to prosecute them, too. One of the worst incidents was the cold blooded execution of Fred Hampton in Chicago in 1968. As far as I know, there was never much official interest in prosecuting that.

I nodded. "You're right. Do you have any idea why they might have been interested in Albert in the first place?"

She thought a moment. "Their file on him goes way back, to the early days of the Civil Rights movement. He was quite taken with the Freedom Riders and corresponded with Dr. King and some of the others. He was at the top of our class in high school and planned to join them after we graduated." She smiled. "He was ready to quit school and take off for Montgomery, but Dr. King advised him to finish school first. Then he was drafted right away and spent four years in the Army. Dr. King's people advised him not to resist." She paused, remembering.

"When he came back from the Army, things had changed quite a bit. He had changed, too. The Army picked him for Special Forces and then kept him in two extra years. When he came out, he was so angry. They released him in Los Angeles, and somehow he met Bobby Seales. That was before the Black Panthers were formed, but Albert met the men who would lead it. He wrote me and told me about it, all about how discouraged he had become with Dr. King's nonviolent movement. He said violence was all the system understood and that black folk would never achieve equality until they took up arms and forced white America to give them justice." She stopped, tears gathering in her eyes. "You know, I didn't care about any of that back then, not that much. All I knew was that the beautiful, gentle man I sent off to the Army came back as an angry stranger, so full of anger I almost left him."

"No wonder they started a file on him," I responded. "He probably scared them to death even talking to Bobby Seales. Do you recall why the warrant was issued for him?"

She looked at me as if I'd asked which way was up. "You just said it," she told me. "They knew how he was trained and what he could do. He frightened them to death like a lot of other people they arrested."

"Yes, I understand, but that wasn't what I was asking. Was there a specific charge mentioned, like illegal possession of weapons or conspiracy or something else? There usually is when a warrant is issued."

"Oh. Well, yes, but it was absurd. They wanted him as a material witness to whatever they were trying to get against the Panthers."

"That was all? A material witness?" She nodded. "Then why did he run?"

"He didn't know that at the time. All he knew was that there was a federal warrant out for his arrest. He ran because people were getting killed in custody, even when the FBI was involved. Or, maybe, *because* the FBI was involved."

"So he came back here to Arkansas?" I asked.

"No, he went to Canada. It was easy to get into Canada back then, and the government there was reluctant to extradite anyone for what they considered a political crime." She smiled. "Canada was good for him…very good. He was able to work his way through college there, and it was during that time he found his faith again. He even went to seminary there."

"He had a conversion experience?"

"No, it was more like a quiet awakening. He never stopped writing to me, you know, even through his angry days in California, and I think I may have had a little to do with his change of mind. I never hesitated to tell him exactly what I thought, either." She smiled. "I can be quite emphatic at times."

I laughed, thinking of the sound of glass breaking in the parsonage the day before. She gave me a sharp look. "My wife, Nellie, can, too," I said, not lying for a minute. "I think it may be gender-related."

"You mean you men can be so pig headed," she scolded, but very mildly. "Albert tells me I was his angel from the Lord, and I think he's right. They are not exactly the gentle creatures most people think."

What Emma was telling me put a whole new cast on things. I wondered if Albert Jones might not fit well as a suspect. One thing was certain. Trained by the Special Forces, he would certainly know his way around the M-14. He would also be a crack shot, even if he had not held a rifle in years. I made a mental note to check where he was when the shots were fired.

"You said he was pardoned. Tell me about that."

"Yes," she said. "Bless Jimmy Carter, even if he was a southerner. It was one of his last official acts as President." She thought for a moment. "There's not much to tell. I got a lawyer with good political connections, and he was able to get it done. Some of the NAACP people were involved. There were some people in the Justice Department who opposed having the fugitive charges dropped, but the pardon took care of everything. I'll show it to you. The way it's worded covers any and all crimes. That was to keep someone later on making a different charge from the same incident. Not that there were any crimes except for standing up for our rights."

I asked her several questions about the day of the shooting and who all she had seen there for the celebration. I ended up with three pages of notes in my steno book. I was sure most of this was duplication, but I knew it might turn up something new, and it never hurts to be thorough.

At some point Emma saw me squinting as I tried to write, and got up and turned on the church lights. "We are probably causing talk," she said with a smile. I suddenly realized we had been alone in the church for over an hour and how this must look to people in Oak Grove It must have showed in my face. She smiled and said, "Don't worry, Jazz. I'm not about to be inappropriate."

I started to say I couldn't imagine her being anything but appropriate but stopped. Crime brings out strange behaviors in otherwise normal folk, and I did not want her taking my words as an insult. Nor did I want her to take it as a challenge, showing me just how inappropriate she could be. "I'm sure you can handle any foolish talk," I told her. "They wouldn't dare."

She laughed, and I asked her about her husband's friends. "The choir boys were not always exactly that," she told me. "There was some devilment they raised around here, too, especially on Halloween.

Mostly they were decent young men, and they were deeply wounded when Goodie died. Wilbur, of course, was about twenty years older than the rest of them and seemed to be the least affected. I don't think he was there the day it happened, but you'll have to ask Albert about that. You have seen for yourself what it did to Luther—Luther Adams—and the other Luther, the one they call Slide, went downhill from there. He was always the wild one, but that seemed to push him over the edge. Come to think, he was a little younger than the rest, too." She stopped speaking.

"I'm not sure what you mean by his being pushed over the edge," I told her. "What did he do?"

"Well, I'm not sure I know everything, but if half what I heard was true, he went pretty bad. Nothing violent, but dishonest. He was always a bootlegger, but mostly for himself and his friends." She nodded. "Yes, I'm talking about the choir boys, including Albert. He's no stranger to hard spirits, and it was Slide who supplied them. After Goodie was shot, he started supplying anyone who had the money, and I understand he got pretty big. I heard he got involved in other things, too…stealing and then drugs. Then he had to leave the state for a while. Seems he got some of the wrong people mad at him, and he had to leave town rather suddenly. He only came back a long while after they were dead."

She looked at me. "You read the article about Wilbur, didn't you?" I told her I had. "Well, when the deacons invited Wilbur to leave, it was Slide he went to before he ended up in New Orleans. It may have even been those very same deacons, of this church, mind you, that Slide angered. They were known as moonshiners, and he probably didn't pay them. Anyway, it was Slide got Wilbur his job with the carnival. I think he decided he could starve to death just as fast playing piano as working as a roustabout." She smiled. "Wilbur really wasn't a physical person. Moving his fingers was about all the exercise he cared to get. It didn't seem to matter whether it was with a piano or one of the ladies."

I laughed. "What about the deacons? Any of them or their kids still around?" It was a stretch, but like human memory, motive for murder is not bound by time. Sometimes it is not even tied to people still living.

Emma Jones shook her head. "They died out years ago and their children all moved away. I can give you their names, but it'll be a waste of time. They're all respectable people now, and they never came back...ever."

"Why don't you tell me, anyway? Then we can cross them off the list." I was thinking of Spinks when I said that. I didn't think there would be any fruit from this line of investigation, but it was something that would keep him busy in Little Rock for a couple of extra days. With luck, it could take him a week.

Emma gave me seven names. She thought four of those lived in or around Memphis, but was not sure where the others were. That was even better. Spinks might have a difficult time tracking them down. Nor could Lonnie say I wasn't keeping the Bureau actively involved.

I looked over my notes. I saw two things I needed to ask and decided to take the easy one first. "There was a sixth member of the choir: Edward Posey. Do you know whatever came of him?"

"Poor Eddy," she said. "He was the youngest one by three or four years. I think the others picked on him pretty bad, especially Slide. Wilbur was his hero, at least at first, and he was standing next to Goodie when he was shot." She shook her head. "I don't know what ever came of him. His family moved away five or six years after the accident, and we never heard from him again. I heard he was drafted and sent to Vietnam, but I have no idea what happened to him after that. He was one of those people other folk never notice. When they did, they thought he was Slide or maybe Wilbur's younger brother. He looked exactly like them."

I did some mental arithmetic. Smiley Jones was celebrating his eightieth birthday when he was shot, which would put Pastor Jones somewhere in his middle seventies. It didn't add up, and I asked Emma about it.

"Wilbur was old enough to be their dad," she told me. "I know Albert must have told you different, but he sees himself as much older than he is. He is still on the prime side of sixty. Even so, Wilbur looked younger than him."

"So Edward would be in his middle fifties?" I asked. Emma nodded. "Then Smiley was old enough to be his father," I said.

"That's true," she said. "There was even some talk that he was. He sure looked enough like him. Back then, Wilbur was a real heartthrob, even to the younger girls." The way she looked at me said she was speaking from experience.

"What do you think?" I asked. "Was Edward his son?"

She frowned. "I really don't think that matters. Let's not go there."

"All right," I agreed. "You told me Smiley was Edward's hero at first. What happened?"

"I'm not sure," she said. "After the accident Edward kept more and more to himself. He still came to church and sang in the choir, but I didn't see him with the others much any more. Wilbur had left town by then, and I know Edward must have missed him. But when Wilbur's name came up, he never had anything to say. The one time I remember, he looked angry. Even bitter."

"Maybe he felt abandoned," I suggested. "Kids do that."

She shook her head. "Maybe so. Who knows?" I had the impression she thought there was more to it than that, but she fell silent.

I decided it was time to ask the tough one. "I need to ask you some things. I am just trying to be thorough. There is one thing I do need do know. Were you and Albert in the community center when the shooting happened?"

"Of course," she said, surprised. "We were talking to a group of people when someone came in and told Albert that Wilbur was shot. Albert was the first one out the door."

"Do you remember who it was that brought the news?"

"Yes. It was one of the children. I told the other policemen this." She was beginning to grow uneasy. "Where are you going with this?"

"I'm just trying to get a clear picture," I said. "Police reports don't always give enough details. Or the right details." That was an understatement. Police reports are often barely literate. There were sharp complaints when I put some of the CID investigators through a course in remedial writing, but it paid huge dividends in clearing cases. It paid off even better in court.

Emma nodded, but she was not convinced. "Please bear with me," I said. "Were you and Albert in the community center the whole time the celebration was going on?"

"Yes. I told the other officers that, too. Neither Albert nor I left the center from the time we came in until the news came Wilbur was shot."

"Neither of you left at all...not even to use the privy?"

I expected her to get angry, but she laughed. "No. Albert would tell you that two things are necessary for the ministry with all the pot luck suppers and long board meetings. One is a brass stomach and the other is a cast-iron bladder. We are very careful to watch our intake at things like that." She looked at my watch. "We better wind this up soon, or there *will be* talk."

I thanked her for her time, and she walked me to the church door. "There is one other thing," I asked. "Are there any other Luthers around here?"

Again, she laughed. "No, praise God. Three of them has been confusing enough. Especially with Slide being mistaken all the time with Wilbur." Then her fact took on a mischievous look. "There *was* a Luther Anne, but she always went by her middle name."

"You've got to be kidding!"

"Not for a minute. She used to live in Nashville, but she grew up here. She married and moved away."

I turned to leave, but stopped. "Where does Luther live?" I asked. "I want to make sure he's all right."

"Thank you," she said. "It would save me a trip. Albert usually checks on him." She gave me directions.

Luther's place was in the deep woods behind the store, not far off the path Dee and I followed that morning. Even though we passed within fifty feet of it, the brush was so dense we never saw it, and I would have missed the turnoff if I had not been watching carefully. It was getting late and light was fading fast in the deep woods. Without my flashlight, I couldn't make out more than the dim outline of the path.

When I first saw Luther's shack, I thought I had taken the wrong turn. It was low and badly weathered with ill fitting boards nailed at odd angles to cover places the wallboards were missing. I found out later it had started out as a barn before being converted into a chicken shed and then a hay barn. At some point, it was abandoned, and later on Luther bought it for next to nothing. There was no power and no plumbing, but it was home to him, and he had lived there for more years than anyone could remember.

There was no light showing when I got there, and I almost went back to the parsonage for better directions. Yet, there was a hint of wood smoke, and I could see faint tracks in the grass by the door. So I knocked loudly. There was no answer, and I turned and was half way back to the path when the door creaked open. I looked around just as Luther stuck his head out. He was holding up a coal oil lantern in one hand, and I saw a stout length of an oak hoe handle gripped in the other.

When he saw who it was, Luther pushed the door farther open and waved for me to come in. I had to duck my head to enter, and I was surprised by what I saw. I found myself in a very comfortable room. Despite the outside appearance, Luther had carefully covered the outer walls with board and batten and had done the same with planks for a ceiling. The floor was made of what looked like old paving bricks laid tight against one another and held in place by sand. His bed was a simple iron Army cot covered with what looked like an old bedroll, and a rough table with two old chairs stood next to a small iron cookstove toward one corner. An old army locker at the foot of his bed apparently served as his dresser, and a small wooden crate stood by his bedside. A worn Bible lay open on it.

Luther offered me a chair, but I told him I was just checking to make sure he was all right. I told him he had a nice place, and he seemed pleased. Then my eyes caught a familiar shape in the dim yellow light and I felt a chill run up my back. There by the door, leaning next to his length of shovel handle, was the unmistakable outline of an Army M-14.

Luther seemed puzzled when I quickly stepped to the door and grabbed the rifle. "Is this yours, Luther?" I asked, and he nodded. Since the shovel handle was behind me, I glanced at the rifle. Even in the dim light I could see it was in very rough shape, and, when I tried to clear the chamber, the bolt was stuck solid in locked position. The same was true of the safety which was on. "Where did you get this?" I asked.

"I found it," Luther told me. "It don't work. Rusted shut. I tried soaking it with kersene, but dint work."

"Where did you find it, Luther?"

"In one of them empty buildings. You know, next to the store."

Suddenly, the mystery of the missing floor boards I'd seen in the back of the blacksmith shop was solved. I pointed to the walls. "Is that where you got some of this lumber?" The way Luther nodded it was clear he did not consider this to be stealing. To him he was simply recycling what others abandoned, and I had to agree. Better it be used for a purpose than left to rot. "That's where you found this," I asked, holding up the rifle. "Under the floor?"

"Yessuh," said Luther. "I found them there, too." He reached to the back of the table and picked up a stained cardboard box about the size of a paperback. He handed it to me, and I looked at it. Sure enough, the lettering told me it was military ball ammunition, caliber .223. It would fit the M-14. I opened the box and counted the shells. From what I could tell, there were about a dozen missing. The markings on their bases were exactly the same as the one Dee had found by the blacksmith shop.

"I am going to have to take this with me, Luther," I told him. "Our lab will have to look at it. It may be evidence."

Luther looked sad, but said nothing. He stood up and held out his hands, as if he expected them to be cuffed. "I'm not going to arrest you, Luther," I said. "You haven't done anything wrong."

He looked surprised and sat down. "Did you find anything else in there?" I asked him. He shook his head, but I could tell he was lying. I decided not to push him at the moment. For one thing, I was alone and without backup. I had no warrant to search nor the authority to enforce one even if I had. Yet, more to the point, I did not think even the rifle had anything to do with our case. Luther was welcome to whatever else he had found as far as I was concerned.

"Will you show us where you found this?" I asked Luther. He nodded. "All right then, I'll see you tomorrow." As I turned, my eye caught something in the shadows on the table. I reached out and picked it up. It was a military commando knife, still in the case. I pulled it out. The blade was bright, clean and sharp. I looked at Luther. "This is what you didn't want to tell me about, isn't it? You found this under the floor, too, didn't you?" He nodded glumly, and I understood. The rusty gun was of no use to Luther and no great loss. The knife was a tool he could use every day and probably did. It would be a big loss.

I slipped the knife back into its case and laid it on the table. "Well, I won't mention this if you don't," I told him. "It will be our secret, between me and you. Thanks for your help."

Luther looked like I had just given him the moon. He jumped up and shook my hand, then insisted on walking me back to my car. The last time I saw him alive was in the rear view mirror as I drove out of town, a sad old man standing there in the rain with a lantern in his hand.

CHAPTER FOUR

SLIDE JONES

There was a note from Dee waiting for me when I got back to the motel. It said something came up that required his presence in Little Rock the following day and that I would be on my own. It also gave me several numbers where I might reach him. I wondered what could be so important to pull him away in the middle of a major murder investigation, then remembered the same thing happening to me when I was at CID. More than likely it would turn out to be something that could have waited or someone who considered themselves too important getting impatient. I hoped it was not something that grew out of my crossing swords with Lonnie.

I changed clothes and headed to the drive-in for a burger and some fries. I love fried food which Nellie never fixes at home mostly because it doesn't love me. It plays havoc with my system, but I have trouble remembering that in the middle of a chicken fried steak. So I get my quota when I am out of town on trips like this one. That's when I use up my quota of seltzer tablets, too.

I swung by the county jail to drop off the M-14 I found at Luther's place. I didn't consider it an important piece of evidence, but it wouldn't hurt to have the state crime lab check it out. Taking it to the county evidence locker would create more paperwork, but it would preserve the chain of evidence if the rifle or the ammunition led us anywhere. Cases can be won or lost on such decisions.

While I was filling out the papers, the deputy in charge of the locker looked over the rifle. "Someone did a piss poor job of camouflage on this," he remarked.

I nodded and kept writing. Then the significance of what he said struck me, and I looked up. "Camouflage? That's rust, isn't it?"

He looked at it closely, then handed it to me. "Nope. It looks like brown paint to me. Or some kind of lacquer."

It only took a glance in the bright fluorescent light of the evidence room to see the deputy was right. What I thought was rust in the light of Luther's oil lamp was some kind of light brown coating smeared over the black matte finish of the bolt and barrel. I scraped it with my thumb nail and a thin sliver peeled off easily. "That's not even paint," I told the deputy. "It's probably something like Cosmoline. With a heavy coat of dust."

I examined the rifle more closely and tried to open the bolt again. It would not move, and rattling it back and forth did not work, either. "Let me show you something," the deputy said, grinning. I handed him the rifle, and an instant later the bolt was locked open. "There," he said, obviously pleased with himself.

"How did you do that?" I asked, feeling stupid.

"There is a little catch here," he said, showing me. "You push that, and it opens even if it's locked."

I tried it and it worked. Then I checked the chamber which was clear. I held my thumb in the breech and looked down the barrel. There was no trace of rust or Cosmoline or gunshot residue, and I could see the lands and grooves quite clearly. I handed the weapon to the deputy and asked him to look and tell me what he saw. "It looks good to me," he said. "Hasn't been fired in a while. There's a light coat of dust near the muzzle, so it's been a while since it was cleaned."

"So it's ready to go?" I asked.

The deputy nodded. "You might need to take the bolt apart and clean the firing pin hole. Sometimes that gets crud in it and the pin doesn't hit the primer hard enough. I think they had some trouble with that in Vietnam. Other than that, it looks ready to fire."

I thanked the deputy and checked the weapon in as evidence, making note of the serial number in my notebook along with the date and place I recovered it. Lab results might take a while to get back, but with the serial number, we could at least start a trace on the rifle itself. I tried to call Dee to set this up, but there was no answer on his cell. So I headed for the drive-in.

While I was eating my burger, I wondered if I was making a mistake in not bringing in Luther Adams. The sheriff would send along a deputy to make the arrest if I asked, but I decided against it. I thought it could wait until I talked to Dee. The old man had been through enough that day and I was pretty sure he had little to do with the shooting. There might be more he could tell us, but it would take patience to get it. Nor did I see any reason for him to run. There was no place for him to go. Now I wished I had decided to bring Adams in. It might have prevented another death.

I tried Dee's cell phone again after supper. There was still no answer, so I left a message for him to call back at two of the other numbers he left. I didn't know who might retrieve the messages, so I simply let him know I needed to talk to him fairly urgently. Then I changed shoes and set out on another walking tour of Nashville.

The message light was blinking on my phone when I got back to the motel. It was Dee calling back, and I dialed the number the clerk gave me. It was not one on the list he left.

A woman answered on the second ring and told me to wait when I asked for Dee. I wondered who she was, though her voice sounded vaguely familiar. After a few moments the woman came back on the line again and asked if Dee could call me back. I told her I was at the motel and would wait there for the call. She asked for the number and I gave it, wondering what was going on.

Ten minutes later the phone rang. It was Dee and he sounded completely exhausted. He told me I had caught him in the shower. My silence must have been rather eloquent because he laughed and explained the woman was his sister. I couldn't remember her name, but I remembered meeting her several times in Little Rock. She was very good looking and very quiet, and she and Nellie hit it off right away.

At that moment, I was more concerned about Dee than about the case, and I asked him if he was all right. That has to be about the dumbest question in the world. We only ask when we think something is wrong. Yet, it did get him talking. He told me things were not good at home. So he had been staying with his sister the last few months until they got things resolved. One of the issues was his work and the long hours it demanded. I thought it was little wonder Dee seemed to stressed. It sounded like his whole life was falling apart.

I told him this and suggested he might want to consider emergency leave. Doing so is frowned on in the macho world of police work, but at this point in his career, Dee had nothing to lose.

When I suggested this, he brushed it off, as I knew he would. Nor could I argue. I would have responded the same way. I know because I have. "What would help me most right now is closing this case," he said. "Your message said it was urgent. What do you have?"

I told him about Luther Adams and the rifle, and why I was reluctant to have him arrested. He agreed with my assessment, and we talked for several minutes about how to cover our choice if we guessed wrong. He suggested I talk to Kruger and see what he had to say. I agreed. That would make the decision a team choice.

We talked for a couple of minutes more. I wanted to ask Dee what was so important for him to do in Little Rock, but I was not sure I wanted to know. Nor did he volunteer the information. So I let it go and asked whomever might be listening to watch over my friend. I am not a religious man, but things were far beyond my power to help, and I figured it couldn't hurt.

I called Kruger next, but there was no answer at his room. Thinking he might be at the jail, I tried there, too. The jailer told me he had seen Kruger an hour or so before I stopped by to check in the rifle. After a couple more dead ends, I gave up and left a message with the desk clerk. I asked Kruger to call me if he got in before midnight. Then I went to bed. I don't sleep well away from home and my own bed, but that night I dropped off right away.

———

I woke early the next morning feeling rested and refreshed, and I surprised myself by singing in the shower. Then I realized something was different. I had not experienced my normal after effects of eating fast food. Whether it was the water in Nashville or the new antacid Nellie and the doctor insisted I take, I was pleased. There may be life after giving up fast food, but it's one of the joys that makes getting up in the morning worth the effort.

I was dressed and filling my pockets when I heard a knock on the door. I looked out the peephole and saw Kruger looking tired and worn. His suit was pressed and his shirt fresh, but he looked like he had been run through the mill. He wanted to know if I cared to join him for breakfast and we headed for the café.

While we were waiting for our food, Kruger filled me in on what had been going on the night before and why he had not called back. The arrest of Albert Jones apparently set off a political fire storm all over the District of Columbia. For, rather than simply showing up today with her husband's pardon in her hand, Emma Jones had made some phone calls before she talked with me. Some of them were to important people Albert had known from the early days of the civil rights movement. Needless to say, they were outraged by his arrest and they began to make calls, too. The result was that no fewer than eight senators from both political parties had called the director at home, setting off tremors up and down the chain of command.

Even though he did not make the arrest and had tried to stop it, Kruger had spent several hours the previous night going through an inquisition. The good news was that Albert Jones had been released in the early hours of the morning, and it looked like Ken Spinks was headed for Butte regardless of his connections. The bad news was that Lonnie was taking all this very personally and blaming me, even though it was his agent who screwed up.

Nor would this be good for Kruger's career. Despite the fact he was the junior agent and tried to talk some sense into Spinks before it went down, he was hit by the splatter. He told me it was so bad he was seriously considering an offer from a private security group.

When I told Kruger about Dee being called back to Little Rock the day before, he agreed it was probably over the Spinks tempest. He brightened up when I suggested we spend the day working together, and he agreed with my decision not to bring Luther in the night before. There was a potential witness he needed to interview that morning in Nashville, and we decided to talk to Luther Adams after we were done with that.

To tell the truth, I was not disappointed to be working with Kruger rather than Dee. I love Steve DiRado like a brother, and we work together so well it is sometimes scary. I often know what's going on in his mind before he does, and I'm sure it works the other way. Yet, I also know there's a liability with this. We think so much alike we sometimes come to exactly the same wrong conclusions, and we can reinforce bad decisions. With Kruger, I would get a fresh perspective, and given the political minefield this case was moving across, we needed every edge we could find.

Kruger told me the witness was a lady who believed in rising late, so we took our time over coffee and swung by the jail on our way. Kruger looked over the rifle carefully and popped the action open without a moment's hesitation. He made note of the serial number and examined the box of shells I brought in with the rifle.

Like the deputy the night before, Kruger mentioned having the lab check the firing pin hole for crud. Then he threw the weapon up to his shoulder and took aim at a spot high on the wall. "I love these old military designs," he said. "I put a lot of rounds through a rifle like this in basic training."

"Old?" I asked, then realized he was right. I remember when the M-14 first came out. I was younger than Kruger then. Old military design to me is the 1903 Springfield or the Garand used in World War II. I grew up hunting with a Springfield A3 my dad liberated from an unnamed source when he came back from the Pacific, but it was older than me. To Kruger, a Springfield would seem as ancient as a flintlock. I wondered how I looked in his eyes. I decided I did not want to know.

The lady Kruger needed to interview was named Anne Smith, and she now made her home in Charlotte, North Carolina. I could tell she had lived there a long while. There were still traces of southern

Arkansas in her voice, but she spoke with that soft, mellow Carolina lilt that falls so gently on the ear. I could have listened to her reading a dictionary for hours.

Like so many other folk who grew up in Oak Grove, she had come back to Nashville for Smiley's birthday and then taken emergency leave to stay for his funeral. She had spent the last two weeks helping the aunt who was clearing up Smiley's estate, which was not that simple. Now she was due to fly back to North Carolina from Little Rock in three days. She was a teacher there and needed to get back to her classroom. Her principal was very understanding, but there was a limit to how long she could be gone.

I listened as Kruger led Anne Smith through the basic questions and I was impressed how quickly he established rapport. The Bureau would lose a valuable asset if he went to the private sector, but Kruger himself would gain. To put it in a nutshell, he was out of their league, and if he stayed on, his career would be one of constant frustration. I made a mental note to bring this up with him when the time was right.

Anne Smith told us pretty much what everyone else had said. "I grew up with Wilbur," she told us. "He was old enough to be my daddy, but he was like a big brother to me." She smiled. "He was like that to all the kids in Oak Grove, and we worshiped the ground he walked on." Tears gathered in her eyes. "I cannot imagine the world without him. He was the best man I knew."

Kruger looked at me. It was an invitation and I took it. "I don't suppose you were in the choir, were you?"

"Are you kidding?" she laughed. "Of course, I was in the choir. Wilbur was the choir master and the piano player, and I had a terrible crush on him."

"So you must know Albert Jones and the three Luthers pretty well then?" I asked.

"Of course, I do! And there were four Luthers, not three."

This was not new information to me, but it was to Kruger. It confirmed something Emma Jones told me in passing but I had not mentioned it to him. I realized we were talking to the fourth Oak Grove

Luther, and my ears must have stood up like a terrier because she laughed again. "I don't know who you've been talking to, but they told you wrong. There were four of us."

"Four of *us*?" Kruger asked.

"Yes, it was so funny. All of our mothers were carrying us at the same time. They all grew up together and had a singing group, a beauty shop quartet. They called themselves the Grove Sisters and I guess they were pretty famous around here. One day they were talking about names for their babies, and one of them said she favored Luther. I don't know exactly who it was, but one of the other mothers said no, she already picked that out if her child was a boy. Then one of the others said she liked it, too, and was going to use it if her child was a boy and was born first. That was May Adams, Luther's mother, and, sure enough, she delivered her baby first. That made the other three mothers mad, so they named their babies Luther, too. That's how Oak Grove got four Luthers."

"Wait a minute," Kruger said. "I 'm confused. You have a brother named Luther, too?"

"No, I'm the fourth Luther," she told us. "I go by my middle name now, but I grew up being called Luther Anne Williams. I didn't think anything of it until I had a friend in college from Minnesota, and she almost died laughing when I first told her my name. I went by Anne after that." She smiled, but there was hurt there, too, and I didn't know how to respond.

Kruger tuned the conversation gently. "You know, everyone tells us what a great man Wilbur Jones was. No one can imagine who might have done this. Do you have any idea who we could talk to that might know? Anyone at all?"

Anne Smith looked at us a long time. "What folks are afraid of is someone knowing they talked," she told us. "People in small towns have to live together for a long time, so they're careful what they say. Particularly to outsiders."

Kruger smiled. "I'm not asking you to rat anyone out," he told her. "We just need to be pointed in the right direction." I don't know how he did it, but Kruger looked like a choir boy himself at that moment, or maybe a hungry street urchin.

Ann looked at him and raised an eyebrow. She thought about it for a long moment and I appreciated how intimidating her students might find that. That reminded me of Robert's dad and I wondered if they were somehow related or if this was a habit black folk in rural areas developed in self defense. "Well, you might talk to Slide," she told us. "He walked on the wild side a long time, and if anyone would know, it would be him."

"By Slide, we're talking about Luther Jones?" I asked. She nodded and I went on. "Can you tell us anything about Slide?"

She sighed. "I can tell you more than you want to know. He and I were sweethearts once. It didn't last long, and it ended because of his wild ways, but he sure could dance." She smiled again. "That was scandalous back then. We were all Baptists here, and the preacher thought dancing was the work of the devil. You know, it was Albert's dad who was our preacher back then. I never will forget the look on his face the day Slide asked how come the Bible talks about David dancing before the altar if it was so bad. You've never seen a black man so dark turn so red—purple as a blood blister. He looked like he was going to pop and spew all over us." She shook her head. "That Slide. He always had more brass than brains. I could have tolerated that, but he was a skirt chaser, too."

"Why was he called Slide?" Kruger asked.

Anne snorted. "Believe me, the name fits him. He was always trying to slide by on style, but he didn't have the sand to do it." Then she shook her head. "That's not why he was called Slide. We called him that because he used to play the trombone. Or, maybe I should say he tried to play. He was never much good at it, but he sure made a lot of noise for a while. He used to brag he was going to be some big time musician. The sad thing is, he might have done it if he stuck with it." She shook her head. "Slide was not much for sticking with anything except his vices." There was an edge of bitterness in her voice.

I nodded but said nothing. Nor did Kruger. After a moment Anne went on without prompting. "Of course, I'm biased when it comes to him. I guess you could I say I'm a woman scorned, but I don't feel vindictive. Mostly, I feel sort of sad. He had so much going for him, and he threw it all away."

"How long has it been since you've seen him?" Kruger asked.

"He was here for the birthday," she told us. "I saw him then, but we didn't speak." She frowned. "It was odd. He was carrying that old trombone of his and I thought he was going to play or maybe do something funny like he used to do when we were kids. Only, he didn't."

I looked at Kruger and he nodded. We were thinking the same thing. An old trombone case was exactly the right size and shape to carry an M-14 carbine. The molded nest the instrument rested in would have to be taken out, but that was not hard to do. It was a perfect disguise for a murder weapon.

"Do you remember how Slide was dressed?" I asked.

She started to answer, then thought a moment. "That's odd. The first time I saw him he was in a dark brown suit. He was wearing a light brown shirt and a multi-colored tie. That's when he was carrying the trombone. Then later when I saw him at the picnic, he had on a beige suit, just like Wilbur, and a different colored tie. As a matter of fact, I actually thought he was Wilbur for a while. Then I saw the two of them together and I realized it was Slide. I couldn't figure out why he changed his clothes."

"Did they look that much alike?" Kruger asked.

"Yes, they did, especially when they got older. When they were younger, people used to tease Wilbur by asking if Slide was his son or his younger brother." She shook her head at the memory. "They looked enough alike that Wilbur got blamed sometimes for some of Slide's mischief. Only, it wasn't mischief later on. It was downright criminal."

"It sounds like you avoided a lot of heartache," Kruger suggested,

"Yes," said Anne Smith. "I suppose I did. My husband is a fine man, and we have a good life and a wonderful family. But I wonder sometimes. I know it's fool talk, but I wonder if I had stuck by him and made him fly straight, maybe Slide might have turned out differently."

I shook my head. "You're better off the way things are," I said. "I can't be absolutely sure, but I would almost guarantee you he wouldn't. My experience is that guys like that take a lot of good people down with them."

"Yes, but you're a policeman. I'm a teacher. Our whole profession is built on hope. I've been around long enough to see that come to fruition many more times than not, even with kids with a lot to overcome."

We talked with Anne Smith a while longer, but she didn't have much else to tell us except that she had not seen Slide in the community center. When she saw him with Smiley, they were at the picnic under the oak trees. She was very sure of this.

After we left, Kruger and I talked about it and were in agreement. Each of us thought Slide Jones was probably the shooter. We debated what might be the best way to go after him. There was not enough evidence at that point to hold him without bail, and arresting him could precipitate flight. While that in itself would be good evidence of guilt, I was reluctant to push too hard. It may be more difficult to disappear these days than it was forty years ago, but it is still possible, and Luther Jones had all the right connections.

We decided to go with a low key interview. This would mean driving sixty or eighty miles to Hot Springs since that was where Slide lived, but there was no way around it. We decided to take off after we talked with Luther Adams. Taken with what Anne Smith told us, it was entirely possible Adams was telling us the truth when he said Luther did it. He might well have been talking about Luther Jones, commonly known as Slide, and it was possible Adams might give us what we needed to arrest Slide and hold him without bail.

What neither Kruger nor I could figure out was why someone else had not come across this information already. The way it looked then, the case should have been a slam dunk even for a rookie fresh out of detective school. The only reason we could think of was that the case had gone so political so fast. As they say, it's hard to drain the swamp when you're ass-deep in alligators. That's as good a description as I know for politicians trying to run the show.

We got to Oak Grove a little after nine and Kruger parked by the store. We headed straight for Luther Adam's shack, but there was no one there. The door was sealed with a padlock and chain, and the panels shuttering the screen vents that served as windows were secured from inside. We knocked twice, anyway, but there was no response. The place felt empty.

Robert's mother was behind the counter of the store when we walked in, and I introduced myself and Kruger. Out of the corner of my eye I saw Robert watching us, and I turned and waved to him. When I asked if they had seen the old man that morning, Mrs. McNutt told us she had not. Nor had Robert and we thanked them and headed for the parsonage.

A few moments after we left the store, I heard the door slam behind us and turned my head to see Robert loping after us. I told Kruger about my deals with Robert and he smiled. He seemed to get a kick out of my unorthodox methods. I guess there was reason for it. Within forty-eight hours my methods, such as they are, had produced more solid information than the previous two weeks' effort. We had the shooter's nest and a very strong possibility for the shooter himself. All we lacked was motive, but with people who have known each other as long as Smiley and Slide, there was a world of possibility.

This time it was the Albert Jones himself who answered the door when we knocked. He smiled at me, then spotted Robert. "What is he doing here?" Jones demanded.

I smiled back. "He's keeping an eye on us. A Baker Street irregular."

Jones chuckled. "Well, he's good at that. What can I do for you?"

"I went by to check on Luther Adams," I told him. "He wasn't there and I wanted to talk to him. Have you seen him?"

The pastor shook his head. "No, I slept in this morning. Luther's probably wandering around here someplace. Did you look in the church?"

I told him we would try that. Then something struck he. "You know, his place was locked up tight. Does he usually lock up when he's not there?"

Albert Jones frowned. "Locked up? No. Luther doesn't even lock up when he goes out of town. What do you mean, locked up?"

I told him about the padlock and chain on the door and the window vents pulled tight from the inside. By the time I was done, Jones was very concerned. "Let me get my jacket," he said. "That doesn't sound good."

We searched the church and the outhouse on our way by, then went over the crest to the cemetery. There was nothing there but weathered grave stones, not even tracks in the sandy soil. Then we went to the community center and checked the outhouse there. By the time we got to Luther Adams' shack, Albert Jones was clearly worried. When he saw the lock and chain, he shook his head. "This is not like Luther," he told us. "Not at all."

We spread out and searched the area around Adams' place, and then spoke with neighbors to the north. No one had seen Luther since the day before, and a couple of men joined the search. I borrowed Kruger's cell phone, which was one of the new satellite jobs, and called the sheriff in Nashville. I filled him in and asked him to send a couple of deputies to help search. I asked him to send along a search warrant for Luther's place, too.

"You think Luther Adams had something to do with the shooting?" the sheriff asked.

"No, I don't. I think we may find a crime scene in his place, and I want us to be covered, no matter what we find."

"What's our probable cause?" Tanner asked.

"The rifle and ammo I found there last night," I told him.

"What rifle and ammo?" the sheriff asked.

I filled him in quickly. The deputy on duty the night before had not put my visit in the night log. Nor had he told the sheriff about my coming by to check in the weapon. I gave the sheriff the serial number of the rifle and a brief description of it and the ammunition box. When Sheriff Tanner hung up, I was glad I was not in the deputy's shoes.

Kruger looked at me gravely. "Don't tell me they lost the rifle."

"I hope not." I told him what happened. "It could be the deputy just forgot to log me in. That's what I'm hoping. I'm glad I wrote the number down."

"No shit." It was the first time I heard Kruger swear. "Does anyone else know about it besides us?"

"Yeah," I told him. "DiRado started a serial number trace last night. So it's in the system."

Kruger took out his notebook. "Well, just for luck, let me check it against my notes. The way things seem to be going...." He left the thought unfinished and I watched as he took out his notebook and carefully double checked it. "That's the number I have, too," he said, looking very troubled.

We looked around a bit more and were headed back to join the others when Kruger's phone chirped. He answered, then handed it to me. It was the sheriff calling back. "Go on in," he told me. "Cut the chain. We have the warrant. I'll have it there in thirty minutes."

"That was fast. Even for Arkansas."

Sheriff Tanner laughed. "I got lucky. I ran into his honor right after I talked to you, and he was in a good mood. The Razorbacks are in first place, and his daughter was elected homecoming queen."

"Let's hear it for the coach," I said. "You don't want us to wait until the warrant is here?"

"No, I have a bad feeling about this. That lock and chain doesn't sound like Luther Adams to me." I had the impression he wanted to say more but didn't.

I hung up and asked Kruger if he had a chain cutter in his car. He didn't, nor did Robert's dad, but when we asked Albert Jones who might have one, one of the men helping search told us he did. When he met us with it at Luther's shack, it turned out to be an industrial bolt cutter, so old and rusty it took two men and some oil to get it to work. Even then, it was designed for cutting steel bars and was almost too big for the chain on the door. The harder they tried to get it to cut the worse things got, and by the time we got the chain cut, a Cub Scout could have sawed through it with a nail file.

When we opened the door, Kruger and I slipped on latex gloves. I asked the men gathered outside to wait there while we went in to look. By then most of the men in town had joined the search and were standing around watching. I asked the pastor to keep everyone out until we were done.

We looked around for a few minutes, but I could not see anything different from the night before. There was no blood and no signs of a struggle, but I did see a shelf full of pulp westerns I had not noticed by the bed. They were old and worn with use, stained from many readings. Yet, what surprised me even more was a worn hardback copy of *Hamlet* standing by them. The name written in the front was not Luther Adam's name, so either he, or someone else, had picked this up at a garage sale or from a used book store. I wondered whose fingers had marked the edge of the pages with a dark stain.

We checked the books, but there was nothing there. People sometimes use books to hide things, but there was no money and no papers. The exception was the Bible by the bed which had Adams' name written in the front and contained a black and white snapshot of a young man. I went to the door and showed the photo to Albert Jones. He told me it was Luther Goodman and looked like it was taken about a year before he was shot. When he asked me where I found it, I told him, and he nodded and turned away.

Kruger and I looked around some more, but we didn't find anything out of the ordinary. Luther Adams didn't have many earthly possessions, so it didn't take us long. When we were done I asked the pastor to come in and see if he saw anything unusual or out of place. He looked around quickly and told us that was the way Luther kept it. He looked around again, then mentioned something I had noticed, too. The commando knife Luther prized so much was gone.

"Would Luther have taken it with him?" I asked.

Jones shook his head. "I guess he might have, but I can't think why. He has a good locking blade knife he carries in his pocket. Mostly he uses the other one around the house like a butcher knife."

I wondered what the makers of the commando knife would think of that for an endorsement. I doubted they would have been amused by their fine weapon being used in the kitchen. *Cuts throats and dices potatoes well.* "Luther seems to be quite a reader," I said. "Do you have any idea where this came from?" I held up the copy of *Hamlet.*

Albert Jones smiled. "Yes, I gave it to him. He asked to borrow it so many times I finally just gave it to him. Next to his Bible, it was his favorite book." I must have looked surprised because he added, "Luther is a well-read man, Jazz. He is not formally educated, but he is much wider read than I am." He pointed to the pulp westerns. "Those are like favorite television shows to him. He reads them to fall asleep."

"That surprises me," Kruger said. "What else can you tell us about him, Reverend?"

"Well, he can fix just about anything. That's the way he earns the little money he needs to live—by fixing things. All he has to do is see someone else do something once and he has it down."

"You mean like appliances and cars?" Kruger asked.

"Yes, he fixes that kind of thing. Where he is really good, though, is with farm machinery. He could work for just about any implement dealer around here when he wanted. All you have to do is show him a piece of machinery, and he can tell you exactly what it came from, not only the kind of machine, but the maker and model."

"So he was able to work regularly?" I asked.

"Well, yes and no both," Albert Jones told us. "He's able to do the work, and he's a hard worker when he can work, but he has these spells from time to time. When he does, it's about all he can do to get out of bed and cook for himself. Sometimes he'll be like that for a week and sometimes longer. So you can't always count on him."

"These spells are related to the Luther Goodman shooting?" I asked.

"To that and some other things that have happened over the years. But, yes, the spells began with that. This time he's been in one ever since Wilbur was killed two weeks ago." He looked at Kruger. "That's why I was so upset when the other agent arrested Luther. I was afraid it would make him worse."

Kruger nodded. "I'm sorry I couldn't head that off."

"You tried," Wilbur Jones told him. "I know you had to support him, but you did try, and I appreciate it."

"Thank, you," Kruger replied. He as clearly uncomfortable with the way the conversation was moving. "You mentioned some other things that happened to make Luther the way he is. What other things were you talking about?"

"The usual things that happened in Arkansas forty years ago," the pastor told him. "Racial incidents. There was a lot of trouble around here over all the things that were going on in Little Rock. Luther was the target of a couple of vicious attacks. He got beaten pretty badly."

"You don't think he's having a flashback, do you?" I asked. "That might account for his being gone like this. Post traumatic stress."

Pastor Jones thought this over a moment before answering. "I am not sure I can make an intelligent response to that. I suppose it is possible but I don't know enough about such things to dare to guess. I did see a lot of it after Vietnam and also with some of the folks here. What I have read fits Luther pretty well. Yet, I'm not comfortable saying more than that. I'm not a doctor."

There was the sound of someone arriving outside the shack and a moment later one of Tanner's deputies stuck his head in the door. "I have the warrant for you, Dr. Phillips," he said, handing me a folded legal document.

"What warrant?" Wilbur Jones asked. His voice was like ice.

"We didn't know what we were going to find here, Pastor," I told him, folding the warrant again and tucking it in my hip pocket. "Luther had a rifle here last night that might turn out to be the murder weapon. He had some ammunition, too. So I asked the sheriff for a warrant in case we needed one."

Jones was angry. "You mean that rusty old rifle he had leaning up next to the door? That's ridiculous. The whole thing's rusted shut. Luther didn't shoot Wilbur. We straightened that all out last night."

"Then Luther must have fixed it," I told him. "It was working fine when I showed it to Kruger this morning. There were some shells missing out of the box of ammunition Luther had, too."

"Pastor, we are not looking for evidence against Luther," Kruger asserted. "The only reason we searched this place was because we thought something might have happened to him. We didn't call for the warrant until we were sure he was not around here somewhere."

Albert Jones wasn't mollified and I couldn't blame him. I probably wouldn't have been as calm as he was in his position. I made a decision to bend the rules. We needed his cooperation. "Did Luther ever tell you where he found the rifle and the knife?" I asked him. He shook his head. "He told me he found it in the old blacksmith shop," I said. "That's where we think the killer shot from to kill Wilbur Jones. It was that caliber rifle."

Suddenly the logic of what I was saying got through Jones' anger. I could see the next question forming. "So why didn't you arrest Luther last night?"

"I don't think he's the shooter," I replied. "I didn't last night and I don't today. DiRado and Kruger agree." Kruger nodded. "He didn't act guilty when I talked to him about the gun, so I let it rest. I thought he had been through more than enough yesterday. I wish now I had taken him in."

Albert Jones nodded. Then the implication hit full force. His face lost all its color. "So you think ... you think the killer...." He choked.

Kruger nodded. "We're not sure. Hopefully, Luther will come wandering in on his own, and we'll be wrong. Yet, it's possible the killer came after Luther. He may think Luther saw something and kidnapped him."

Albert Jones looked around wildly. "There's no blood!" he protested.

"That's a good sign," Kruger assured him. "There isn't sign of a struggle, either, which is good, too. On the other hand, from what you told us, it looked like someone else locked up here."

"I'm almost positive of that," Jones whispered. All the fire had gone out of him now. He turned away, his shoulders quaking.

Kruger and I waited until he turned back to us. When he did, it looked like he had aged years in those few moments. "So what do we do now?" he asked.

I looked at Kruger. When it comes to kidnapping, the FBI has the experts and the experience. "First, we organize a wider search around here," Kruger said. "We also put out an all points bulletin for Luther as missing and a possible kidnapping victim. Then we wait. While we do, Jazz and I will continue work on the homicide. That's all we can do."

"What can I do?" Albert Jones wanted to know. "I can't just sit here. I need to do something."

"You can help the search by calling around to see if anyone you know has seen him," Kruger said. "You can also write down a list of places he might have gone on his own, and check those out. Is there anyone he might have gone to visit. Any friends or relatives?"

"Not really," Jones told us. "The only people left he was close to from the old days was me and Luther Jones. Most everyone knows him as Slide."

"We'll talk to Slide," I said, trying to keep my voice casual. "We needed to see him about something else, anyway."

"He might not be at home yet," the pastor said. "You might want to call first. After the funeral, he told me he was going to spend a couple of weeks with a friend of his in Texarkana."

"You don't happen to have the name and number of the friend, do you?"

Jones shook his head. "The fellow's name is Early. At least, that's what he's called. I can check with my wife. She might know." He thought for a moment and added, "I bet the police down there would know. Early was a friend of Slide's from his bootlegging days."

I borrowed Kruger's phone again and made the call while Kruger and the pastor went to talk to Emma Jones. I was in luck. One of the people I knew from way back when was still on the police force on the Texas side—Denny Slade—and he knew exactly who I was talking about. It turned out he knew Slide Jones, too. Early Andrews was one of those people police keep an eye on, and his connection with Slide was well known. So when Slide turned up and the police caught wind of it, they were interested. Even though both men were believed to have retired from bootlegging and drug running, the department on the Arkansas side of Texarkana kept them under casual surveillance.

When I told him Slide was at the top of our suspect list, Denny offered to pick him up. I explained why we didn't want to do that just yet and asked if he knew of another, older man with Jones. I explained what was happening with Luther Adams, and Denny promised to call me back right away and let me know if Slide was still in Texarkana.

Kruger was happy with the news when he got back to his car. While she didn't know his last name, Emma Jones did tell him that Luther knew the man through Slide in the old days. On one occasion, Luther had been one of Slide's drivers making the liquor run into Texas from Louisiana.

That cast a whole new light on the case, and Kruger and I decided to head out for Texarkana right away. The day was getting away from us. Even if Slide wasn't there when we arrived, we wouldn't waste much time going there first. The road from Texarkana to Hot Springs is interstate almost all the way, and we could make up a lot of lost time there if necessary.

Kruger was reluctant to let me drive the Bureau car, even though I knew the roads much better and could get us there more quickly. So he drove and we talked about the new developments on our way. At one point I asked him, "What if we have it turned around?" What if the real target was not Smiley but Slide?"

Kruger gave me an odd look. "You know, I wondered about that," he said. "I wasn't going to mention it until we ran out of better theories. It would give us a whole lot more to work with."

"I think it makes more sense," I replied. "Slide had lots of enemies. Smiley didn't. They were both dressed about the same on the day of the murder and they looked enough alike to fool someone who knows them well until she saw them together."

"Someone who *knew* them well," Kruger corrected gently. "It may not be someone who was part of their lives now."

"That's a good point. I'm not saying we should change direction, but I do think we need to keep that possibility in the back of our minds just in case."

Kruger nodded. "Of course, that raises some new questions. Who would be the shooter then? That's the main problem. Who was it who was carrying the trombone case?"

I thought about it a moment. Then I saw something that could blow the political top off this case if it were true. I looked at Kruger. "I just had the most awful thought. Are we sure the victim was Smiley Jones?"

Kruger looked at me as if I had lost my mind. "What do you mean?"

"I don't think it fits that well, but what if there was something Smiley Jones had against Slide. What if he was the shooter? Think about it a minute. The two of them look enough alike to fool a good witness. They're dressed alike, and there's blood all over the corpse. With the head shot, the features would be distorted. So maybe we should go back a few steps and ask how Smiley Jones was identified. Even if I'm wrong, it would close out that possibility."

Kruger thought about that for a couple of minutes. Then he pulled over to the side of the road and opened the trunk. He pulled out a briefcase and opened it. Taking a document out, he returned to the driver seat and began to look over what I could see was a coroner's report. "All it says here is that the victim was identified by his pastor, Albert Jones." He looked at me and started the car. "What about fingerprints? Surely they printed the corpse."

"Yes," I told him. "I'm sure they did. That's been standard procedure for quite a while now, but rural counties can get a bit lax. Even if they printed the corpse, they may not have done a comparison or run them through your data bank. That's expensive and with positive identification by a trusted witness, it may not have been done."

"Shit!" Kruger said. "We could do it now, but how do we even approach this without precipitating a political shit storm?"

"We could pass it off as routine," I suggested. "We do need a set so we can eliminate suspects if we turn up prints at Luther's, so we can ask for one if it's not with the autopsy report. I'm sure Smiley must have paid him a visit at some point. I'm also sure Slide must be in the system, too."

Kruger's phone rang and he pulled over to answer it. The call was from Denny Slade telling me Slide's car was still in Texarkana. He gave me a street address and promised to have someone keep an eye on it until we got there. I thanked him and told him we were about an hour away. I knew I could have us there in forty-five minutes, but Kruger was driving.

Kruger made it in forty minutes flat. When I told him what Slade said, Kruger dropped the car in gear and stepped on the gas. The Bureau puts special agents through a rigorous driving school and that day it showed. Nor was there any further conversation. Kruger was completely focused on the road, and I shut up and let the man concentrate on getting us there.

When we got to Texarkana, Kruger asked me where we were going and I navigated us through the back streets. I spotted the unmarked police car about a block away from the address Denny had given me and pointed it out to Kruger. We stopped, and I was surprised to see one of the officers was Denny himself. The other was a fellow I'd known on Highway Patrol. The last time I had seen either of them, they were still in uniform.

I introduced Kruger. Denny told me the house across the street from the car belonged to a lady Slide was known to visit from time to time when her man was out of town. That was good to know. It gave us some leverage.

I thanked Denny, and Kruger parked close in front of Slide's car. As we got out, I saw Denny's partner pull in close behind, blocking the vehicle in. Denny grinned and gave me a thumbs-up. I thought things must be pretty slow on the Arkansas side for them to take the time, but backup is always welcome.

The woman who answered the door was still in her bathrobe. Kruger showed her his identification and introduced me. "What you want with me?" she demanded rudely.

"We hate to disturb you, Ma'am" Kruger told her. "We need to speak with Luther Jones. Slide."

"No one that name lives here!" the woman snapped and tried to slam the door in our faces.

Kruger blocked it open with a shoulder. "That's his car across the street and he is known to visit here," he replied. "All we need to do is talk with him."

The woman looked across the street and saw the unmarked cars. "Why you come here making a raid?" she whined. "We ain't done nothing wrong."

"Is he here, Ma'am?" Kruger insisted.

"Don't see that's any of your business," she retorted. There was no way she was going to be helpful.

"Maybe we should talk to her husband," I suggested to Kruger. "Maybe he knows where we can find Slide."

Fear replaced the outrage in the woman's face, but she held on. "I ain't got no husband. I ain't married."

I shrugged. "All right, maybe we need to talk to your live-in boyfriend."

"Why you want to do that? He don't know no...what's his name?"

She was good. I have to admit that. For a moment I wondered if we had the right house. Then I glanced back at the unmarked car and Denny nodded. I spoke to Kruger. "Maybe I should ask those officers over there. Maybe they can help straighten this out. Or we could ask the neighbors."

The woman looked at me with pure venom in her eyes. I think she would have held out longer, but someone inside spoke to her softly. She moved aside and the door opened. A grizzled, thin black man stood there. He was dressed in jacket and a tie and freshly shaved. "I'm Luther Jones," he told us. "What can I do for you gentlemen?"

At that moment, I couldn't tell who we were talking with. The man was a dead ringer for Smiley Jones, and I couldn't be sure it wasn't him. He exuded a quiet dignity I associate with old men at peace with the world. There wasn't one thing about him that suggested a con or any fear of the police.

Kruger was just as taken aback. People who have reason to fear the police show fear or some sign of psychopathology. Sometimes it's bravado and at times it's simple tension, but it's almost always something, and experienced police can sense it. This man gave us nothing but a profound sense of sadness.

The man in the door spoke up again. "Come, now, gentlemen. You barged in on my visit with these dear friends. What do you want from me?"

"We're looking for Luther Adams," I told him. "Have you seen him?"

There was something in his eyes for a moment when I asked that. "Luther? Goodness, has he done something wrong?"

"He's missing," I told him.

The man smiled and chuckled. "Oh, Luther, he probably just wandered off somewhere. He does that from time to time."

"We think something may have happened to him," Kruger said. "So does Pastor Jones. The whole town turned out to search, but we couldn't find him."

"Goodness. That sounds serious. I hope he's all right." The man's eyes didn't match the emotion I heard in his voice, and I was sure then we were in the right place. This man might be a dead ringer for Smiley, but this was Slide. He was telling us the truth about that.

"May we come in and talk?" Kruger asked.

"This isn't my house or I would invite you in," Slide said. "You seem to have upset my host, so I think we better talk out here."

"All right," said Kruger. There was steel in his voice and he pulled out a set of handcuffs. "We can talk at the police station."

I heard the doors of a car open behind us and knew Denny and his partner had seen the cuffs and were on their way to us. "There's no need for restraints, officer," Slide said as Kruger took his left arm and slipped a cuff on. "I'll come quietly." Kruger ignored him and spun Slide around, quickly cuffing the other hand. I could see he had some practice doing so. I could also see this wasn't a new experience for Slide, either.

"Everything under control?" Denny asked from behind us.

"I think we've got it," Kruger told him. "You mind us using your station for an interview?"

"Be my guest," Denny said, stepping aside to let Kruger by with Slide. At that moment, the door behind us flew open, and the woman we had talked to threw herself on Kruger's back, cursing and clawing at his face with her nails.

Denny grabbed her while his partner reached for his handcuffs. Even though she stood five foot four and weighed less than a hundred and twenty, it took all four of us to hold her down. By the time we were done, the robe was wide open for the world to see she was wearing nothing under it. In the background, I could hear Luther laughing.

"A visit to dear friends?" Kruger asked Slide as the Texarkana officers shoved the woman into their car. "Is her sister here, too?"

"Goodness, no," Jones cackled. "Her sister is ugly as a bulldog. I believe you must have seen the friends I was visiting during the...ah...scuffle."

There was no denying the man had charm. Nor was he short on *chutzpah*, either. He was enjoying this. "You may have some trouble explaining this to her boyfriend when he gets home," I told him. "I'm sure the neighbors saw the 'scuffle' and your two friends, too."

Slide laughed again. "They've seen it before. She's always getting drunk and running around the neighborhood more or less dressed. I'll tell him I came by to see him. After all, that's what brought me here in the first place."

"Right." I opened the rear door of Kruger's car. There were a couple of things there, and I cleared them out. "Want me to ride in back with him?"

Kruger shook his head and helped Slide into the rear of the car. "The police station here is so depressing," Slide said. "Why don't you take these cuffs off and let me buy you the best cup of coffee in town?"

"New rules," Kruger told him. "We can't even take a cup of coffee now."

"I could suggest a place where we might find some stronger beverages."

"I'm sure you could," Kruger said. Then he turned to me. "Which way do I go to get there?"

Slide Jones kept up his banter all the way to the station, but once we were inside, he quieted down. "I believe I need an attorney," he said casually as we sat down in the interview room.

I shook my head. "You're not under arrest, Slide. Not yet. Help us out and we'll see about making the 'scuffle' go away." I looked at Kruger and he nodded. "Otherwise, your friend is looking at assault on a federal officer, and you will be up for obstruction of justice."

"I don't think you can make that stick," he said. "At least, not mine."

"A real gentleman, aren't you?" Kruger said. "Bailing out and letting your girlfriend take a fall."

He shrugged. "I didn't ask her to attack you or even suggest it. You will remember, I also came along quietly when you cuffed me."

I found it odd playing good cop to Kruger's federal asshole. "Look," I said. "We're getting way ahead of things here. All we want is some conversation."

"Otherwise we can have them hold you as a material witness to homicide, if nothing else," Kruger interjected. "With the attitude we're getting, there won't be bail. You'll stay here until we let you go."

Slide Jones shook his head. "I prefer to talk with a lawyer present."

"Look, I can talk to you alone, if necessary," I told him.

Slide chuckled. "Yes, an all the time he'll be watching from the other side of that mirror and taping the whole thing. No, sir. I want a lawyer."

Kruger shrugged and left the room. "You're sure you want to do this?" I asked Slide. "Once Kruger books you, it'll be out of our hands. Montana gets kind of cold this time of year."

"Montana? What in the world has Montana got to do with this?"

"Just this. Kruger will charge you with a federal crime which means you can be held in any federal detention center. I understand the one up in Butte, Montana, is pretty basic. It gets pretty cold there, too." I had no idea if there was a federal detention center in Butte, but it sounded good, and Slide didn't know if there was, either.

"What do you want to talk to me about?" he said. "And how did you know I was here?"

"All we want to know about is Smiley's murder," I told him. "Someone in Oak Grove told us you might be here." I shook my head. "You're making a big deal out of something very simple, Luther. Tell me what you know and you can walk out of here a free man."

"What about Louella?" he asked. "My friend."

"Kruger's a reasonable man. He's just torqued right now. Believe me, we can work something out. Maybe Louella will agree to recovery instead of jail time. It sounds like she could use it."

"You won't be talking to her boyfriend?"

"I don't see how he needs to be involved at all."

Slide nodded. "All right. As long as you are not charging me, I'll tell you what you want to know about Smiley."

"Why don't you start with the day he was shot? When did you get there?"

Kruger later told me it was one of the most skillful interviews he had ever seen. I don't know about that, but Slide gave us a lot of information. By the time we were done, I still considered him our best suspect. Yet, in my estimation, the probability had slipped from ninety-five percent to about sixty. There were still some gaping holes in his alibi, but it was quite possible he was telling us the truth.

Slide told me he arrived early in the morning on the day of the celebration so he could spend some time with Smiley before other folk got there. He wanted the two of them to do something together, but Smiley was against it.

"Was that why you brought the trombone?" I asked.

"What trombone? I haven't touched a trombone in years and years," he said, clearly surprised. "Why do you ask?"

"Someone mentioned they saw you carrying a trombone case," I said.

"Well, they're wrong. It must have been someone else." The way he said that told me he was telling the truth, but I reminded myself this man had fooled me before without uttering a single word.

"So you didn't bring your lunch in your trombone case?" I asked lightly, smiling.

"No, though I've been known to carry some excellent spirits in one on occasion. Not that day, though. No money in bootlegging any more."

That was a blatant whopper and we both knew it. I decided he was baiting me gently and let it go. I asked him to take me through his day there, and he did, giving me thirty or forty names of people he'd visited during the day along with a little background information on each of them. None of this seemed germane to the case, but one never knows, and I dutifully took notes.

The only thing Slide told me that had direct bearing on the shooting was that he was not there when the murder happened. "I was on my way here, as a matter of fact. Louella can tell you when I got here. That is, assuming she was sober enough to notice. My impression is I got to town about half past four, but I wouldn't swear to that. It's been a day or two. The man at the liquor store might know."

That was interesting. It could be force of habit, but Slide Jones was giving me his alibi without my having asked for one. I decided to respond with my own mild deception. "I didn't mean to imply you were the one who murdered Smiley, Slide. After all, you've been friends all your life."

"Yes, but then, friends have been known to kill one another, have they not, Dr. Phillips? Even life long friends," he added dryly.

"When did you first hear about it?" I asked, changing direction.

"It was two days later when I first heard the news on the radio. When I did, I called Albert Jones right away and talked to him. Smiley and Albert and I were all close way back when."

"Not now?" He shook his head. "What happened?"

"One of our good friends was killed in a hunting accident when we were in high school. Luther Adams was the one who shot him. It was a terrible accident, and we all seemed to drift apart after that. Then we grew up and had less and less in common. As I'm sure you are aware, bootleggers and Baptists may be in coalition to keep a county dry, but they don't mix socially."

What fascinated me most about Slide was his pedantic Southern manner of speech. Were I listening to him on tape and unable to see his face, I would have sworn I was speaking to one of the white Catfish Aristocracy of south Arkansas. I wondered what it would take to make him revert to his native Oak Grove patios.

"You and Smiley were still close enough for him to turn to you when he had to leave town," I observed. "Tell me about that."

"The media got it close to right for once about that," he said. "Their only serious omission was mention of the time Wilbur spent with me at the carnival. Yet, he may not have thought it fitting to mention that." He shook his head sadly. "Not to speak ill of the dead, but that was Wilbur's one flaw. He was a first class hypocrite. Once he got on a person's case, there was no getting him off it."

"Tell me about it," I murmured, and he did. I'm not sure why, except that I may have been the one person he could tell who might believe him.

"Smiley Jones was a living saint in the minds of most people," Slide told me. "I knew him as Wilbur, or Willie at first, and he was slick. Not unlike our former governor. He had to be slick. He had all those folks at church believing he could walk on water, and all the time he was playing piano at taverns and houses of ill repute. Not knowing him as I did, folks thought he couldn't say 'shit' if he had a mouthful." Slide shook his head. "Understand, I'm not condemning him for that. Or even the other petty dishonesties, like the song Eddie wrote that Willie passed off as his own. What I have against him is his condemning others for doing exactly what he did himself."

I asked him which song it was, and he told me. When he did, I was shocked. Not only was it Smiley's first big hit, but it also was the signature song his bands used for forty years. I think it was at that point the interview changed. I lost all awareness of time passing or where we were. At that point, the whole universe was made up of just the two of us and Wilbur Jones, and I bored in like a boll weevil. When I came back to the present, I had an aching back and a legal tablet half-filled with notes. The clock told me three hours had passed.

"One last question," I said as I stood and tried to work the kinks out of my spine. "Whatever happened to Eddie Posey? No one seems to know."

"I don't either. Eddie and I were close for a while there, even after Luther shot Goodie. At least, we were until I became known as a boot-legger and his mama told him not to hang out with me. Even still, we talked from time to time when she wasn't looking. When his song became Wilbur's big hit, he came to see me. He was so proud. He was sure Wilbur would send for him and make him his song writer. I did-n't have the heart to tell him not to hold his breath. By then Wilbur had done a few numbers on me. I was aware of not only his dishon-esty, but his hypocrisy." He sighed. "Eddie held out hope for a long time, but Wilbur never answered his letters. After a while he figured it out. Not long after that, he was drafted and sent to Vietnam, and no one has heard anything from him since then. As I recall, his mother died about then, and he didn't come home for the funeral. I know, because I was there. The word then was that he was killed in action, but I think he may have been among the missing. Otherwise, he would have come to lay her to rest." He shook his head sadly. "I believe that was what I held against Wilbur the most…how he treated that boy."

I nodded and went to the door then turned back. "Why did you come to Smiley's celebration, Slide?"

"You mean, feeling the way I did?" I nodded. "I hoped we might reconcile. We were both old men now, and there's a time for all things. I had hoped it was a time to forgive and be forgiven." There were tears in his eyes, and I think they were real. "Wilbur wouldn't hear of it. He refused. Now he's dead and it's not possible. Yet, I did offer."

When I entered the observation room, Kruger gave me a long look. I took my time responding, turning to look at Slide Jones through the one way mirror. "What do you think?" I asked Kruger finally.

"I don't know what to think," he told me. "It sounds like he believes what he told you. Who knows if it's true. How about you?"

"Pretty much the same. We need to check out his alibi. It's your call, but I'd let Slide go for now. He's still our best candidate for shooter, but if he is, we just witnessed Academy Award level acting." I looked at Kruger. "Did you get it on tape? I'd like to listen to it again tomorrow."

"Even better," he told me. "We have it in living color. Videotape."

I nodded, thankful for modern technology. Nonverbal signals are just as important as what people say and can be more so. Watching the interview again might help me see something I missed. "You don't think it's admissible, do you?"

"Well, he did ask for a lawyer and we didn't give him one, so it's probably not. On the other hand, we do have one helluva lot of information we can use to chase down leads. Just to be safe, we probably need to keep the fact it exists to ourselves." Kruger was excited, like a hound that's just caught fresh scent.

We talked about it and decided Louella needed to stay in custody, but we drove Slide back to his car. Kruger was cool to the idea but gave in to my insistence. When we got there he told Slide to remain available in case we had more questions. When I asked where Slide would be, he told us he was headed home to Hot Springs and was going to be there for a while. I took his address and phone number then thanked him for his cooperation and offered my hand. He was surprised, but he took it and smiled. When I got back into the car, Kruger gave me an odd look. "It's the oldest trick in the book," I told him. "Put him at ease. Let him think he has us fooled."

"Right," Kruger said. He didn't buy it for a minute. "You just keep in mind that the hand you just shook may have pulled the trigger."

We decided to have supper in Texarkana and I suggested one of the catfish places on the Texas side. I knew I was pushing the limit with fried food, but there's nothing better than good catfish, and I knew the place was one of the best. So I compromised by staying away from the hushpuppies and the fries and loaded up on catfish and cole slaw. It was as good as I remembered, and I was surprised how much Kruger put away.

When we got back in the car, I was glad Kruger was driving. Between the good food and the intense interview with Slide, I was beat. I got Kruger to the highway and pointed in the right direction, then told him I was going to catch a quick nap. The next thing I knew, Kruger was shaking me awake. I glanced at my watch. I saw an hour and forty minutes had passed since we left Texarkana. Then I looked around and saw we were in Nashville, parked by the jail.

We went in to see the sheriff and caught him still there. I let Kruger take the lead bringing him up to speed. I was still groggy from the nap and not firing on all cylinders. Tanner told us there was still no sign of Luther Adams, and while Kruger was writing up his report, I borrowed a phone and called Dee.

Dee answered on his cell phone, and I brought him up to date quickly. He laughed when I told him Kruger's response to my shaking hands with Slide. "What he doesn't know is you've done that with just about every murderer you ever busted."

"I have?" I asked, surprised.

"Well, you have since I've known you. It's your signature. When you shake hands with a suspect, the rest of us know who did it."

"You're jerking my chain!" I laughed. "I shake hands with a lot of people, including some politicians we both know."

"I hope you wash your hands afterwards," Dee laughed. "Especially with the politicians."

I was curious at his change in mood from the night before. "What's made you so bright and cheery? Did Barton kick the bucket?"

"Don't we all wish," he snorted. Then he got serious. "I decided to take your advice, Jazz," he told me. "So I pulled the plug. I decided to take terminal leave and turned in my papers today. Amazing what it did for my mental state. I may even put in for medical retirement while I'm at it. The doctor said he would recommend it."

I was shocked. I had no doubt this was the right thing for Dee to do, but the fact he had to see a doctor concerned me. "What doctor?" I asked.

"The doctor who saw me in the emergency room here in Little Rock," he said. "That's why I had to leave Nashville. I was having chest pains."

"You were having chest pains and you drove yourself all the way to Little Rock?" I was angry at the risk he had taken. "Are you out of your mind?"

"Don't be pissed, Jazz. I didn't see much alternative. I'm not even sure the hospital in Nashville has a regular doctor. Besides, it wasn't a heart attack. It was acute gastroenteritis and angina precipitated by stress, mostly job stress. The doctor said it was quit or die."

"You didn't know that!" I protested. "You could have killed yourself and someone else, too!"

"I drove very carefully, Jazz," he protested. "I pulled over every time it started to hurt. But, you're right. I guess I wasn't thinking very clearly."

My anger faded as quickly as it arose. I could see myself doing exactly the same. "All right," I said. "Thank God you got away with it. Where are you now, in the hospital?"

"No, the doctor let me come home if I agreed to take the day off. There was no problem with the heart they could find. It was my stomach, the worst case of heartburn you ever saw. They want to check me for a hiatal hernia."

"Good," I told him. "I'm glad to hear it wasn't worse and even more glad to hear you're getting help. Who's going to cover the case now from CID?"

"I will, mostly from here in Little Rock. The doctor wanted to put me in the hospital for a couple of days, but he agreed to very limited desk duty. He said they need to run a bunch more tests, but I can drive in for that. He talked to the boss and as of five o'clock today, I'm only assigned to this case. When we close it, I'm out of here." He laughed. "The boss man didn't like it a bit, but the doctor didn't give him much room to wiggle. I heard the doctor's end of it, and he laid it on thick. I wish I could have seen the boss' face!"

"Well, let's hear it for the good doctor," I said. We talked about the case a bit more and set up a flexible schedule for my checking in. I asked if there was anything on the rifle yet, but he said not.

I heard something in the background and asked what it was. He told me I caught him in his hot tub which he had not had much time to enjoy. "I should be so lucky," I groused and told him to take care. Then I hung up.

Kruger was still writing his report, so I told him I'd walk back to the motel. I ended up walking a lot farther, clearing the circuits of the day's garbage, and working out the tension in my back. It was just after nine when I showered and fell into bed. Something tickled the back of my mind when I did, but I didn't even try to figure it out. Ten seconds later I was out for the count.

DOWN BY THE RIVERSIDE

I was awakened by the phone at half past seven the next morning. It took me a moment or two to figure out where I was before I answered on the fifth ring. It was Kruger and he sounded worried. He wanted to know if I was all right. He had knocked on my door twice without getting an answer.

This worried me more than it did Kruger. Nellie tells me my hearing is not what it used to be, and I guess she's right. I probably need to check it out at a clinic and do something about it. Knowing this is one thing, but accepting it is a different matter. I can't seem to remember to make the appointment.

I took a long, hot shower and was glad to find the tension in my back was gone. When I got to the cafe, Kruger was finished with breakfast and eager to get on our way. Crime Scene was due to meet us that morning in Oak Grove to go over Luther's shack and tear up the floors of the blacksmith shop. I thought that Weaver and company would be glad it wasn't another outhouse. While I hated breaking in on their Saturday plans, I knew they would be glad for overtime.

Kruger was genuinely sorry to hear about Dee, but glad that we'd be working together on the case. At this point, Lonnie would normally assign an agent to replace Spinks on the case, but a couple of situations in other parts of the country had pulled away most of his people. Kruger was left in place because the case was so politically sensitive. This told me we needed to get this case cleared up as quickly as we could. The last thing we needed was to be swamped by an influx of special agents when other crises were resolved.

The rainy weather had passed with the front the night before, and the day was bright and clear, the way it is after a storm. As we drove to Oak Grove, the colors were completely out, brilliant in the clean air. It's on fall days like this in Arkansas I find myself most grateful to be alive.

We arrived in Oak Grove about thirty minutes ahead of Weaver's team. I was about to suggest we talk to the pastor when Kruger's phone rang. "I bet it's for you," he said. When he answered, he was right. It was Sheriff John Tanner asking to talk to me.

"Jazz," he said when I got on the line. "I have some bad news. Luther Adams is dead."

I wasn't surprised by that, but I found myself with a sense of loss. "What happened? Where did you find him?"

"I didn't," Tanner told me. "The Highway Patrol said a fisherman found him along the river down by Wilton. It was a fluke. Where he was dumped no one would have ever found him except that was the guy's secret fishing hole and his dog smelled him out."

"We better get Weaver and his crime scene guys down there," I said.

"I guess," said Tanner. "But I don't think they'll find much. Highway Patrol said it didn't look like he was killed there."

The whole world is a forensic expert these days. "Yeah, but our guy may have gotten careless. Maybe they'll find some tracks or something."

"Maybe so," he said. I knew he wouldn't be betting on it. "By the way, I did talk to Leslie yesterday. We have the rifle. I saw it myself. The number matches. He just forgot to log it in."

"Maybe Weaver can pick it up on his way through," I suggested. "Thanks. I appreciate it."

"They found Adams?" Kruger asked and I gave him the details. "How do you see it?" he wanted to know when I was done.

"Someone must have seen us together," I replied. "Either in town at the drive-in or here. We weren't exactly inconspicuous." I told him about Luther singing. Then it hit me. "We better check out the blacksmith shop."

"Someone needs to tell Pastor Jones," Kruger reminded me. Seeing my face he added, "I will if you want me to. Adams was just another guy to me."

I thanked him and told him that in Arkansas we're raised to shoot our own dogs. He nodded and followed me to the church where we could see Jones talking to two other men. I waved to get his attention, and he hurried to me.

There's no easy way to pass along news of the death of a loved one. Even though he was around death all the time, Albert Jones took the news hard. At first he said nothing, just turned to one side and looked down. Then tears began to roll down his cheek. By now the men Jones had been talking to had gathered around, and seeing the pastor's face, they knew without a word being passed. "Poor Luther," one of them said. "Well, he's with the Lord now."

Albert Jones was facing me when the man said this. I saw a blaze of anger flare in his eyes and for a moment I thought he would strike the fellow. Then he forced it down and let out a deep breath. He turned and patted the man on the shoulder. "Yes, LeRoy, he is. Luther is at rest now." Then he looked back to me. "Please excuse me, Dr. Phillips," he said. "We can talk later, if you don't mind. There are things I need to do right now."

Kruger and I walked back to his car. "What do you think?" I asked as he dug a couple of flashlights and a camera out of the trunk.

"About the pastor?" he asked. I nodded. "He's for real," Kruger said. "No one can fake that kind of grief. But I think he knew before you told him. Not knew for sure, maybe, but he had a good idea."

"I think he knew the minute he saw the lock and chain yesterday," I said. "I think there's a lot Pastor Jones isn't telling us."

While we were there, we took a quick look around the blacksmith shop. Kruger had thought to bring along a pry bar, but we needed to get to Wilton and decided to wait and let the crime scene people take up the flooring. With all the traffic in and out the day before, I couldn't tell if there were any fresh tracks in the dust and neither could Kruger. There was nothing more to see, so we took off for Wilton and I called the

Highway Patrol and asked for one of the officers who recovered the body to wait for us out on the highway.

It wasn't far from Oak Grove to the Millwood River near Wilton. Yet, the road is narrow and full of curves, and Kruger didn't push it today. The trip took us the better part of an hour, but I was able to get in touch with Weaver. I called on Kruger's phone and told Weaver about Luther Adams. I asked him to skip Oak Grove until he was headed back and join us at the crime scene near Wilton.

When we got there the state trooper was someone I knew and he was glad to help us out. It was his last week on patrol before retirement, and the last thing he wanted was excitement. He told us the other officer who answered the call was back on patrol but available if we needed a statement. When he showed us where the body was found, I was glad to see he had sealed off the area with yellow crime scene tape.

We looked around a little, but there wasn't much to see. Luther's body lay behind a bush to one side of a little used path at the edge of the water. I didn't look that closely, but there was nothing along the path, and when I touched Luther's face, it was cold. What got me was the expression on his face. He was smiling the way he had while singing the hymn at the drive-in.

"Jesus," Kruger murmured from behind me. He was not being irreverent.

"Something like that," I answered. It wasn't obvious how Adams died, but the old man had left this world in peace.

There was nothing to do but wait for Weaver and his team, so I spent the time going over the autopsy report while Kruger caught up on his paperwork. I turned to the very last page to read the pathologist summary and discovered two pages stuck together. When I gently peeled them apart, I discovered one of them was a fingerprint chart. The name at the top was Wilbur O. Jones and the date was about ten days before.

I mentioned this to Kruger, but he was deep into something and simply murmured and nodded. When I chuckled, he looked up. I told him we must have been working together too long since his answer to me had been much like the old standard, "Yes, dear." He smiled and nodded, but gave me an odd look. It was clear that he was not amused.

Reading through the slice-by-slice autopsy report, I came across something else. As Pastor Jones told us, our killer had won out over mother nature by just a few weeks or months. Smiley Jones had stage four colon cancer and he had not received treatment. This time Kruger was more attentive when I told him what I found, but he didn't see the significance.

"He was aware of his cancer," I told him. "Albert Jones told me so. But there was no sign he had been treated."

"I still don't see the connection," he replied.

"Well, if he knew, maybe he wanted to spare himself some pain."

"You mean, he arranged his own murder?" Kruger looked at me as if I had lost my mind.

"It happens, but I wasn't thinking along those lines," I replied. "What if he knew someone was after him and simply didn't do anything about it?"

This got Kruger's attention. "You don't suppose he left a message, do you?"

"I hadn't thought about that, but it's something to keep in mind. You know, as one of those back-burner possibilities. Or, maybe he knew someone was after him, but he didn't know who. Maybe he just accepted it."

Kruger thought about that a moment, then shrugged. "You would think it would show up in his behavior somewhere. None of the witnesses I've talked to noticed any difference in his behavior or his mental state, and I haven't seen it in any of the reports, either."

"Well, it's definitely back burner, but it would be interesting to know if he was settling his affairs."

"As far as I've been able to discover, he didn't even leave a will," Kruger told me. "He had some savings and a few residual royalties he used to support himself, but nothing worth hiring a professional hitman. He was comfortable, but not wealthy."

I asked how much the estate was worth, and Kruger gave me an estimate. "You've seen Oak Grove," I told him. "While a couple hundred thousand dollars might not seem like wealth to you, to black folk in rural Arkansas, it could seem like all the money in the world."

Kruger thought about it for a minute. "I wonder who went through his stuff? Or if anyone looked at his bank records. I didn't see anything mentioned in the reports. Did DiRado say anything about it to you?"

I shook my head. "Not a thing. I don't even know where Smiley lived. I think maybe you and I ought to go through his place."

"Maybe we need to go back to square one," Kruger suggested. "Maybe we need to approach this as a fresh homicide. Not much has really gotten done until the last few days, and we're the ones who did it."

Weaver and his team arrived about then. He told us he had left one of his team in Oak Grove to begin work on Luther's shack while he and the other two handled the crime scene here. Normally the four of them worked in two separate teams with Weaver floating between, but this case had top priority and the guys liked working together.

There wasn't much at the river for Weaver and his people to find. They determined rather quickly that the cause of death was probably a single deep wound entering just over the left kidney. Weaver guessed it was made by a knife with a seven or eight inch blade which penetrated the heart, causing immediate arrest and almost instant death. There was very little blood around the wound and only a few smears on the leaves and grass behind the bush. Nor was there any sign of the murder weapon, even though they searched the brush along the trail carefully.

"I don't think you'll ever find the murder weapon," Weaver told me as he nodded toward the river. "Most likely it's out there somewhere, but it'll be a miracle if you find it. I guess you could fish with large magnets."

I told him about the commando knife, and he nodded again. "That would do it, all right. As a matter of fact, the placement of the wound suggests that the killer knew what he was doing."

"You mean, like a professional?" Kruger asked.

"More like a commando," Weaver told him. "This is how they teach the Marines and Special Forces to do it: quick and silent. The poor bastard never knew it was coming."

"Then we may get lucky," Kruger said. "Those guys are attached to their weapons, particularly blades. He may have kept the knife."

"Then he may have kept the rifle, too," I added and Kruger nodded.

"The other thing is that Adams wasn't killed here," Weaver added. "I bet you already guessed that, but it's for sure now. I didn't see any sign he was killed between here and the van, either, and I looked."

I nodded. "So he was killed somewhere else and brought here," I said softly, talking to myself. I looked around. "I wonder if the killer knew about this spot. He took some trouble to hide the body. Any idea of when it happened?"

Weaver shook his head. "I would guess at least twelve hours and no more than twenty-four. On the other hand, it's been cool. It could be a little longer."

I glanced at my watch. "No, not really. I left Oak Grove at a quarter to nine last night. So we're looking at fourteen hours at the most. Ask the Highway Patrol when the body was discovered. I expect it was fairly early this morning."

Weaver nodded. "Will do, boss." Somehow, I missed the irony.

"Well, keep an eye out around Adams' place in Oak Grove when you go over it," I added. "I doubt he was killed there, either, but he might have been. You might keep an eye out for a likely place between here and Oak Grove, too."

Weaver gave me a look that was eloquent, but said nothing. It was a very gentle reminder that I was no longer in charge of CID. "Never mind," I said. "I guess I'm being unreasonable, aren't I." Weaver answered with a smile and left to supervise his team.

Once the body was loaded, there was nothing more for us to do there, and we followed the crime scene van back to Oak Grove. About halfway between Ben Lomond and Mineral Springs, we were crossing the Saline River when something caught my eye. It was a turnout on the north side of the road, the kind that fishermen use to get to the river, and I could see two trucks through the brush about fifty yards off the road.

I asked Kruger to stop and go back. He gave me a strange look but did so, and I directed him down the primitive road until we came to a clearing. I asked him to stop before we got to the trucks. I got out and looked around the clearing and Kruger joined me.

I was about to give up and head back to the car when I spotted what I was looking for. It wasn't much, just a small dark stain on the ground toward the middle of the clearing. I called Kruger over, and when he got there he nodded and handed me his phone. "I'll get the tape. You call Weaver."

I could tell Weaver really didn't believe me when I told him I had a spot, but he humored me and came back, anyway. When he saw the faint tracks by the stain, his attitude changed. He very carefully took a smear of the stain and took it to the van to test it. A few minutes later he came back. "It's blood, all right. Human blood. I can't tell you for sure it's Adams', but it's the same type—O negative—which is pretty rare." He looked at me and shook his head. "I don't know how you do it."

"The secret is mineral water and clean living," I laughed. "Come on, I just got lucky this time, Ben."

Weaver looked at Kruger. "You wouldn't believe how often this guy gets lucky this way. His batting average is over seven hundred."

"I believe it," Kruger said.

"You guys are embarrassing me," I told them. "Let's see if we can get some plaster impressions of these foot prints." I looked around and pointed. "Let's try those tire tracks, too. They look like car tires."

Weaver grinned and spoke to Kruger again. "If you ever want to get Jazz off your case, just say something nice about him."

The crime scene team spent over an hour going over the site. There was more there than at the river side, but none of it was conclusive in pointing to the killer. One set of foot prints matched Luther's shoes, but the others were from a major brand of running shoe sold in every department store in the country. The size was a bit small—nine medium—but that only gave us a rough idea of the size of the man. They could belong to a tall man with small feet, or a short man with feet to fit his stature, or even a woman, for that matter. One thing we did learn was that he was not as heavy as Luther. His tracks were not as deep.

When his team was done, Weaver came over to where Kruger and I were talking. He waved his hands in the air and bowed. "Where to now, oh Great One?" he said. Kruger laughed.

I played along, pulling my fingers together on the bridge of my nose and looking down. "The Force tells me…Oak Grove! I see an old shack and a lonely crime scene technician who wonders where in the hell his boss is."

Weaver took off for Oak Grove, and Kruger and I debated our next step. It would take Crime Scene a while to go over Luther's shack and take up the floor of the blacksmith shop. There was no one in Oak Grove we needed to interview other than the pastor, and he would be busy with his flock for a while. There was little else we could do and I suggested that we might head back to Texarkana and check out Slide's alibi since we were so close. Kruger thought that was a good idea, and I called Ben Weaver on Kruger's phone to let him know.

"Don't tell me that you've found another one," Weaver said when he heard my voice. I laughed and told him what our plans were and how to reach us.

Kruger was in a much better mood as we drove south. He even told me a little about himself, and I told him about me and Nellie. He was from a large family in a small town in North Dakota, the first in his family to go to college. He had been with the Bureau five years and was still unmarried, a point I asked about since Nellie would want to know. While he was not sure why; he was sent to Arkansas since his performance reviews were always excellent, he was glad it wasn't Mississippi.

Since it seemed an appropriate moment, I told him what I thought about his doing better in private industry. He agreed and told me he was hoping to be able to take leave from the Bureau to complete law school soon. Once that was behind him, he thought he might find a place he liked to live and think about a family. Seattle interested him, as did Anchorage. He also liked Little Rock, too, but wasn't used to the heat down here.

It was noon by the time we got to Texarkana, and I took Kruger to a little cafe in the original downtown business district that served good Cajun fare. He was fascinated when a table of young businessmen and women ordered boiled crawdads, or mud bugs, as they are also known, and the waitress poured them directly from the pot onto a sheet of newspaper in the middle of the table.

"I've heard of this, but I've never seen it," he said to me quietly when one of the men made a production of sucking the juice out of the heads. There was a roar of cheers when one of the young women did the same with much more flair. When she was done, she raised an eyebrow and said something to the man that brought a round of laughter and teasing by the other men.

The new law enforcement center was just down the street from our cafe, so we walked the two blocks there. The center is unusual in a number of ways, one being that the state line runs down the middle. This joint effort required several special laws from both state legislatures before the building was occupied, and the building took several years to complete. One of the major issues which had to be resolved was jurisdiction. Under the old laws, it was foreseen that an inmate could simply cross a hallway and demand extradition proceedings before being moved back to the other side. Technically, an inmate could become a fugitive without knowing it, too.

It took a while before we could see Louella Smith. The problem was that neither Kruger nor myself knew her last name and the jailer wouldn't let us see their census. It took me a while to run down Denny Slade by phone, and when I finally got him, he was torqued.

"Those dumb sons of bitches!" he said. "Just a minute. I have my copy of the arrest record." A minute later he gave me not only Louella's full name, but her date of birth and the report number, too. "Call me back if they give you any more shit, Jazz," he told me. "I'll rip those dumb bastards a new one! We have had nothing but trouble since they went with this new center."

When the matron brought Louella Smith to the interrogation room, our prisoner was dressed in orange coveralls with an attitude to match. Nor did the jailer cuffing her to the table improve her disposition much. When he did, she started cursing the matron in a loud and shrill voice. "I'll be in the observation room," the matron told us, pointing toward the large mirror along one wall.

When the matron left, Louella turned her attention on us. Nor did she recognize us right away. When we got across who we were, Louella turned even more surly. "What you have them peckerwoods bust me for, anyway!" she demanded, glaring at Kruger.

Their dislike was mutual. Yet, Kruger's way of showing it was to become very formal and very polite. "You assaulted a federal officer, Ms. Smith," he said quietly. "You also resisted arrest. You're here on several serious charges."

"That was your fault!" she shrilled. "You come to my house, busting in with no warrant! What you expect!"

It went on that way for a while. The more strident Louella Smith became, the more correct Kruger was, which only egged her on. Subtlety was lost on the woman, and Kruger finally looked at me, got up, and left the room. "Where you going!" Louella demanded, but Kruger never looked back.

"What with him?" Louella demanded, turning her attention to me. I didn't respond… just sat there looking at her. That precipitated a full rampage, but after a while, she fell silent and sat there glaring at me. "Who you? The fucking Sphinx?" she said.

It was too much. I started laughing. That inspired Louella to even greater efforts to offend me, but the more creative she became, the harder I laughed, and, at one point, I could see she was working hard at hiding a smile.

"You're very good," I told her, wiping my eyes. "You're also very smart." She started to frown and I waved it off. "Come on, Louella. It takes a good mind to cuss that well. You're not dumb."

I stopped and she took her time looking me over, evaluating her situation. "So, what is it you want, Dr. Phillips?" she asked in perfect

English, and I was impressed. Hung over as she must have been, she was in complete control.

"Dr. Sphinx," I said and a grin came and went quickly. "All I want is some information. It won't cost you a thing, and it can get you out of here."

"I see. What about the 'serious federal charges?'" she asked, matching not only Kruger's voice, but also his polite tone perfectly.

"You've got a good talent there," I observed. "The charges can go away, but there'll be a price over and above your cooperation."

"I'm listening," she told me. Had I not been looking right at her as she said this, I could have sworn I was hearing Kelsey Grammar.

"You agree to thirty days in rehabilitation and six months making two AA meetings a week when you get out."

"Who pays for the rehab?"

"You do," I told her. "It'll take you a while, but you won't have a booze bill then."

She thought about this a long time. Then she sighed. "It's more fun being Wild Louella. I don't think I can live without drinking."

"A high stepper like you?" I asked. "I think you can do just about anything you set your mind to, Louella."

"Except stop drinking," she said. "What do you want to know?"

"I need to know when Slide Jones got to town the day Smiley Jones died. I also need to know where he was the night before last."

"So you think Slide may have shot Smiley?" Louella said. Since it was more of a statement than a question, I didn't answer. I just shrugged.

After a moment, Louella told me she wasn't clear exactly when Luther Jones arrived on her doorstep. It was late afternoon the day Smiley was shot, and she had been drinking all day. Her best impression was around four o'clock, and maybe a little later. I took her over this a couple of times, trying to pinpoint the time by asking about radio or television shows she might have been listening to, but there was nothing she more could add.

Turning to the night before last, she admitted she had been in a complete blackout. The last thing she could remember was taking a drink before starting out for a dance hall about six o'clock or seven. The next thing she remembered was waking up in her own bed the next day about noon with a terrible hangover and no memory where she had been or what she had done. When she woke, Slide was at the house but he was already dressed and said he had been up for a while. She couldn't say for sure whether he was with her all night.

I asked for the names of the places she and Slide normally went when they were out, and she frowned, immediately suspicious. "I thought you said that was all you wanted to know, Dr. Phillips."

"Would you think I was doing my job if I didn't check it out?" I asked her mildly. "I don't know if Slide shot Smiley or not, but if he didn't, I need to check him off the list."

"You know, Smiley wasn't the saint people said he was," she told me.

"That's what Slide said. Do you know that on your own, or is that based on what Slide told you?"

"On my own," she replied. "At least, based on what my mother told me. I asked her who my daddy was and he's the man she named. She said she was a virgin until she met him. I was their love child."

I thought about that for a moment. I was convinced Louella believed that was true, and if so, I had just turned up another suspect. Or, at least, someone else with a motive. Yet, Louella Smith didn't fit the picture of our killer that was coming together.

"Look, I don't want to offend you," I said. "But do you think she was telling you the truth?" Louella nodded. "Do you think I could talk to her."

Her smile was bittersweet. You could, but I don't know how much help it would be. She's in a nursing home now. She has severe dementia. Parkinson's."

"I am sorry," I said. "My dad went the same way. It was bad."

We were quiet for a moment. Then she began to speak without prompting, giving me the list of places I asked for earlier. When she was done, she said, "You know, I hope it doesn't turn out to be Luther. That's what I call him even though everyone else calls him Slide. He has lived a pretty rough life and done some bad things, but there's another side to him. He's a very gentle man. I've never seen him raise his hand against anyone, not even when he was armed. One of the reasons I'm cooperating is that I hope you can clear him."

I nodded and started to speak, but she continued. "I hope you'll forgive me what I said before, Dr. Phillips. You're a very good man, too."

"There's nothing to forgive," I told her, not knowing how else to respond. "It was the booze talking. Besides, I sort of like Dr. Sphynx."

I called for the matron, but Louella Smith had another surprise for me. She spoke to the mirror and asked Kruger to come back in, too. When he did, she apologized to him for her behavior earlier and the day before. I could tell he didn't believe her for a minute, and Louella knew it, too. Kruger was very stiff and correct in his response in the way only a career FBI agent can bring off.

"You didn't think she was for real, did you?" he challenged me on our way back to the car.

"I hope so," I said. "Not for my sake but for hers. She has a tough row to hoe ahead of her. I hope she makes it." Then I challenged him right back. "Are you going to take what she said and did personally, Kruger?"

He glared at me but didn't respond. "Come on, Kruger," I said. "This is not about you or me or anyone else. What it's all about is a bunch of really screwed up people doing the best they can but screwing up, anyway. All you and I are is part of the cleanup crew. That's what they pay us to do."

He looked at me as if I had lost my mind, and maybe I had. Yet, the older I get the more I see people as neither good nor evil, but broken folks doing horrible things to one another in their collective insanity. That's not to say they should get away with the things they do, for I believe we're all accountable, including for the way we treat our prisoners. What it does say is that the longer I'm in this line of business, the more I believe punishment is useless. A person like Slide or Louella, or just about every inmate in our prisons, can take all the punishment the penal system can hand out and come back for more. So I believe we need to do something much different if we want them to change. Rigorous rehabilitation is the only thing I see which offers much hope. Nor am I a liberal. Radical is the right word when it comes to the change I see our criminal justice system needs.

Of course, I didn't tell Kruger all this right then. Some things a man has to learn by picking up the cat by the tail, as Mark Twain observed. "We'll see," I said, holding up my note pad. "She gave us a lot to work with."

We spent the rest of that afternoon and evening checking out what Louella had told us. The result was frustrating, not because she lied to us, but because it became obvious we could neither clear Slide nor find a glaring contradiction to his alibi. One of the bartenders we talked to was clear about the time he had seen the two the night before last. "It was six o'clock," he said. "I came on right at six and they were the first people I served."

"How do you remember?" Kruger asked.

"The lucky bastard won the roll and I had to buy their drinks," he told us. "The shift went downhill from there. It must've been a full moon."

I didn't think the moon was full that night, but I didn't correct him. That was at the fourth place we tried, and our prospects were already headed south. I could sympathize. Our luck wasn't much better. I wished the hell there was a full moon to blame. The barkeep wasn't able to remember how long Slide and Louanne stayed before leaving his bar or if Slide was there the whole time.

The high point of the evening came when we decided to call it quits and went to Oscar's for their ribs. I don't go there often, mostly because Oscar won't let me pay when I do. The two of us go back many years to a time when I was able to do him a large favor without violating the law. So Oscar stayed out of prison and that's not something a man forgets.

Oscar joined us at the table and entertained us with his sharp banter until a minor crisis in the kitchen required his presence. When he was gone, Kruger looked at me and said, "That guy is about as straight as a three dollar bill."

"Yeah," I said. "Oscar and his boyfriend are Texarkana institutions. They go back a long way."

"That surprises me," Kruger replied. "I wouldn't have expected that kind of tolerance in a Southern town."

"How long have you been down here, Kruger?" I asked. He told me it had only been eight months.

"A lot of people from other places think the Deep South is a hotbed of total intolerance," I replied. With good reason, given the civil rights reaction that hit national news. What one doesn't hear is about the bigotry in other places. I don't know who the North Dakota bigotry might be against, but I'm sure there's someone. With South Dakota and Minnesota, it's the Indians or the whites, depending on the perspective."

Kruger smiled. "We look down on the whole rest of the nation."

"There you go. The thing is, most folk in Texarkana hate queers. That's exactly how they would express it. Talk to them about Oscar and his buddy, however, and you'll never hear the word used. To them, queers are perverts from someplace else. So Oscar and his partner may be gay, but they're *our* gays to the people who count. The same used to be true of our black people, too."

"They may be niggers but they are *our* niggers?" Kruger asked. A couple from the table next to us looked at him sharply when he said that.

"I wouldn't use that term out loud around here, if I were you," I told him. "Nor at my table. Oscar's partner is a gentleman of color."

"Don't you ever get tired of it?" Kruger asked.

"Tired of what?"

"Tired of the hypocrisy. I mean, look at the way people down here talk. You say a gentleman of color when everyone knows exactly what term you're thinking. I swear to God, I heard someone talking about 'the late War of Northern Aggression' the other day."

"You really have a bee in your bonnet," I told him. "That was a joke you heard, Kruger. We like to use colorful expression down here. Maybe you don't understand that it's considered an art form. We work at being droll."

Kruger shook his head. "Sorry," he said. "That was unprofessional of me."

"Well, kiss my Aunt Sadie's purse," I quipped in my most pronounced delta accent. "You were being human, Kruger. Relax, man. We're taking our repast. You don't have to grind diamonds with your sphincter every minute."

For a moment, I thought I'd gone too far. Then he smiled. "That's a good one. I haven't heard that one before."

"Not to barbecue your sacred cow," I said, "but did your late director not have a gentleman companion of the same persuasion as Oscar?"

"That fact produced a lot of polished diamonds," he chuckled. "Now it's like the cousin families keep locked in the attic."

The ribs were as impressive as always at Oscar's, and when we were done, I used Kruger's phone to call Dee at his cellular number. When he answered on the second ring, he sounded glad to hear from me. Riding a desk with little to do doesn't suit his disposition, and he told me he was going crazy with boredom. He did have a preliminary report from Weaver on the crime scenes and the search and some information on the rifle I found in Luther Adams' place.

The blacksmith shop had yielded little new except a close encounter of the wrong kind with a copperhead taking shelter for the winter. However, it was cool enough that the snake was not up to full speed, and no one was hurt, not even the snake. Weaver said he was holding the copperhead for me to interview as a material witness.

The team did find something that looked like a strip of heavy wrapping paper which might have been used to wrap the rifle at some point. It was either treated or soaked with an oily substance Weaver guessed was Cosmoline, but the lab tests were not back on that yet. There were also a number of fingerprints. Most of those were smudged from handling or age, but there was one clear print that belonged to Luther Adams.

The serial number on the rifle produced more interesting results. There was a hit and an inquiry from the FBI office in Sioux Falls, South Dakota. It was one of three rifles which were missing and presumed stolen from a National Guard armory in Rapid City about twenty years before. Since he had little else to do to fill his day, Dee had called back and talked to the agent in charge of the Sioux Falls office. All he found out was that the FBI was as much in the dark as we were. The weapons turned up missing on routine inventory and there was no report of burglary in the file.

What was strange was the serial number had produced another hit, this time from the Pentagon. Yet when Dee tried to call to follow up, he was shuffled from one desk to another. Finally he hung up in frustration. Five minutes later his phone rang. The caller was a Captain Smith who listened to everything Dee had to say and questioned him about where and when the weapon was found. Yet, when Dee asked for information in return, Captain Smith politely told him that the information was classified. Nor was Captain Smith willing to leave a number where Dee could call him back.

We talked about this for a bit. Then there was a pause in the conversation and I started to say goodbye. Yet, I had the sense there was something else Dee wanted to say. When I asked him, he told me there had been another call from Washington not long after his call from the elusive Captain Smith. It was from an old drinking buddy in the Army Dee had not heard from in years. The fellow knew my name and had asked Dee how he might get in touch with me. He left a number I could call. Yet, when Dee tried to do a reverse trace on the number, the phone company had no record of it.

Dee went on to say he was hesitant to even pass the number along to me. "The guy's name is McKee and he wouldn't tell me what he wanted. Said he wasn't sure about something and wanted to check it out with you. Apparently, he tried your home, and your wife told him to check with me."

"Sounds reasonable," I observed. "What made you suspicious?"

"Maybe I've been around too much. I don't believe in coincidence. His call came in a couple of hours after I talked to the alleged Captain Smith. Back when I first knew him, McKee was a guy I would trust completely, but I heard later on he was involved in some pretty nasty stuff."

"Nasty, like in drugs or arms running?" I asked.

"No, not directly, although there was enough of that going on with the CIA in Southeast Asia. I heard he was involved in some of their dirty operations, even though he was Special Forces. They did a lot of black operations for the CIA and McKee had a reputation for being one of the best. He was just back from Vietnam the last time I saw him, and he didn't have much to say about it, not even when he was drunk. What I picked up, I got from other people later on."

"Maybe he simply needs a forensic consultant," I said. "I wonder how he got my name. Did he say who he is with?"

Dee told me McKee was vague about this, but gave Dee the impression he was in private practice as a lawyer. "Maybe that's it," Dee said. "He's a lawyer and I don't trust lawyers. They always have a hidden agenda."

We talked a bit more and Dee gave me the number. I wrote it on a piece of paper and tucked it in my pocket, intending to call when I got back home. I don't do much business with the private sector, but being an expert witness pays well and it wouldn't hurt to widen my network of referrals.

I hung up and told Kruger about the call from Captain Smith. I asked him if he thought the Bureau had the leverage to pry the information I needed loose from the Pentagon. He shook his head. "I don't think so. It sounds like black operations or CIA to me. It may even be Delta Force or our own Hostage Rescue people. They only give us what they want us to have."

"This isn't exactly a case involving national security," I pointed out. "It's a pretty straight-forward murder case."

"It doesn't have to involve national security directly," he answered. "Our security is so tight these days that the curtain comes down even if it might barely touch someone involved in national security. You wouldn't believe the stupid stuff that gets classified."

"What I can't figure out is the two separate responses," I said. "Why did we get a hit on the rifle at all if national security is involved?"

Kruger laughed. "Someone must have screwed up, big time. Maybe the weapons were on the Armory inventory without ever having been delivered there. Maybe they were diverted to a black operations unit. The computer hit from the Pentagon should have never happened."

"These are not state of the art weapons, not like the ones special weapons teams use now," I pointed out. "The rifle I found is Vietnam era. Even if it was made later, it's an obsolete design. Why all the hoorah over some an old clunker you can buy at any crossroads gun show?"

Kruger shrugged. "I trained on one at the Academy, and I imagine you did, too. There are a lot of them around. Maybe they used this old clunker just because it is old, to point suspicion in the wrong direction just in case something went wrong. Maybe this particular rifle was part of the equipment involved in something highly...inflammatory."

"You mean, something hot like the grassy knoll in Dallas?"

Kruger didn't bother to answer. He just rolled his eyes. "Suppose for just a minute I'm right. The question, then, is how it got to an unused blacksmith shop in Oak Grove, Arkansas. Why was it brought here? That's probably what Smith wanted to know."

"Maybe someone in black ops walked off with it," I answered. "As you said, these guys get personally attached to their weapons."

"So maybe we need to ask who was involved with the military and is from Oak Grove. Of course, if one of them was involved in anything having to do with national security, we'll never know."

I thought about it a minute. "I expect most of the men there were drafted during Vietnam. None of the ones I've met there strike me as someone who could set up this kind of operation. How about you?"

"I don't either, but maybe that's just who we need to be looking for. Aside from Slide, there aren't any other obvious candidates. Maybe we need to look for someone who's not so obvious."

"The man never seen," I murmured. Suddenly, I felt overwhelmed. There were just too many loose ends. "All this is crazy-making," I said. "I mean, I think you're right, but how in the hell do we find out who wasn't seen? Where do we focus? Who do we ask? For that matter, how do we ask? I imitated Jack Webb. "Pardon me, Ma'am, was there anyone you didn't see there?"

We kicked it around for a bit longer and got nowhere. Since it was getting late and Kruger needed to be in Little Rock the next day, we headed up the road toward Nashville. When Kruger yawned, I offered to drive, but he shook his head. He appreciated the offer but reminded me again that the FBI takes a dim view of anyone else driving their cars. The one exception was emergencies, but agent fatigue was not considered an emergency.

When I got back to the motel, the message light on my phone was flashing. I called the switchboard and the clerk had a message. Someone had called and left a number for me to call back at my earliest convenience. While the caller had not left a name, the clerk told me it was a man's voice on the other end. Yet, the clerk could not remember just when the call came. He thought it was after six, but he couldn't be sure.

The number looked familiar, but I couldn't place it. Since it was late, I put it on the dresser and emptied my pockets, intending to call back the next day. I thought about an evening walk, but when I sat down on the bed, even the effort of putting on my running shoes seemed too much. Instead, I stripped and headed for the shower. I don't even remember my head hitting the pillow.

I woke early the next morning and threw on my sweat suit and running shoes. It was a cool, brisk morning, and I set a fast pace, breaking into a trot after warming up. Normally, I walk to save my knees, but running felt right just then, and I headed west along the highway. A couple of miles from town, I found a good vantage point and watched the sun rise over the hills. Our sunrises in Arkansas may not have the bright colors and contrasts one sees in the Southwest, but that morning it was glorious. The air was full of mist, muting the bright colors of the trees, but somehow making them seem even brighter, too. The early light was like radiant gold shining through the mist.

When I got back to the room, Kruger was there waiting for me. He wanted to go over a couple of things in his reports with me before taking off for Little Rock. So I skipped the shower and grabbed my wallet, and we headed for the cafe. While we were waiting for our breakfast, I went over his reports and suggested a couple of things he might want to include. He made note of these and asked me what I was going to do that day. I told him I would probably head for Oak Grove and talk with the pastor. Then, if the sheriff would lend me a deputy, I might go through Smiley Jones' place to see what turned up. Failing all else, I would come back to Nashville and go over the case files at the jail.

"Sounds exciting compared to the meeting I have on Monday," Kruger told me. "Is there anything you need from the big city?" I asked him to pick up any reports Dee might have on our various crime scenes, along with Luther Adams' autopsy report if it was ready.

Kruger was in a hurry to get going. He had plans to spend the afternoon with someone in Little Rock and wolfed down his breakfast before I was half through. I told him not to wait, that I would pay the check. He agreed so long as he could get it next time. When he took off, I could have sworn I saw a dust trail swirling in the sunlight cutting through the side window. It must have been a hot date, and I wondered what kind of woman would be Kruger's type.

As Kruger was going out the door, the sheriff was coming in, and I invited Tanner to join me at the table. We sat there for the better part of an hour talking about fishing, hunting, everything else but how the case was going. Only when we walked out onto the sidewalk did Tanner ask me to come by his office before getting away that morning.

When I got to the sheriff's office, we talked about the case for a while. I told him about the FBI report on the rifle, but not about Captain Smith. Though he was a bit short-handed, Tanner agreed to have a deputy meet me at Oak Grove to go over Smiley Jones' place. "Just keep in mind that there may not be much left there now. I tried to seal the place off, but you know how it is. Once a man passes on, a lot of his stuff seems to walk off on its own."

I was surprised that when we were done, Tanner walked me out to my car. Glancing over toward the cafe, he said, "You know, Louise, our waitress over there, is the best-hearted woman you would ever want to meet. She would give you the coat off her back, but she's not exactly the soul of discretion. You might want to keep that in mind, and pass it along to Kruger."

I felt a cold prickle at the nape of my neck. "You mean, she's been passing along what she heard us discussing?"

The sheriff shrugged. "I don't think she's said anything that will damage your investigation so far, but you've got to understand. Something like this murder is better than soap opera to a lot of folks around here. They don't mean no harm. They just want to know what's going on."

"I take it the reason you're telling me this here is that she has connections in the jail, too," I said.

Tanner grinned. "You city boys catch on real quick."

As disturbing as this was, it was good to know. Nor was it a total liability. I've been known to use misinformation on occasion to provoke someone to rash action. Doing so has broken more than one case, and Tanner had just given me the key to the Nashville neighborhood telegraph.

Back at the motel, I showered quickly and dug out a fresh pair of chinos to wear. As I was filling my pockets with all the stuff guys carry, I came across the note with the number Dee had given me the night before. I tucked it in my shirt pocket and picked up the note next to it. It was the number the clerk gave me for my caller the night before. Then it struck me why the number had looked so familiar. It was the same as the one I got from Dee.

I started to call from the motel, then remembered my conversation with the sheriff thirty minutes before. So I drove around until I found a pay phone on a relatively quiet wall outside the convenience store. I bought a calling card and punched in a long stream of numbers, adding my caller's number when I was told to do so at the end. It was a touch phone, but when I was done, my arm was almost as tired as if I had been dialing an old rotary set.

My call was answered on the second ring. "McKee. Please hold on a second." The voice was a deep, mellow baritone. Eight seconds later it was back. "Good morning, Dr. Phillips. This is Sam McKee."

"How did you know it was me?" I asked.

"I have a brother who is a technical wonk," he laughed. "That gave me the number outside the Buzz In convenience store, and you're the only person I know who might be calling me from Nashville on Sunday morning."

"I'm impressed," I said. "You did that in eight seconds."

"Well, not to brag, but I also knew who you were by your voice print, too. I have no idea how Jack does it, but I'm not sure I want to know."

"I know what you mean," I replied. "Something to do with cemeteries and arcane rites at midnight. What can I do for you?"

"Well, there are a couple of things. First of all, I'm interested in the item you found in Oak Grove, and I may be able to help you out with that."

"I don't mean to be rude, but I really don't know who you are, Mr. McKee. Any information from my investigation would have to go through the CID."

"I appreciate that. Nor would I want to talk about these things over an unsecured line. What I wanted to do was to let you know someone from our agency will be looking you up in the next few days. I'll talk to DiRado and get his *imprimatur* before our man gets in touch."

"Agency? Mr. DiRado had the impression you're with a law firm."

McKee laughed. "We may be a bunch of brigands, but we aren't a bunch of thieves. No, we're a small government agency no one has ever heard of because we like it that way. Our primary mission is aimed at internationally organized crime. Most of what we do is assess information. Among other things, I serve as our in-house attorney. I think I said something about it to DiRado and that may be where he got that impression."

He told me the name of his organization and he was right. I had never heard of it. "All right," I said. "I'll talk to your guy, but only when DiRado gives me a green light."

"Fair enough," McKee said. "The name of the fellow who will be getting in touch is Willie Dill."

"Dill? Like the pickle?" I laughed despite myself.

"Exactly, though I wouldn't make a point of that with Willie," McKee said dryly. "When you meet him you'll see why. Any questions?"

"Quite a few," I answered. "I would imagine you would tell me the answer to most of them is classified."

"You must have been dealing with the Pentagon or the CIA," McKee told me. "We keep necessary secrets when it comes to operations and personnel, but we're actually rather transparent with people we trust."

"That makes you rather unique in the intelligence community."

"What makes us most unique is that we are almost entirely self-funding."

"I thought you were a governmental agency," I said. "How can you be self funding?"

"We steal, Dr. Phillips. We have license to steal from the bad guys the way the DEA does with drug dealers. They call it confiscation and develop all kinds of legal mythology justifying it. We don't bother. We have guidelines, and we are accountable for them, but we call things what they are."

I was beginning to like the guy. "That's refreshing. You said there were two reasons you want to talk to me."

"Yes. I'm interested in your doing some consulting with us."

This was strange, and I thought about it for a moment. "All right," I said. "But I can't figure why you need a forensic expert."

"Actually, I need your expertise as a criminologist. I believe that's the right term. I need someone with your background. Didn't you write an article on corporate financial crime a few years back?" There was a rustling sound in the background. "Yes. Here it is. Six years ago."

"Yes, I did. That's actually the direction I was moving when I retired, but I didn't find anyone with much interest in pursuing it. I was swimming against the tide. Most of my consulting now is down and dirty crime scene investigation or serial killers or being a forensic expert."

"Given the corporate welfare orientation of our times, I'm not surprised. I only came across the article recently and I was quite impressed. I'm interested in talking to you."

"I can see why, given the way you do things. It's an interesting twist on Robin Hood."

McKee laughed again. "Robin Hood? Don't tempt me, Dr. Phillips. I'm way too good at rationalizing as it is. What we do isn't romantic, not at all. It's as down and dirty as any crime scene. Maybe more."

We talked a while longer After we hung up, I called Dee to let him know what was going on. When I mentioned who McKee was sending out, he knew Dill personally. "Willie Dill? Yeah, I know him. He was the roughest trainer Special Forces had, but he was the best. His training saved my ass more than once. Not that I liked him for it when I was going through."

I had a strange feeling talking to Dee. I told him most of what McKee told me about his agency and the fact he wanted to hire me as a consultant. Yet, I held back why McKee wanted to consult me.

That bothered me. While I knew I was completely within normal ethical boundaries by respecting McKee's confidence, and although it was none of Dee's business what McKee wanted me to do as a consultant, I still had a feeling I was somehow betraying DiRado with my silence. Maybe it was because we were both cops and had been partners so long. Partners spend more time together than husbands and wives, and in some ways, are closer, if not more intimate.

Or maybe it was because I knew how Dee might look at what McKee and company did for a living. To a cop, stealing is stealing, even if the victim is a criminal. I know that, in this day and age, a lot of cops drive cars confiscated from drug dealers without due process of law, so maybe Dee wouldn't have seen it that way at all. Yet, he was as old school as I am, and I think the bottom line was I just didn't want to take the risk. That was a strange decision with someone I have trusted with my life.

I should have known he would pick up on it. "What's the matter, Jazz?" he asked me.

"This thing is getting way too complicated," I answered. "It started out as a pretty standard murder, and now we have spooks involved. I don't like it, Dee. I'm wondering what's going to jump out of the bushes next."

"No shit!" he replied. "You want out? It's no skin off my ass if you do. I'm in the clear now. They can shove this case and the whole frigging CID as far as I'm concerned."

"No," I said. "It just gives me the red-ass. I'll get over it."

"You've been known to do that," he laughed. "Look, you want me to drive over to keep you company?"

"No, I want you to take care of yourself. Your boss might get the wrong idea if you come with us, and I don't want to mess up your retirement. Tanner is giving me a deputy for the day, so I've got help, or at least backup. I'm all right. I'm just blowing off a little steam."

———

The deputy Tanner promised was waiting for me when I got to the jail. It was Leslie Parker, the fellow on duty the night I brought in the rifle and he was dressed in jeans and a faded cotton warmup parka over a black tee shirt. The jacket was hunter green and on the left breast was a golden shield with the words "Sheriff's Department" written in small block letters circling it. The same words were written in large letters across the back of the parka, and underneath that I could see the bulge of a pistol holster on his belt. I suspected his cuffs were looped over his belt in back.

Leslie seemed cheerful and friendly, like a large, overgrown pup, but I wasn't sure just where I stood with him. I decided it would be better to confront any issues he might have before we left town. "I hope I didn't get you in a jam with your boss," I told him, watching carefully.

He seemed surprised I mentioned it. "You mean with the rifle? No sweat. It was my own fault for getting sloppy. He didn't even say much. Just moved me back to patrol."

"So no hard feelings?" I asked.

He shook his head and grinned. "No, I'd rather be out on patrol, anyway. I don't like driving a desk much."

"I don't either," I said. I told him what I had in mind.

Leslie echoed the sheriff's assessment. "I was in on the first search, but there wasn't a whole lot there like there is with some old people. Mostly his clothes and some musical instruments. What there was has probably disappeared by now, but we can give it a try."

It turned out he was right. Smiley had lived alone in his own house, and it was obvious he had taken care of the place. Yet, the front door was missing, as was the kitchen sink and the commode. The place was bare of furniture and the only thing that remained was trash scattered around the polished wooden floor. Not even coat hangers remained in the one closet. "It sure don't take long out here," the deputy observed, looking around. "Unless someone moves in, the floor boards will be gone soon."

The way he was eyeing the oak flooring, I wondered if he was considering it himself. "Not much left for his family, is there?"

The deputy gave me a startled look. "Hell, it was probably his family who done this," he said. "Cousins. He didn't have no kids or even an ex-wife."

"Any evidence he was gay?" I asked, watching the deputy closely.

"Wouldn't surprise me, him being a musician and all, but I ain't heard a word about that. He had the reputation of being a lady's man and I hear a lot of ladies thought he was their man." He laughed.

"Sometimes that's a screen," I said and I could tell he didn't follow. "You know, what people in the gay community call window dressing."

"Window dressing?" he asked, looking at the bare frames where even the curtain rods had been taken.

"It's the way some guys hide the fact they are gay. They have a family or lots of girl friends."

"Jesus!" he said. The look of revulsion on his face almost made me laugh. When the implications hit him he frowned. "Then how do you know...?"

I shrugged. "Mostly, you don't. That's why I was asking."

"Yeah," he said absently, looking deeply troubled. I realized I had opened the door to a vast abyss before him, and there was nothing I could do to close it. "You know, we've got a guy like that in the sheriff's department," he told me. "A real ladies' man. You don't think...?"

"Good heavens, no," I said, improvising. The last thing I wanted to do was stir up trouble in Tanner's office. "Not out here. Smiley was a city guy most of his life. That's why I asked."

"Oh," he said. "Yeah. I see what you mean." It was obvious he didn't see, and it was equally clear he was still troubled. Yet, I hoped I had given him a way back to shore. What he said next told me I had failed. "There are some weird folks out there. Guy has to watch himself."

Out of habit, I sorted through the trash. Most of it was just that, but in one of the back rooms, I turned over what I thought was a sheet of yellowed paper and found myself looking at an old photograph. It was black and white and the paper was stained a bit from age and dust, but the image was still clear. Nor was it a snapshot. It looked professionally composed, almost like a publicity shot, though there was no name of the photographer on the back.

The picture showed six young African American men dressed in their Sunday best. One of them was older and a bit taller and wore a black suit with a white shirt and a wide conservative tie. He looked to be in his early twenties, but he could have been forty or more. There was something that looked like a white carnation in his lapel and he was smiling broadly, his large white teeth as bright against piano keys against his dark skin. It was that famous smile that had given Wilbur Jones his sobriquet.

Directly in front of Smiley was a much younger man about the same age as Robert McNutt was now. He was wearing what looked like a grey blazer and black dress pants and was seated facing the camera directly. His tie was much narrower, but he, too, wore a white carnation in his jacket lapel. What struck me immediately was how much he looked like Wilbur, whose hands rested on the youngster's shoulders. Most viewers would probably think they were looking at a father and his son—a son born in his father's exact image.

The other four men were much younger than the man in the center, in their middle teens and a bit older than the youth. Two of them

stood to either side of Wilbur, and they were dressed the same way as
the young man in front, with grey blazers, black pants, and carnations
on their lapels. They were all grinning, too, and small beads of light
reflected from the shine on their shoes.

While all of these four young men were about the same height and
build, only one of them bore any resemblance to the two in the center. This young man stood directly to the left of the man in the center,
and except for his height and age, could have been the older man's
twin. Or perhaps the youngster's twin.

I recognized the photo as one I'd seen in the article on Smiley.
There, the man in the middle was identified as Smiley, but the other
men were described as members of his church choir. Now I recognized
the man to his left as a much younger Slide Jones, and the man standing immediately to Smiley's right was Luther Adams. Next to him I
recognized the young Albert Jones, and from what I had been told, I
knew the youngster was Edward Posey.

The man I did not recognize, standing next to Slide Jones, had to
be Luther Goodman. Dressed up and posed for the photograph, I
would not have recognized him from the picture in Luther Adams'
Bible. I guessed the photo I was holding must have been taken some
time before his death.

Whether it was the clothes or the formal setting of the photo, all
the young men looked older than I expected. Or it could be Albert
Jones was mistaken about how old they were when Goodie was shot. I
made myself a note to check the date in the county records.

Something at the very bottom of the photo caught my eye. It was
a line of small type and I had to move to better light to make it out.
When I did I saw it said that the photo was by one Jackson Smith of
Arkadelphia. So it was done by a professional, and I guessed it must
have been a publicity photo for the young man's choir from Oak Grove
Baptist Church. Assuming Jackson Smith was still alive, he might be
able to tell me exactly when the picture was taken.

"I hear they were really good." Leslie's voice startled me. He had
come to where I was standing by the window and was peering over
my shoulder.

"They were a bit before your time, weren't they?" I asked, irritated with him for sneaking up on me but trying not to show it.

"My mama used to listen to them all the time," he said, oblivious to my rancor. "She had an old record they made when they first started. It was good but all scratchy."

My rancor turned to interest. "Did she know much about them?"

Leslie laughed. "As much as any white woman, I guess. Her daddy used to get upset by her spending so much time at the n...at their church."

Leslie looked at me nervously to see if I had caught his near slip. I ignored it, more concerned with any information he might have than with his political correctitude. "Do you think she would mind talking to me?" I asked. "It could help our case here."

"I don't see why not," he replied, relieved. "Only thing is, after our daddy died, she went to live with my sister in Orlando. Down in Florida. She won't be home until just before Christmas."

I got the sister's telephone number and asked Leslie to let his mother know I might call in a few days. When it comes to gossip, there's very little crossover between the white community and the black community, and I doubted Leslie's mother would be much help. On the other hand, she might, or she might know someone in the black community who could give me a different take on Smiley Jones and his choir boys. I didn't expect much would come of this, but one never knows. Over the years there have been several times when some of my biggest breaks came from the most unexpected sources. I made myself a note to follow up on this and tucked it in my pocket.

There wasn't much more we could do at Smiley's place. The house was empty and there were no sheds or other buildings to search. I needed to talk to Albert Jones, but I didn't think Leslie's presence would help, so I let him get back to patrol. He told me he was on split shift that day and hoped to get in a little fishing in between.

I watched Leslie drive away, then stood there a while. I wasn't looking for anything or even thinking. I was listening to the silence of the house, like a dog testing the wind with its nose for whatever scent it might bring. I was listening for what the silence could tell me about the man who lived here, about the people he lived among, and for anything this could tell me about why he died.

Yet, there was nothing there. Too many strangers to this place had passed through, raiding the house for its possessions. Their tracks had made this home a public place, and whatever sense might remain of Smiley's presence in this place had been trampled in their greed. I would need to look elsewhere for a sense of the man who lived here.

I looked down at the photo I was holding, now secure in it's plastic bag. As I looked at it, I was overcome by a profound sense of loss. Normally, I try to stay away from such feelings. They can be useful in an investigation, but they can cloud the issues and rob the investigator of objectivity. For such feelings are as much about the beholder as what is beheld.

This time it came on too fast, and I was faced with a difficult choice. I could fight the feeling and risk losing whatever it might tell me, or I could be present to it and enter the fog of crime. I decided to listen to whatever this side of my soul had to tell me, and I fixed my attention on the photo.

The sense of sadness and waste that washed over me at that moment was almost like a physical blow, I was looking at six young men full of confidence and hope. They were full of hope knowing the deck was stacked against them, just as it had been for their fathers. They were male and they were of African descent, and the world they were born in did not prize them. It was afraid of them, and in every generation it ignored those among them who it could not destroy.

Of these six young men, one would be dead within a year or two, taking with him the will to live of the companion whose hand was on the gun. Another would turn to a life of crime, exploiting his own people and providing them with the means of their self destruction. The eldest among them would die a violent death at the hands of an assassin, and the youngest would be sent to die or rot away as a prisoner of war in the jungles of Vietnam.

Yet, as I had this last thought, I realized that I only knew of Edward Posey's death or being missing by hearsay. While I don't hold to the high level of proof the courts require, I do believe in being thorough. I made a mental note to check Posey's family background and military record if I could, but the first thing I had to do was get his full name and date of birth from Vital Records. Then I had the thought it might be easier to check the courthouse records since I was already in the county where he was born. The hospital records might have what I wanted to know, too, as might the church. Baptists are not like Anglicans or Presbyterians when it comes to keeping records, but I might get lucky.

Since I needed to see Albert Jones anyway, I decided to ask him about it. It was just past one and I thought church services should be done. I drove to the parsonage, but no one was there. So I walked to the church. Neither the pastor nor his wife were there, but there was an elderly couple cleaning the place. They told me the pastor and his wife had gone to Nashville, taking Luther Adams' mother to make the arrangements for his funeral. I was surprised to hear she was still alive until I remembered that Luther looked far older than he was. His mother could easily be alive and in good health in her eighties. Most people of color in rural Arkansas don't reach such an age, but it does happen.

On a whim, I asked the couple if they knew anything about Edward Posey or his family, and my luck turned. It turned out they were his aunt and uncle and they were able to give me enough information to save a lot of time with Vital Records. They were even able to tell me just when he was born, dating this the way country people do by connecting it to other events.

I tried to ask them more about Edward, but the man told me they needed to finish their cleaning so the church would be ready for Luther's funeral. I could see there was little use pushing the issue, so I thanked them and asked if I might come back and talk to them when they were not so busy. They looked at each other for a long moment, then reluctantly agreed. When I asked where they lived, they looked at each other once more before the man pointed with a frail, thin arm and told me how to find their place. He said they were usually there in the evenings except Wednesday, which was church night, and Monday night, when their favorite shows were on television.

There was little more I could accomplish in Oak Grove at the moment, so I decided to head back to Nashville, intending to take a shower and review my case notes again. As I drove, I thought about the case. I had a growing sense that the solution lay somewhere in the history of those six young men in the choir. I had no idea what the connection might be, but I had a strong sense it was there waiting for me to uncover. The silence at Smiley's place had apparently told me more than I sensed when I stood listening.

CHAPTER SIX

Vital Records

When I arrived at the courthouse in Nashville on Monday, there was not much left of the morning. Nellie surprised me on Sunday afternoon by driving down from Fort Smith and waiting for me in my room. I was glad to see her and glad for a break from the case. Not much was open Sunday evening, so we drove down to Hope and ended up checking into the motel there. They had a hot tub, and Nellie thought to pack my swimming suit and a change of my clothes along with hers. Nor did we rush our farewells the next day.

I was able to find the office I needed fairly easily, but there my luck turned again. The records were guarded by a curmudgeon with the looks and the disposition of an ill-tempered bulldog. When I asked to see the index of birth records, he demanded to know why I needed the information. I produced a photo ID issued when the CID designated me as a reserve peace officer and told him I was investigating the murder of Wilbur Jones. I also reminded him what he already knew: that the records I needed to see were public records that were available to anyone on request.

He took exception to that and refused to let me see the records. Normally, I would back off and try to work around someone like that, but that day I was fed up. I told him again I was investigating a murder and if he did not produce the records, I would charge him with obstructing justice.

I was very careful to be very polite when I said all that, but it made no difference. The bastard was just being petty, and while that's not a crime, I was fed up. I warned him again, but he dug in his heels and told me not only what he thought of us city boys from Little Rock, but also what I could do with my state ID card. He went on to say that one less black bastard in that county was fine with him.

That was too much. I was over the counter like a cat and slammed him down on his own desk, cuffing his hands behind him before he realized what was happening. I stood him on his feet and walked him out of the courthouse and down the street to the jail, with him cursing me all the way and telling me what he would do when he got loose. As we crossed the street, we attracted a crowd and I spotted several people trying hard not to grin.

It was not one of my finer moments, but it was effective. There must have been fire in my eye because the deputy on duty booked the curmudgeon without question, ignoring his curses and threats and taking him away to a cell. Then, when I got back to the records office, a nervous clerk emerged from a back room and quickly produced the index I requested. She smiled nervously and jumped like a startled deer every time I asked a question.

There were a number of birth records for people named Posey, but none for Edward or Edwin or Ed. Judging from the age of the pastor, I figured Eddie must have been born in the late forties, and there were records of twelve Posey babies born between 1945 and 1950. I asked to see those records and weeded out seven of them right away. Arkansas lists race on birth records, and those children were born to white parents. With children of mixed ancestry, race is always shown as the same as the minority parent, although the race of both parents is given.

I looked over the other five records carefully. I set aside the first three because the name of the mother was different from the one spoken of by Eddie's aunt and uncle. When I saw the fourth one, I felt a rush of excitement. The aunt and uncle had come very close in remembering the date, and the mother's name was the same as they had given me. What was interesting was what they had not said, for on March 15, 1948, a child was born to an *unwed* young woman of fifteen at her parents' home in Oak Grove, Arkansas. The child was named Wilbur Edward Posey, and his father's name was listed as Wilbur O. Jones.

I thought about that for a while, wondering why this information was not common knowledge among people in Oak Grove. Then I glanced at the bottom of the registration and found my answer. The birth was not recorded until three years later, and it was the child's grandfather who had come in to swear to the accuracy of the information given.

At that point, there was no doubt in my mind that Edward Posey was the love child of Smiley Jones. What I did not know was whether Eddie knew this. Were he not dead or missing in action, this would be a classic motive for murder if he knew. So the next step would be to confirm his death.

I thought about that a moment and realized I was feeling very sad. While I was glad to have the information about Edward Posey, the same information was a two-edged sword. Getting it, I lost a personal hero, for I knew a lot more about Wilbur Jones now, much more about the real man behind the famous smile. I know we all have feet of clay, and I try to judge the action, not the actor. Yet, finding this out about Smiley was like finding out about Santa Claus. It left an empty place inside me.

It also changed the way I looked at things. I found myself giving a lot more credence to what Slide had told us about Smiley's theft of the song Edward had written. Nor did I think that knowing Eddie was his son would have made much difference. Like any other habit of soul, crime grows out of human character and reinforces the very traits that give rise to it. So it was not surprising that Smiley did the same to his son as he had done to his son's mother. He was consistent in his *modus operandi*. He gained their trust as children then betrayed them and destroyed their innocence.

With Eddie's mother, his crime was rape of a child. There was no other way of putting it. Whether that was statutory rape or actual sexual assault did not matter. Wilbur Jones had violated his victim, and with Edward, it was no less a violation. It struck at his sense of being. So in my eyes, this made Smiley Jones the worst kind of criminal, and I wondered what the response would be if that was made public. There would be outrage and then denial. Then the messenger would be pilloried by character assassination. I had no doubt of that.

Then another thought struck me. Assuming Louella was telling me the truth about being Smiley's love child, Smiley had done the same to her mother. This also meant Louella and Edward Posey were siblings.

The clerk coughed nervously. I suddenly realized I must have been sitting there like a statue for some time, frowning at Edward's birth certificate like a God of wrath, lost in those reflections. I thanked the nervous clerk, causing her to jump again, and walked out of the records room. As I did, I ran into Sheriff Tanner who greeted me politely and asked if we could have a word in private.

When we stepped outside, Tanner grinned. When he did, his kinship to the Jones family was evident. There are people who would kill for teeth that bright and perfect. "You sure do pick them, Jazz. It's been a long time coming and way overdue, but no one around here had the balls to bust Jim Smith." He laughed again. "Don't get me wrong. You done the right thing, but I just think you ought to know who it was you busted. I'd like to know what happened, too. You know folks will ask."

I told him how it went down, stressing the fact I had tried very hard to be courteous the whole time. When I told him what catapulted me over the counter, Tanner's smile disappeared, and his face grew grim. He nodded. "That fits, all right. What you probably don't know is Jim Smith is one of the head dragons in the state Klan. I come across it myself by accident just recently. I don't think no one knows. Not even CID."

"Why not make it public, then?" I asked. "These guys are cowards. They're nothing but terrorists. They operate in the dark with hoods. Take away the hoods and you take away most of their power."

"Too dangerous. Remember, we all have to live around here. If I leaked it, Jim Smith would know by morning, and you'd be here investigating my killing next. Maybe some of my family, too." John Tanner's face was as solemn as a grave.

"Are you saying Smiley's death was a Klan killing?" I asked. "That would fit the facts we have very well. It would also explain why the killing looks like a professional hit. Some of those guys are professional."

Tanner shook his head. "No, that's not what I'm saying. All I'm saying is *my* leaking his being in the KKK would be dangerous for me and for my family, too. They's no connection I see to Smiley getting killed. Smiley didn't get crossways with the Klan. Least, not so far as I know."

I looked at him. "Well, since I'm out of the good graces of Jim Smith, already, maybe I can be the one to leak it. I could do it so no one would find out where I heard it."

"That's up to you," Tanner told me. "For us here, it would probably be best if you made the leak in Little Rock."

I gave him a grin. "John, I would be honored to take a leak on Little Rock any time." He laughed more than the quip was worth.

We talked about this some more, and then he asked me where the case stood at the moment. I told him that Slide Jones was still my favorite for the shooter, but that Edward Posey would interest me if he were still alive. I told him why.

"Eddie's dead, Jazz," Tanner told me. "At least, that's what I think. They was some kind of news story few years back, about them MIA guys. He was listed as one of them that got took prisoner. He never come back. I think they must of buried him at Arlington or some place like that if they brought the body back at all. It sure wasn't around here."

I made myself a note to check this out with the cemetery register and then stuffed the note in my pocket. Tanner chuckled when he saw me do that. "Short pencil better than a long memory?"

"This time of life, it sure is," I agreed. "Look, I don't really want to pursue the charge against Jim Smith unless it would be helpful around here."

"Wouldn't make no difference here," Tanner assured me. "Wouldn't get no conviction, noways."

"Yeah, I didn't think so. With his connections, he's probably out on bail by now, anyway."

"Nope," Tanner grinned. "Won't be 'til late evening day after tomorrow, neither. His honor went up fishing on Buffalo River. Said he was on the way when I got Luther's warrant. No phone, no radio, no contact for three days. Told me if somebody died, don't send no posse. Pack them in dry ice!" He laughed.

"Well, it's good to know Smith won't beat the bust. Like I say, it's not such a big deal except for his connection to the Klan. Maybe that's how to handle it—let DiRado report the arrest."

Tanner looked at me levelly. "You know, you may have some trouble with them boys in white," he said. "When you gets home."

I shook my head. "No way. Nellie would kick their ass from here to Hope!"

Dee expressed the same concern when I talked to him later that afternoon, but he agreed the two of us had been on the Klan's spit list for a long time. He also told me the information about Smith's ties to the Klan was news to him. He said there had been a revival of Klan activity in the Nashville area and repeated his unease about my safety.

"I don't think they would want the kind of heat going after me would bring down," I reassured him. "They wouldn't cry over it if I stroked out tomorrow, but I don't think they will make a move on me up north. There are a lot of other folk we put away I worry about much more."

"Watch your back," he said. "They might not wait until you get home. I'd be happy to send someone else out."

"I charge extra for house-breaking your new investigators," I told him and he laughed. "Besides, Kruger will be back tomorrow."

I gave him my laundry list of things to check out and he told me what he had learned, which was not much. McKee and company were legitimate but not well-known by his sources in Washington. "The word I have is that they go after corporate crime mostly, but I also hear this gets rough sometimes. Their agents are armed, and I hear they're very well trained. They would be if Willie Dill has anything to do with it."

"Makes sense," I told him. "You know how it was when some of the Mafia went legitimate. It didn't mean their attitudes changed, or even some of their basic techniques, for that matter. They still found a use for muscle."

We talked some more and Dee agreed to put a priority on Edward Posey's military records and anything else we could learn about him. I could tell he wasn't that enthusiastic, and I couldn't blame him. I knew

I was probably chasing a dead man, but he went along with my request. He also agreed to do a check on the Arlington National Cemetery burial records and to dig up anything else he could find on McKee.

I looked at my watch after I hung up. We were well into afternoon in that part of the world, and I had missed lunch. I decided to spend the rest of the day going over the growing case book and taking inventory of where we were. There was a preliminary time line for the shooting and immediate investigation that Dee had put together, but someone needed to plug in the new information we had dug up in the last three days.

It was too late in the day to get going on much else, and working with the time line might point me in a useful direction. Right then, I had no idea where the case was going. All I had was a jumble of different pieces with no idea of what was important and what wasn't.

I dug a set of index cards out of the trunk of my car and headed for the cafe. When I asked for a large table, Louise told me I could use the one in the meeting room and led me there. It was perfect. Unlike the jail, I could work there with no interruption from telephones or people coming and going. So I ordered a chicken fried steak plate, complete with cole slaw and fries and two large glasses of tea. Then I set to work.

The first thing I did was to review everything that had taken place since I arrived and to chart my work log. This may sound redundant, but it does help me catch things that may have slipped through the cracks. I made up a separate index card for each event and piece of evidence then spread them out on the top of the table. As I looked them over, I moved them around, making notes in a spiral notebook as I worked.

What emerged was a clear picture of the investigation. I took this as far as it would go and came up with several questions I needed to ask different people. These might turn out to be important or they might not, but they needed to be asked. Even negative answers would tell us something.

Then it occurred to me that it might be useful to do a rough life-line with the young men in the choir. Doing so made sense if that was where the roots of Smiley Jones' murder lay. So I started to block that out, working from memory and intending to correct the dates later. The only dates I was certain of were Smiley's birthday, the date of his death, and the date of Edward's birth. Yet, that didn't have to be exact. What I was after was a general picture, but what I came up with looked more like a skeleton.

Sept. 1920	Smiley Jones born in Oak Grove
1939/1940	Albert Jones born in Oak Grove
1940/1942	The four Luthers born in Oak Grove in the same year
Mar. 1948	Edward Posey born at home in Oak Grove
1955/1956	Luther Goodman shot by Luther Adams
1959/1960	Slide Jones leaves town in hurry (*what did he do then? carnival?*)
1961/1962	Smiley Jones invited to leave town – joins Slide at carnival – *doing what?*
1962/1963	Albert Jones drafted after finishing college – goes to Canada
late 1963	Smiley Jones goes to New Orleans – starts band when? (relevant?)
1966/1967	Edward Posey drafted – sent to Vietnam (when was he reported missing?)
Sept. 2000	Someone mistaken for Smiley seen behind blacksmith shop in Oak Grove wearing vest (carrying trombone case?)
Oct. 2000	Smiley Jones shot in Oak Grove in early pm (.223 casing found by Robert – when?)

Nov. 2000	CID calls in JSP / FBI jumps in, arrests Albert Jones & Luther Adams
	Luther Adams released – killed same night near Winton

There wasn't much meat on those bare bones, but it helped to set things down in black and white. It also gave me a clear idea of where I needed to go to flesh out the complete picture. I began making a list of the people I needed to talk with and the questions I needed to ask.

At the top of the list was Slide Jones. There were only one or two critical pieces of information I needed from him, but driving to Hot Springs and back would eat up a whole morning. Nor could I do that by telephone. Slide Jones was too smooth a liar to not look for non-verbal cues. I would have to make the trip, but maybe I could tie it in with a conference with Dee in Little Rock. I decided to try to see Albert Jones first thing in the morning and then head for Hot Springs.

My thoughts were interrupted by Louise, asking if I wanted to order some supper before they closed the kitchen. I looked at my watch and was surprised to see it was half past six. I was still full from lunch, but I asked her to bring me a salad followed by a piece of peach pie a la mode when I was done. She laughed, but wrote it down and headed for the kitchen.

I gathered my stuff and when I finished eating, I headed for the jail. I was sure the parsonage must have a telephone, and I found a listing for the reverend. It was Albert Jones himself who answered, and I asked if he could spare me some time in the morning. "The funeral is tomorrow afternoon," he told me. "There will be all kinds of people coming and going in the morning. Why don't you come on out now?"

I told him I would be there within the hour and quickly revised my plans. I didn't realize Adams' funeral would be so soon, and I needed to attend. I wanted to pay my respects. Yet, I also needed to see who showed up. With any luck, Slide would attend and save me a trip to Hot Springs.

I called the motel to see if Kruger was back yet, but he wasn't. I left word with the desk where I was headed and asked for him to call me. I thought I would be back by ten-thirty or eleven at the latest. I also told the deputy on night duty at the jail where I was going and who I was going to see. Then I checked out a riot gun from the sheriff's arsenal and asked for number seven shells. While I was not expecting trouble, I was going out alone and Tom Tanner's warning weighed on my mind. Nellie would never forgive me if I got myself killed and if some dumb peckerwood decided to come after me, I wanted artillery to back up my pistol.

"Little late in the day for quail, isn't it?" the deputy quipped when I asked for number seven shot.

"This is for polecats," I assured him. "Two-legged or four. I hear they been really bad lately. Stealing sheets."

The deputy gave me a strange look. In the light of the armory, his eyes were as dark as his face. "Just a minute," he said. He disappeared into the vault and came out holding a bulletproof vest and a German assault rifle with doubled thirty-shot clips. "Sure you don't want these? They'll definitely level the playing field."

"Thanks, but I'm just being cautious. Not starting a war. I appreciate the thought, but I'm not expecting any trouble."

"You want me to close up and back you up?" he asked. "Sheriff said to give you whatever you asked."

I started to tell him not to bother, then stopped and thought about it. It's almost always better to have someone else present at an interview. Aside from an obvious legal advantage, adding a second pair of eyes and ears gives a better perspective and greater objectivity. Nor did it hurt that the deputy was a man of color. From the way he talked, he sounded educated, too, and I thought that might play well with Albert Jones.

"Thanks, Mason," I said, glancing at his name badge. "Do you go by your first name or do we have to play deputy and doctor?"

Mason smiled. "My given name is James. Not Jim, but James." He saw my surprise and laughed. "Yes, like the actor. Mother really liked him. They call me Mason around here, but I prefer James."

I told him to call me Jazz and asked if he minded changing into civilian wear. Ten minutes later he was dressed in tan chinos with a powder-blue oxford button-down shirt over his body armor. His feet were cased in Hush Puppies, and he was wearing a light-weight brown leather jacket. Had she seen him, Nellie would have called him a total stud muffin.

On our way to Oak Grove, I told Mason what I wanted. He was to listen and watch carefully and to follow my lead. I also wanted him to take careful notes so I would not have to, and if he had any questions himself, to make a note of them to ask when I was done. He was also to keep as good a distance between me and himself as he reasonably could.

He frowned when I mentioned that last one, and I asked if he had a question. He hesitated before asking about the distance. I liked the way he asked, not using his question as a challenge, but as a request for information. It raised my confidence in him. I told him so, then explained. "I don't expect to get shot at, but it makes a harder target if we're not close together."

He nodded. "Makes sense to me." Then he laughed. "I hear getting shot at isn't the danger at the parsonage. I hear the danger is flying glassware."

I asked him about that. He told me Emma Jones was well known for going through sets of dishes quickly. "The pastor is lucky she's not a very good shot," he laughed, tapping his bullet proof vest. "We might need hockey helmets more than these."

"So you heard about our experience, Kruger and me?"

He nodded. "Oh, yes, but that's not the first time, and I doubt it'll be the last. Mrs. Jones has a volatile nature."

"You realize, she may have much better aim than she lets on."

We laughed a good bit more about this and other things, but when we got out of the car in Oak Grove, Mason was completely professional. His eyes were moving constantly as we walked up to the door, and there was little he missed. He also kept good distance, but it wasn't obvious.

Albert Jones answered my knock himself. He was surprised to see Mason with me but greeted him by name. He invited us in, leading the way to the den and offering us comfortable chairs. I noted that while Mason sat casually, he was positioned to move quickly if needed.

I asked about Luther Adams' funeral, and we talked about that for a couple of minutes. I saw out of the corner of my eye that Mason had begun taking notes unobtrusively and without looking down very often. Nor did he show surprise when I asked the pastor if he would mind Mason's being there for the funeral. I was surprised by the pastor's chuckle.

"He won't be unobtrusive, if that's what you're looking for, Jazz," Albert Jones told me. "James is the best gospel tenor around and if he shows up, he'll probably be asked to sing."

I looked at Mason, who shrugged and nodded. "Well, I guess that gives him a good reason to be here, doesn't it?"

Albert Jones frowned. "May I ask why you want him here?"

"To keep his eyes open," I said. "It's not uncommon for killers to go to the funerals of their victims. I plan to come and pay my respects, too."

"I doubt the killer will have a scarlet 'M' on his brow," Jones murmured.

"I wish it were that easy. The point is, Mason is a trained observer and has a policeman's instincts. He may spot something I might miss."

"Will he be armed?" The pastor's voice was deathly quiet. I understood he was also asking if I would be armed.

"That's up to him and the sheriff. Normally, he would be."

Albert Jones' frowned deepened. "I don't like guns in church," he told us. "I haven't cared for them since Goodie was shot, but I particularly don't like them in church."

"It's all right, Jazz," Mason said. "I can leave it locked in the car. I was planning to come to the funeral, anyway, and that's what I would do."

I nodded and the issue was settled. Then Jones spoke. "You didn't come all the way out here to just talk about this. How can I help you?"

"I need information," I said. I told him about my sense that understanding the murder meant knowing something about the history of the young men in the choir. "With Luther dead, that gives me only two sources of information: yourself and Slide Jones."

The pastor nodded. "So is Luther—Slide—a suspect?"

I told him the truth. "Yes and no. I tend to believe him when he said he didn't do it, but I can't clear him, either."

Jones nodded. "That's the sad story of his whole life, I'm afraid. I believe Slide is a good man in the depths of his heart, but I can't prove it. He's done some evil things. Yet, I wonder if his circumstances had been different..." He broke off. "That's idle speculation. He did what he did and is who he is, and only God is wise enough to judge him. What do you want to know?"

"Why don't you start with what you know about him? Not just what you know for sure growing up together, but what you may have heard and believe to be true."

A look of distaste crossed Jones' face. "I really don't care to pass on gossip, Jazz. It's murder by character assassination."

"Well, why don't you stick to what has a high probability of being true and label speculation as just that? Maybe start by telling me if you're kinfolk."

The pastor nodded. "That sounds fair enough. Luther Jones and I are first cousins. Our fathers were brothers, and mine was the elder. We're also distant cousins to Wilbur Jones—Smiley. You wouldn't know it to look at us, but Luther bears a much closer resemblance to Wilbur's side of the family."

He started to say something else, then stopped. I asked what it was, but he shook his head. "No, that was pure gossip and not worth being repeated. Even though we were first cousins, I didn't have much to do with Slide or any of the other Luthers until later on when we were in the choir. I was almost three years older and had my own friends. Like all kids, I didn't really want to hang around with brats younger than me."

I nodded and he continued. "Slide—I don't like the name, but I'll call him that to save confusion—Slide was the one in his family who was always getting in trouble. I can tell you his daddy didn't like him much. There were reasons for that, and I'm not going to get into that. The point is, he got acquainted quite early with his daddy's belt, and there was a while when he seemed to need to get reacquainted more than once a week. He was also his mother's favorite, so you can see how confusing it might have been for him. I think it got better after he started school. He did very well there, and he was able to stay out of his father's way. When his mother got sick, it was Slide who took care of her and his younger brothers and sisters. That's something that's not commonly known."

Albert paused to collect his thoughts. "So things started to go better for Slide, and when Wilbur put together the young men's choir, he was included. As small as he is, he had a very deep, clear voice when he sang, and he was our lead bass." Tears gathered in the corners of the pastor's eyes. "It still moves me to remember him singing 'Go down, Moses,' though the one the white people we sang for always asked for was 'Old Man River.' He could rattle the windows."

The pastor sighed. "Then Goodie was shot. He was Slide's closest friend of any of us. There was something between them…something special. Goodie was a baritone, and when they did duets, it was like one voice singing two parts. When Goodie was killed, it was like something died in Slide. He never sang again to my knowledge, though he was asked. He wouldn't even sing at the funeral, and he could hardly stand to be around Luther Adams. Wouldn't even look at him."

The pastor lapsed into silence, and I felt Mason's eyes on me. When I looked his way, I knew he had the same question I did. I nodded, and he spoke up softly, so softly I could barely hear his words. "Do you think Slide killed Luther?"

Albert Jones didn't answer right away. A long moment went by, and then another. Mason was about to ask it again when Jones finally spoke. "I have to admit, I wondered that. I wondered if he shot Wilbur, too. There was bad blood between them, though I believe Slide tried to reconcile." He looked up. "What I cannot understand is why he waited so long to act."

"Sometimes resentment grows with age," I suggested. "Maybe it just got unbearable. Maybe he went off the deep end."

"The thing is, I've been talking with Slide for the last couple of years," the pastor told us. "I can't say much about it, except to say that Luther Jones—Slide—is not the same man he was even a year ago. Yes, he still has bad habits like we all do. He still drinks and smokes and hangs out with loose women. Yet, he is trying to forgive and be forgiven and to set things as right as he can. That's about all I can say."

I looked at Mason and saw the same reserve in his eyes that I imagine was in mine. There are a lot of jailhouse conversions, and while Slide had not gone to jail, this seemed a little like that to me. Oddly enough, the one thing that made me believe that might possibly be real was Slide's obvious lack of concern with trying to conceal his faults that remained. A hardened felon becoming a goody two-shoes overnight bears the burden of proof with me. I've seen far too many of them repent of their repentance and return to their old ways once they are out of prison or off parole.

"Tell me more about the accident," I asked. "Did all of you go hunting together very often?"

"Yes, we did," Albert Jones said. "Nor was it for sport. When we went out it was for the meat, and we had to be careful with our shells. They cost money." He thought a moment. "Normally, we'd let the best shot take the game, but that day we'd done well. We had six squirrels and two rabbits. Like I told you and everyone but Luther had bagged something. Luther wasn't very good, but it was an easy shot, and Goodie handed him the gun and backed off. Luther tried to shoot, but the gun was on safe and when he took it off, the squirrel moved. Luther was looking up, moving around and trying to sight him when he stumbled. The gun went off when he fell, and Goodie was standing in exactly the wrong place. He must have been dead before he hit the ground."

"So Goodman had the rifle," I said. "Was he the best shot?"

Albert Jones shook his head. "No. The best shot among us by far was Slide. He was the one who took all the hard shots, and he almost never missed."

Whether he knew it or not, Albert Jones was building a strong case against his cousin. What I couldn't understand was my own reluctance to believe that Slide was the shooter. All the evidence seemed to be pointing that way.

As if he read my thoughts, Albert Jones nodded. "I know it must sound like I'm in denial, but I can't believe in my heart Slide killed Wilbur and Luther. He's done some wicked things, but he's not an evil man." He sighed. "Maybe I just don't want to believe it."

"The man's your friend, pastor," I heard Mason saying gently. "Of course you don't want to believe it. I wouldn't, either."

"Had it been a crime of passion, then I could understand him doing it. At one point, he had a terrible temper, but this was a cold, calculated killing. It just doesn't fit with what I know of Slide."

"I have a couple more questions about Slide," I said. "I understand that he had to leave town quite suddenly. I understand he had a falling out with some of his partners in crime."

"You're thinking someone else may have mistaken them?" Jones asked. I nodded. "Well, I had the very same thought," he told us. "With each passing year Wilbur and Slide looked more and more alike, and it's possible someone mistook Wilbur for Slide. Some of the people he used to deal with were certainly quite capable of something that cold-blooded. They're very wicked people. Some of them I would call completely evil." He shook his head. "I've never understood why our Father allows such folk to walk the earth."

"Can you give me names?" I asked.

The pastor nodded and rattled off a list of a dozen names. "Some of them are dead now, of course, but those who are have children who would take delight in killing a black man. Any black man. They take great delight in selling our children poison, and I can't imagine them hesitating to eliminate one of their distributors who quit."

"You are sure that Slide quit?" I asked.

"He told me he had quit long before he ever came to talk with me the first time," Albert Jones said. "I suppose that's breaking a confidence, but not to his detriment. He wasn't there every time the church doors opened, but I'm given to understand he began to attend regularly in the last two years. That wasn't here, of course, but in Hot

Springs." He shrugged. "That information didn't come from Slide, either. It came from one of my colleagues in Hot Springs."

Mason caught my eye and raised an eyebrow. I nodded. "These people he used to distribute drugs for, do you know if they were connected to the Klan?"

"I have no proof, but it's my belief that most of them were. I think their intent was to make a profit destroying young black men. I also think the Klan may have provided some protection for them doing so." He shook his head. "God forgive me, but if one of those man ever walked across my sights..." He left the thought hanging.

I nodded. "I understand your sentiments, but none of them are worth it, Pastor," I told him.

"I don't even have a gun," he told us. "People tell me I'm a fool, but I won't have one in the house. After what happened to Luther Goodman, I never have." He sighed and shook his head.

"Please, bear with us just a bit longer," I asked him. "This is very helpful. Is there anything else you remember about the people Slide dealt with? Do you know who was in charge?"

"Slide mentioned one other name. He didn't say much, but I could tell it was someone he really feared. He said it was an evil old man named Smith—Jim Smith. Those were his words, not mine, 'an evil old man.' However, I don't know who he was talking about."

James Mason gave me a grim look. I nodded back. Albert Jones saw the exchange and asked about it. I told him about the incident in the records office and what I had learned from Tanner, but not revealing the source. "That old man?" the pastor exclaimed. "I knew he has a reputation for being unpleasant, but he's always been courteous to me. Not cordial, but polite. There are many who make no effort to disguise their contempt."

"Then you're among the privileged few," I replied. "With the rest of us, Smith is downright nasty." I told him the last thing Smith said before I arrested him, and the pastor shook his head.

"Well, it is a common name. I just never put the name with the face." He looked at Mason.

"I've seen him with his sheet on," the deputy told him. "Just before he put on his hood. It's him."

My jaw must have dropped. James Mason smiled at my consternation and shrugged. "A sheet and a hood covers a multitude of diversity," Mason told us. "It helps to scout out the enemy."

"What about your hands?" Albert Jones demanded.

James Mason laughed. "With doe skin gloves, who can tell the difference?"

"You're crazy," the pastor said. "You could get yourself lynched."

"I've saved some other folk getting lynched," Mason answered. "Man can get lynched minding his own business."

I admired his courage, but wondered why he was breaking cover. This was apparently John Tanner's source of information, and the first rule of undercover work is staying hidden. I could understand him trusting the pastor, but not why he chose to reveal himself in front of me.

The pastor was thinking along the same lines. "This information needs to stay in this room," he said. "James, you could get killed shooting your mouth off like that in front of the wrong folk."

James Mason nodded and glanced at his watch. I took the hint, wondering if he needed to get back to town. "How about Edward Posey?" I asked. "What can you tell me about him?"

"As I told you, I don't know what ever came of him. I know he was drafted and I heard he was sent to Vietnam. I think that was in the paper. Later, I heard he was missing in action, but no one really knows for sure. I do know he wasn't there for his mother's funeral, and I think he would've been if he were alive. I suspect he's most likely dead, but I don't know for sure."

I nodded. "I realize that, but I need to understand the choir. Can you give me a sense of him as a person?"

Albert Jones nodded. "Edward was our tenor. He had as fine a voice as Art Garfunkel, in my opinion. He and Slide used to sing that *Scarboro Fair* rendition Paul Simon made famous. Some people thought he was doing lip-sync."

The pastor sighed. "Edward was the child nobody ever saw and everyone forgot about. He was very good-looking but he had a way about him of not being noticed, and he was never one to blow his own horn. Unless you paid attention, you would never notice him. I used to think he was shy, but now I know it was something else. It was Edward's way of protecting himself. His father was a terrible alcoholic and a violent man. He mistreated his wife and his children all the time, and they learned to stay out of sight when he was drunk."

Albert Jones paused, collecting his thoughts again. "Edward was incredibly bright, and he did well at school. I always wondered why he was always third or fourth in his class until I realized it was deliberate. The other kids weren't as quick as he was, but he always saw to it they did better. As a matter of fact, the valedictorian that year later told me that Edward tutored him." He paused. "Is this what you wanted?"

"Yes, thank you," I answered. "Were you aware that Edward was Wilbur Jones' love child?"

The pastor nodded. "I'd guessed that. I didn't mention it because it didn't seem relevant. Do you think it is?"

"Only if someone was offended by it and acted on his feelings. More than anything it opens up a line of investigation."

Albert Jones looked at me as if he was seeing me for the first time. "So you do have reservations about Slide being the killer, don't you? My experience is that most police go with the obvious solution and inconvenient facts be damned."

I shrugged. "That's why they hire me. I seem to think outside the box. It may be Slide, but it doesn't feel right to me. All the facts have to fit. That's why I like a Klansman for the killer."

"The white folk who were at Wilbur's birthday celebration struck me as being anything but the right sort of folk to kill that way," Jones replied. "Of course, the killer wouldn't wear a sign around his neck, either, would he?" He shook his head. "I'm glad you have your work and I have mine."

"What about Eddie's family?" I asked. "What can you tell me about them? Were they there the day Smiley was shot?"

"Goodness, you are persistent, aren't you?" the pastor answered. "But to answer your question, no. The children scattered after Edward's father—step-father—died. Edward was long gone by then.

What surprised me was that only one of them came back for the funeral. She told me she couldn't reach the rest of her brothers and sisters." He shook his head. "That whole family was so sad."

"Eddie's got an aunt and uncle living here," I responded, mentioning their names. "Maybe they'll know something."

The pastor shook his head. "I doubt it. They're not related by blood or in law. I know that may seem a little confusing, but they were close enough friends to Edward's mother to be called that. They were very much like what Catholics call godparents. Edward grew up calling them aunt and uncle, but he was never close to them later on. They knew him as the child, not the man."

"Well, 'the child is the father of the man'," I quoted.

To my surprise, Albert Jones nodded and recited the poem by heart. "Yes," he added when he was done. "It's a wonderful way to approach life. Yet, there's a more excellent way."

We talked for a few more minutes, but there was nothing useful that Albert Jones could add to what he already had told us. I thanked him for his time and for his candor, and he asked if I would keep him informed. I told him I would as much as I could, but not to expect much. I told him I was in as much a fog as everyone else on this case.

"I suspect what you call clear as high noon on a dry day is about like fog to the rest of us," he answered. "I wish you well in your investigation, and I'll pray for your success. Regardless how it may turn out."

James Mason and I drove back toward Nashville in silence. About halfway there, I asked him why he had broken cover. "I thought it might give us some leverage with the pastor," he said. "I think it did. He seemed to join with us after that. Before, he seemed adversarial."

"I didn't pick up on it, but you may be right," I replied. "But what about me? I could be the guardian of the grand lizard's balls in the Klan."

"I guess you could," he said, "but you aren't. Cowboy would know. He told me to let you in on who I was, and that seemed as good a way of breaking the ice as any. I wish you could have seen your face."

"Cowboy? You mean John Tanner? Is that what you guys call him?"
Mason laughed. "No, I mean Sam McKee. I work for him."

I kept silent. McKee had not mentioned James Mason at any point when we talked. As a matter of fact, he had said I was the only person in Nashville who would be calling him.

"Don't take my word for it," Mason said. "Call him at the number he gave you when we get back to town."

"You say you work for this Sam McKee. Does Tanner know?"

"Yes. That's how Tanner can afford me. McKee pays my salary. I'm a federal agent." He looked at me. "I even have a DEA card, but that's about as real as a four dollar bill. I work for McKee."

I nodded. "It's hard to imagine what a federal agent would be after here in Nashville, Arkansas."

"I'm after the Klan," he told me. "What the pastor said about them using drugs to kill our kids was right on the money. They've been doing it for a long time now. I'm here to put a stop to it."

"No disrespect, but I think you may be outnumbered," I replied.

Mason laughed. "It sure looks that way, doesn't it? When you consider the Klan is now connected to the cartels in Asia and Latin America, it's scary just how outnumbered we are. On the other hand, we're in the right, and I believe we'll ultimately prevail."

That last was said with the fervor of a preacher at a country revival, and I found myself both admiring Mason's passion and fearing for his disappointment. I envied the passion. I remembered those feelings from when I was a young man, clear in my mission and out to kick criminal ass. Yet, I also remembered the first time I understood how corrupt our criminal justice system can be. I almost quit, and I'm not sure to this day why I didn't. Maybe I was just too dumb or too pigheaded to let the bastards win.

"I'll sleep on what you've said," I temporized. "Are you going to be around tomorrow? I'd like you to brief Kruger on your perspective. Why don't you have breakfast with us? The three of us can talk afterward."

"Are you sure you want to do that?" James asked me. "It might not be too good an idea."

"Wear your uniform," I replied. "Everybody will think Tanner assigned you to be our driver."

"Yazzuh! Sho will Boss!" Despite myself, I laughed. Among other things, James Mason was a first-class ham.

Kruger was back when I arrived at the motel, and I spent the better part of an hour bringing him up to speed. When I was done, he sighed. "Your day was a whole lot more interesting than mine," he said. He told me about his meeting, and I had to agree.

"What do you think about Mason?" I asked.

"I don't know. What he says makes sense, but I don't know if it's for real. Are you going to call McKee?"

I looked at my watch and shook my head. "No, it's almost midnight there. I'll call first thing in the morning. It's a nice night. I'm going to stretch my legs and think about it."

———

I was up again before the sun the next morning. A front had come in, and the sky was overcast and heavy with moisture. The air was cool, but so thick it felt like I was wading through water. By the time I got to the convenience store, I was soaked with sweat, and I knew if the sun broke through, Nashville would be like a broiler.

Dee answered my call right away. He sounded worried. "When you didn't call last night, I got concerned," he told me. "So I called Tanner. He told me you were out with his best deputy."

I told him about James Mason and our visit with Albert Jones. I also told him about the McKee connection. "I don't know," he said. "I don't like it. Sounds like McKee is playing things awfully close to his vest."

"I know, but you can't blame him," I answered. "No one knew about the James Smith connection until Mason sniffed him out. I'm afraid the days of the old Klan are over. That was simple and pretty direct. This new strategy of theirs is pretty sophisticated. If it's true, that makes them a lot scarier."

"No shit!" Dee exclaimed. "Next thing you know, they'll be into major corporate takeovers. If they're not already."

When I asked about Posey's military records, Dee uttered a harsh laugh. "What else is new? I got two responses back. One told me the records I want are classified. Then another one came in telling me the man never served. On a whim, I called Arlington Cemetery. they told me the only person by that name who was buried there died in 1944. He was killed on Saipan."

"That doesn't necessarily mean anything," I answered. "Assuming he was killed and his body brought home, he may have been buried in another national cemetery. Or even a private one."

"Or maybe he never died. I called all the national cemeteries I could think of within five hundred miles and no Wilbur Edward Posey. I tried plain Edward and Edward Wilbur Posey, too, but no soap there, either. Then I checked with the state burial registry here and in Texas. I got nothing."

"So you think he's alive?" I asked.

"Not really. That would be too easy. I think the records got screwed up, and he's rotted away in some jungle in Vietnam. Or maybe Laos or Cambodia. I think Posey was working for the CIA and never came home."

I thought about that a moment. "Well, one thing's for sure. No one missed him when he dropped out of sight. He was perfect for black operations from that point of view."

"I think the word is expendable," Dee replied. There was ancient anger in his voice. "There was a lot of that going around back then."

"Is there something you're not telling me, or is this a gut feeling?" I asked.

"Just a smell," he replied. "Too many things lining up in a strange way. I think we're chasing a dead man, but someone is trying to cover their ass thirty years too late. It's just a hunch."

"Well, I think you're right about the cover-up. It may be a loose end we never tie down. I guess this means we focus on Slide. Kruger and I will pay him a visit this morning."

When I got back to the motel, there was a message waiting for me. I saw it was from McKee, but I didn't feel like swimming back to the convenience store to call. So I walked down to Kruger's room to borrow his cell phone. Someone at the other end answered on the second ring, but it was a woman's voice, and I hung up right away.

I was handing the phone back to Kruger when it rang. He answered, then gave it to me. "Jazz?" came McKee's voice. "Sorry I missed you. That was my wife who answered."

At the time, I thought it was strange McKee's wife would answer his work phone, but I later found out he was her deputy and only acting as head of agency while she was on family leave. McKee's bunch was sounding more and more strange all the time.

I admitted it was me he was talking with, and McKee went on. "One of my friends told me about your visit with him last night. I wanted to let you know he's one of mine. Anything you can do for him, I would appreciate."

"Seems like a good man," I replied. "He seems well-trained."

"He also grew up around there, which made him particularly useful to us. He said he told you who we're after and why."

McKee was being very circumspect, and I guessed he knew he was talking on an FBI line. Remembering what I had read about FBI ties to the Klan, I knew why and responded the same way. "It sounds pretty nasty. I'd like to know more about it."

"Willie will fill you in. These phones are supposed to be scrambled, but I don't trust anything more complicated than a number-two pencil. I just wanted you to know we're all singing from the same page. There doesn't seem to be any overlap between our separate investigations. On the other hand, we'll do what we can to help you all you can stand."

"All right," I said, chuckling. "There's something you could do that might help me with my case. One of the suspects I would like to clear from my list is a veteran named Wilbur Edward Posey. From what I've found out here, he was drafted and served in Special Forces. He's thought to have been killed or to be missing in action in Southeast Asia. Yet, I can't find any record of it, not even his name on the Memorial Wall. We got one call back saying there was no record of him and then another telling us his military record is classified."

McKee laughed. "Sounds like the standard Washington run-around waltz. Let me see what I can find. If there's anything, I'll send it along with Willie."

I got off the phone with a deep sense of foreboding. This case was getting ever more complex, and it felt like I was getting farther and farther out of my element. There are exceptions to the rule, but things are fairly clear cut in basic police work. Sometimes the cops turn out to be robbers, and there can be shades of gray in the choices we make. Yet, most of the time the boundaries are fairly clear. To this policeman, the wonderful world of spooks seemed to be composed in subtle shades of black.

Once again, I considered turning it over to the FBI and bowing out. Were it not for Kruger and the prospect of going after criminal corporations with McKee, I think I might have done so. There comes a point where I get tired of running in seemingly needless circles, and the closer I get to the sunset, the less willing I am to tolerate foolishness. What keeps me going is the memory of just how tired I got of fishing and puttering around the house after the first six weeks of retirement. When I mentioned going back to work again, the way Nellie lit up with a smile told me her prayers had been answered.

Kruger sensed my mood and asked about it. When I told him what I had been thinking, he nodded. "Law enforcement is getting that way, too. At least, it is in the Agency. The rule these days seems to be that politics comes first." He grinned. "Of course, some of the lifers tell me it was worse under Hoover."

"Well, then maybe we should do something radical, like solving this case like a regular crime," I answered. "Let's go talk to Slide Jones."

The road between Nashville and Hot Springs is not the best in Arkansas, but we made good time and were there by ten thirty. I called ahead and asked the local officers to keep an eye on Slide's car and to pick him up if he left home. I gave them half an hour to get in place before I called Slide and told him I was to talk on my way over to him. I told him I would be there soon and to wait for me. Even though I woke him up, he was polite and told me he would be there when I arrived.

Kruger smiled at me when I was done. "Very interesting," he said. "Quite sneaky, too. Even if he goes out to buy a paper, you can claim he was running."

I shrugged. "He's probably too old a dog to fall for it, but who knows? He may try to run. It would simplify things if he did."

"Yes, but would that satisfy, Jazz ?" Kruger murmured, surprising me. We had only been working together three days, and he had me pegged.

Slide Jones met us at the door, freshly shaved and dressed in dark slacks and a dress shirt with vest and tie. There was a delicious aroma of fresh coffee, and when he invited us in, he offered us some. "I'm afraid it is chicory," he told us. "But if you can stand that, it's not bad."

That was an understatement. The coffee was excellent, ever though I don't normally like chicory. Once we had sipped and made appreciative noises, Slide leaned back and smiled. "Well, gentlemen," he said. "As good as the coffee may be, I don't suppose you drove all the way over here to discuss chicory. Do I need to have my lawyer present?"

I decided to play it straight. "I have to tell you, Luther, you're the most likely candidate we have."

"Luther," he said softly. "Thank you. Very few people call me that besides Albert Jones. So you're here to build a case against me?"

"My preference would be to clear you," I told him.

Slide laughed. "I bet you tell all the girls that. On the other hand, I may be able to help you do just that." He reached into his shirt pocket and pulled out a piece of paper. He was holding it between his thumb and a forefinger along one edge. "Please be careful handling that, if you will. I don't want to destroy any finger prints you might find there."

I pulled out a plastic case and opened it for him to drop the slip of paper. I looked at it once he had and saw it was a Texas lottery ticket. "I found that in my vest pocket after I talked with you," he told us. "At the time it skipped my mind. I believe you'll find it to be my winning lottery ticket."

"You didn't turn it in?" Kruger asked.

"No, the numbers were all wrong," Slide laughed. "I swear, I could make a living telling people what numbers to not buy. Of course, the numbers that will matter to me on that ticket are all right."

Kruger frowned and shook his head. "I don't follow you."

Slide smiled again. "Look at the date and time it was issued. I believe those numbers will clear me."

Kruger looked and nodded. "Yeah, they might. How do we know you got this yourself and not from someone else?"

"Elementary, my dear Watson," Slide told him. "When you run it for latent prints you should only find two sets. One will be mine and the other will be those of the store clerk. To my knowledge, no one else has touched it."

I took the plastic bag, dated it, and put it in my pocket. I looked at Kruger. He shrugged, and Slide laughed. "Forgive my enjoyment, gentlemen. It's not often one is able pull a rabbit out of the hat like that."

"You do understand that this takes away any reason you might have to keep silent, don't you?" I asked casually.

Slide nodded. "As it pertains to the murder, I agree. However, this does not give you license to fish other waters."

"Fair enough," I told him. "Why don't you tell us about when you left Oak Grove? " Slide started to object, but I held up a hand. "Suppose for a moment that Smiley was not the target. Suppose you were. Suppose someone mistook him for you. You looked enough alike to fool Luther Anne. Who might be out to kill you, Luther?"

The smile left his face. "Most of those people are dead now. The rest are in nursing homes or soon will be. The young ones have moved away. I don't think you'll find much there."

"Do you owe them any loyalty?" Kruger asked. "They were out to kill you, weren't they?"

Slide nodded. "Yes, and rightfully so. I'm afraid I cheated them rather badly. Were they honest people, I would feel awful about it. As it was, I took from them what they gained from the pain of others."

"Sounds like a strong motive to me," Kruger said.

"We reached an understanding," Slide replied. "I documented quite a bit of dirt against several of them and made sure they knew exactly what I had. We reached a truce. They left me alone, and I stayed out of their territory. I was very careful not to cross their paths again." He shook his head. "My, some of that's been more than forty years ago."

187

"I'd like to see your documentation," Kruger said.

"That would be my death warrant. Even though the statute of limitations has long passed, it would embarrass some powerful people." Slide pulled a pack of long, dark cigarettes out of his vest. "Would you gentlemen mind if I smoke."

I could see Kruger start to object, but I jumped in quickly. "Of course not, Luther. It's your house."

"Yes, but you're my guests." Slide lit a cigarette and took a deep pull. "It's a dreadful habit. The problem is, it's one of the few vices I have left." He smiled. "That and Louella."

An idea began forming in my mind. I asked a couple of questions and Slide answered them at length, lighting another cigarette when he was done with the first. The information wasn't new, but it confirmed what we had heard earlier.

"Tell me about when you were with the carnival," I said. "How did you happen to end up with them?"

Slide smiled. "I knew them from the circuit. They used to come through from time to time, and I had done some business with them." He shook his head. "I'm not going to be more specific than that. They moved around quite a bit over a large area, and that was useful to me."

"So they were your suppliers," Kruger said. I could have kicked him for the way he said it. There was no misunderstanding the contempt in his voice.

Slide did not respond in kind. "I am who I am, Agent Kruger," he said so softly I had to strain to hear. "Not all of us are fortunate to be born white and in the Midwest. I was supporting myself and a rather large family, and I did what I thought I had to do. I might not make those same choices today, but I refuse to condemn myself. Some of my suppliers, as you call them, are your masters now. I don't serve them any more. You do."

A deep flush moved up Kruger's neck, but he had the grace not to respond. "I see how your insurance could be embarrassing," I said. "I don't think we need to get into that. Tell me, what did Wilbur do at the carnival when he came to you for help?"

"Well, for a while, he helped me out at the shooting booth. He never had to work as a roustabout like I did when I first got there. He didn't like the guns, but he had that beautiful smile, and that drew the ladies like a magnet. Not many of them cared to shoot, but their boyfriends did, and business was good while he was helping me. Then one of the musicians ended up in jail, and Wilbur started filling in as a vocalist. I think he saw the light then, so to speak, because the next thing he did was teach himself to play the guitar. He was far enough along by the time the circuit got to Baton Rouge to make his break and head to New Orleans." He chuckled. "He never repaid me the three hundred dollars he borrowed to do it, either. Once he got famous, every time I showed up it was 'Who you?' It's too bad that article writer didn't talk to me, isn't it? Not that he would dare publish what I had to say."

"So you ran the shooting booth." Tuner observed. "You must know your way around guns. Are you a good shot?"

"I was one of the best in Howard County," Slide answered evenly. "And I do know my way around firearms. I'm always very careful with them, and I always have been, even before Goodie was shot. Had that rifle been in my hands, he would not have died."

"So you held that against Luther Adams?" Kruger persisted.

"No," Slide said quietly. "That was a terrible accident which should never have happened, but there was no fault in it. Nor did I punish Luther for it. Over the years, he punished himself far more than I ever could. I hope he's at peace."

I picked up my coffee cup and drained the last few drops. "I don't suppose you have any more of this?" I asked. "It's very good."

"Of course," Slide said, stubbing out his cigarette and getting to his feet. "I get to running on like an old man and become remiss in my hospitality. Agent Kruger?"

Kruger shook his head, and Smiley took his cup and mine and headed for the kitchen. When he was gone from the room, I reached for the ash tray and retrieved the last two butts. I replaced the ash tray and sealed the butts in a plastic evidence bag. Kruger looked at me curiously but said nothing.

Slide was back with our fresh coffee a moment later. "You know, I'm still curious who might want you out of the way," I told Slide. "What about enemies you might have who were not connected to business."

"You might not believe me, Jazz, but outside business, I have tried to live by the Golden Rule." He smiled at Kruger's frown. "I'm not claiming virtue so much as convenience, you understand. Treating others as one would like to be treated is a very practical way to live. One does not make unnecessary enemies. You'd be surprised how many people would sing my praises for what I have done for them in times of need. Again, I claim no virtue in it. I was simply making markers I could call in later."

"How about jealous husbands or brothers of women scorned?"

He laughed. "That was more Wilbur's game than mine. He was awful, but the poor dears put up with him. The magazine writer didn't know this, but that was one of the main reasons Wilbur was invited to leave town. They could have worked out an acceptable *detente*, but one of the elders didn't want that. He knew Wilbur's reputation with the ladies." He shook his head. "It is amazing how unfaithful husbands suspect their wives of infidelity, too. I've had my moments, but Louella is the closest thing to a married woman I've ever had."

Suddenly, I understood this man. "You know, Luther, if word about any of this gets out, it might ruin your reputation."

For the first time, there was something like fear in Slide's eyes. It was not much, just a hint. "What on earth do you mean, Jazz?" he asked. His eyes told me he knew the answer already.

"I suspect that under all that bad-ass bullshit, there's a decent soul. Am I wrong?" Out of the corner of my eye, I could see Kruger looking at me as if I had lost my mind.

Slide was quiet for a long moment. He lit another cigarette and cleared his throat. "Will there be anything else, gentlemen?" he asked. "I will need to leave soon if I'm to be on time for the funeral."

I looked at Kruger and he looked troubled. He shook his head. "You need to be available until we talk to the clerk and check prints on the lottery ticket," I told him.

"I hoped to attend Luther's funeral this afternoon," Slide said. "It would mean a lot to me. Albert asked me to deliver the eulogy."

"All right," I said. "But just go there and back. No side trips to Texarkana. "Are you all right with that? He nodded, reluctantly.

"Warning noted, though. I cannot imagine why anyone in their right mind would flee to Oklahoma," Slide said. Then he frowned. "By the way, you may find Louella's prints on the lottery ticket, too. Not that she bought it. She has a bad habit of going through my pockets when she thinks I am asleep."

CHAPTER SEVEN

DAY OF REMEMBRANCE

Kruger was silent as we started our trip back to Nashville. I thought I knew what was on his mind, but I held my peace. Sure enough, I was right. When we were a couple of miles out of Hot Springs he spoke up.

"You really believe that, don't you?" he asked.

"About Slide being a decent soul?" I asked. He nodded. "Yes, I do. Oddly enough, I understand Slide Jones in a way I never could Smiley."

"Care to share your thoughts?" he asked.

"I will, but I'm not inviting argument," I told him. "Discussion is invited, of course, even lively discussion, but not argument. You may not agree with my conclusions, but I ask you to respect them."

"Fair enough," he said.

"Despite what the psychologists say, my observation is that character can be changed. At least, it can change direction. The same traits may be there, but the way they're expressed can be different. Where I have seen it happen most often is with alcoholics. People who are totally irresponsible become pillars of the community. I've also seen it happen with addicts and compulsive gamblers. They're still the same basic people, but they respond to things differently. What I don't understand is why it happens with some people and not with others."

"You think this has happened with Slide?"

I nodded. "Slide is one of the best cons I've ever seen, so I may be wrong. I may be seeing what I want to see. From the evidence we have, he looks like the best candidate for our shooter. He's one of the best shots around. He has plenty of motive, and if it weren't for that lottery ticket, I would have brought him in and charged him. Even feeling the way I do."

"That lottery ticket may fall apart as an alibi," Kruger replied. "If the woman's prints are on it, she could have bought it for him."

I thought about that. "Yeah, but then we have conspiracy. Louella would have had to be in it with Slide. She would have needed to know when to buy the ticket, which sets up all kinds of complications. We need to check it out, but I'd lay odds the store clerk will say Slide bought the ticket. I don't think he would be foolish enough to depend on Louella. He strikes me as crazy like a fox."

Kruger thought about that. "I see your point, but I hope you're wrong. We're running out of suspects. I think Slide is our man. We have enough for a search warrant."

"What would we be looking for?" I asked.

"The rifle. Ammunition. The commando knife. Something belonging to Luther Adams. Old love letters. Blood. Anything." Kruger ticked these off on his fingers.

"I think the judge would call that a fishing expedition," I said. "The first thing he will ask is if we have bullets to match with any gun we found, and we don't. The crime team cannot even swear what caliber weapon was used. We think it was a .223, and that may be what the evidence *suggests,* but the rifle could have been .243 or a .257. The best we have is a weak circumstantial case."

Kruger growled, but nodded. "Yeah, you're right. This whole thing is starting to get to me. There are too many loose ends." He shrugged. "There's a lot of pressure from Lonnie, too. He wants it wrapped up by the day before yesterday." He looked at me. "That's what our meeting was about yesterday. That and other things."

"Well, maybe we can. We may turn up some DNA from that soda can in the blacksmith shop, and it may match what's on these cigarette butts," I tapped my pocket. "We could get lucky, and that would give us enough for a warrant."

"Shouldn't we be getting those to the lab in Little Rock? And the lottery ticket, too?" Kruger asked. He looked at his watch. "We could be there in less than an hour." He pulled off to the side of the road.

"I want to be there for the funeral," I told him. "I want to see who shows up and hear what Slide has to say."

Kruger gave me an evil grin. "Well, you could catch a ride with him," he said. "At least to Nashville to get your car. I can run the evidence to the lab."

"We'll never find him going back," I said. "He's probably left by now." I looked at Kruger. "Besides, he's a suspect."

"What better way to keep track of him?" Kruger answered. He looked at his watch. "We'll give him ten minutes. If he's not along by then, I'll take you to Nashville myself."

I've done stranger things in the course of an investigation. Putting my life in the hands of a suspect was not one of them, but Kruger had a point. If I didn't really think the man was our killer, then I had nothing to fear. "All right," I said. "But don't tell Nellie." Kruger laughed.

Four minutes later, Slide pulled over and agreed to my request. I was very careful to make sure he understood it was a request, and he laughed. "I would be glad of the company," he said. "However, I am curious why Agent Kruger isn't able to take you himself."

"He needs to get to Little Rock, and I want to go to the funeral," I said. "I didn't know Luther well, but..." I shrugged.

"Yes," Slide said. "Luther often had that effect on people. He embodied goodness itself. Get in."

I spent much of the next hour listening to Slide reminisce. A lot of what he had to say went into the eulogy and had nothing to do with the case, but I also learned some interesting things about the people he grew up with in Oak Grove. Among other things, I learned that Emma Jones, the pastor's wife, never missed when it came to her throwing arm.

"That girl was the best baseball pitcher in the county," Slide laughed. "She could throw left handed or right. When she and Albert came to visit the carnival, they wouldn't let her throw balls at the milk bottles. She was too good. I've seen her pick up a rock and knock a squirrel out of a tree."

I mentioned her reputation for going through dishes, and he laughed again. "The only reason Albert Jones is alive is because she never wanted to hit him. I would hate to be in his shoes if she ever got mad enough to do so."

Even though I enjoyed his company, I felt relieved when Slide dropped me at my car in Nashville. He offered to take me on down to Oak Grove and drop me off later, but I declined. "I've enjoyed this," he told me. "I hope we can talk again under happier circumstances." I told him I would like that, and I was a bit surprised to discover I really meant it.

Even though I was there on business, the funeral of Luther Adams was an incredible experience. No fewer than four gospel choirs showed up, complete with their sound equipment, and the small church was packed. I got there early enough to get a seat but gave it up to an old man who looked so frail he might not make it through the service.

Albert Jones saw this and smiled, inviting me to take a seat beside him in the chancel pew. "I don't have to preach, do I?" I asked, and he smiled again.

"I hope you used the outhouse before you came in," he said. "This may be a while."

While the place I sat gave me a good view of every face in the pews, I felt rather conspicuous. Yet, when the first choir fired its opening slavo, I was carried away with the singing. I hoped someone was recording this so I could get a copy to take to Nellie. As I said, I'm not a religious man. Yet, when I die I'll know I'm at the Pearly Gates if I hear a choir like those singing that day.

Even so, there was a part of me watching the crowd. The habits of being a policeman don't go away with retirement, and there were two people there that caught my attention. One was a tall black man in a conservative suit cut too well to be from anywhere in Arkansas. He stood quietly at the back, listening to the music with complete concentration. What startled me was that as soon as my eyes spotted him, he looked directly at me and nodded so slightly I doubt anyone else noticed. Then he looked back toward the choir, standing with an air of quiet authority that told me he was a cop. I guessed he was FBI, though that didn't seem to fit that well. He looked more like Secret Service.

The other man I only saw once. He was standing in the foyer looking into the sanctuary, and my eyes moved by him before the image registered. When it did, I looked back, but someone else was standing there. What had caught my attention was how much the man looked like Slide Jones, but that was true of at least a dozen men there. Seen from one angle or another, each had caught my attention for a moment until they turned and I saw the differences.

I had to smile at myself. I really didn't want Slide Jones to turn out to be the killer. I liked the man, and that was affecting my judgement. Since Edward Posey was the perfect suspect, I was seeing him everywhere, as if I could wish him alive so I could arrest him.

Then another thought struck me. I wondered if all the men I noticed were love children of Smiley Jones, too. It almost gave me a headache thinking how many suspects this would add to our list.

When the funeral was done, I found myself uplifted and also a bit sad it was over. I looked at my watch and was surprised to find two and a half hours had passed. Albert Jones saw my surprise and smiled. "How time flies, doesn't it?"

I walked over to the community center where food was prepared for those who attended. I was halfway hoping to spot the man I glimpsed in the foyer just to make sure it was not Edward, but he wasn't in the crowd. So I joined the line waiting for the outhouse. As Albert Jones predicted, it had been a good while.

I was on the way back to the community center when I heard someone call my name. I looked around, and it was the tall man from the back of the church. He walked toward me with the grace and assurance of a jaguar, and I had the thought this would not be a good man to have as an enemy.

"Dr. Phillips?" he asked, offering a hand. It wasn't so much a question as a statement. "My name is Dill. Willie Dill. I think you're expecting me."

I shook his hand. His grip was firm but not the crushing grip of someone with something to prove. "Mr. Dill," I answered. "Do you have some kind of identification?"

He looked amused. "Do you really want me to do the full federal flash?" he asked. "Right here in front of God and everybody?" I noticed a subtle bulge under his perfectly cut jacket that told me he was armed.

"Just a moment," I said. "I'll be right back."

I spotted James Mason and made my way over to him. He was talking to a stunning young lady who was obviously taken with him. I apologized for the intrusion and told him there was someone who admired his singing and would like to meet him. He glanced in the direction I nodded and excused himself. The young lady looked, too, and I could see she was impressed by Dill.

When we arrived where Dill was standing, I asked James if I needed to make introductions. He extended his hand to Dill. "Doctor Livingston, I presume."

Dill laughed easily. "Hello, James. That was a marvelous solo you gave. I had no idea you sang so well." He looked at me. "I appreciated what Dr. Phillips had to say, too."

"I could have hit Pastor Jones for putting me on the spot like that," I said. "I had no idea what he was going to do."

"You did very well," Mason assured me. "It's the price of the seat." We all laughed. "Now, if you don't need me any longer, Jazz, there's a young lady who needs my attention."

"Looks like she has all the attention she needs," Dill said, looking over at the striking young woman who was now surrounded by young men.

"That's what I mean," said James Mason, hurrying away.

"He's a good man," I said to Dill. "McKee said you'd be down this way. Are you just passing through or do you have a stake in this case?"

"We need to discuss that," Dill said, looking around. "I'm not sure where we can talk with more privacy around here. Why don't we take a drive? My car, not yours." Seeing the look on my face, he explained. "I know mine's not bugged, Dr...."

"That doesn't do much to reassure me," I said. As a matter of fact, the whole drift of our conversation bothered me considerably. Nor did the prospect of being alone with Dill please me. While we were both armed, I suspected I was no where near his class. Nor was I completely sure we were on the same side.

Even so, I nodded, but suggested we eat first. Dill agreed, and when we sat down, we were immediately joined by Slide Jones. "Thank you for your kind words about Luther, Jazz," he said. "You may not have known him long, but you had a good sense of who he was."

"I suspect that's true of everyone Dr. Phillips meets," Dill said. When Slide looked at him in surprise, he added, "We only met today, but I'm a student of his work. He's a remarkable man."

"Sounds like you're reading my eulogy," I growled. "And, please, call me Jazz. Dr. Phillips sounds like a brand of shoe powder."

"He is, indeed," Slide answered, ignoring me. "And I hope what you say is right. I'm the best suspect in their murder case here. I, like everyone in prison, am innocent. So I'm depending on him to prove it. Are you here on the case?"

Dill smiled at him and shrugged. He was saved from any further answer by Robert who popped up just then. "Who this?" he demanded of me, speaking with a pure Oak Grove accent.

I introduced them. "Dill?" Robert said. "You mean like pickle?"

"Yes, but I try not to be too sour," Dill laughed. He turned to me. "Who is this? One of your Oak Grove irregulars?"

"I ain't troubled by irregularity!" Robert exclaimed, and we all fell apart.

"Robert's a friend of mine," I said, still laughing. "He's been showing me around and supervising. He's a lot of help."

"You a cop?" Robert asked Dill. Dill nodded, and Robert sat down by him. "Show me your gun!" he demanded.

"I can't do that," Dill told him solemnly. "I can't take my gun out unless I intend to shoot somebody."

Robert considered that. Then he spotted something on the other side of the room. "Ice cream!" he said and was gone as suddenly as he appeared.

"Who said good help is hard to find?" Slide murmured, and we chuckled.

Dill and I took our leave and drove south toward Hope. As he drove, he told me about the agency McKee headed up. While it had nothing to do with the case, I was intrigued. The Agency, which is what people who work there call it, got its start before World War II as a covert military group gathering intelligence and making preparations for what they saw as an inevitable war. How that special operations group avoided being incorporated into the OSS, or later the CIA, was due to the evolution of its particular mission and the fact it remained completely covert. It was also due to an initial strategy of gathering critical information and covertly turning this over to other agencies for action.

"What we're up to these days is tracking connections between cartel drug money and multinational corporations," Dill told me. "There's a cooperative network between such diverse groups as certain white supremacist groups and Asian trading companies with close ties to the drug trade."

"I didn't realize the Klan was involved," I said. "That brings the whole thing pretty close to home."

Dill nodded. "To give the devil his due, most chapters of the Klan are not involved in this. Yet, enough of their key people are connected that we began to come across them in odd situations. So we began to look more closely."

"With people like James Mason," I said and Dill nodded. "The question that comes to mind is why you're telling me all this."

"We would like you to work with us. McKee was impressed with your grasp of the general situation and would like to talk with you."

"All right, I'm interested, but I'm in the middle of a case at the moment. I'm not sure just when we will be done."

"We'd be willing to offer any help we can," Dill said. "What we have to offer is access to information."

I thought about that for a moment. The offer was tempting. Yet, accepting help might mean giving McKee a personal marker in his mind. "All right," I told him, "but only as a gesture of good will. There can't be any strings attached. No markers."

Dill laughed. "Fair enough. We're not above using that kind of leverage, but not with our own people. What do you need to know?"

I mentioned the trouble I was having getting Edward Posey's military file, and Dill's smile faded. "Yes, Sam told me you wanted to know about him. The official word is that he's dead. We haven't been able to get details just yet, but we will. When we do, we'll pass them along."

I noticed the way he said that. "All right," I answered. "So what's your unofficial take on it?"

Dill sighed. "I know Eddie Posey. I trained him, and he was one of the best, though I had to get on his case about that. He was always hanging back at show time, letting other people come in first and second when he was best qualified. When I heard he was killed in action, I had trouble believing it, and when he turned up on the missing in action list, I wondered. As far as I know, he never made it back from Southeast Asia."

"You mean, he's dead? Or still a prisoner?"

"No, although I have no hard information." He gave me a stern look. "What I'm about to tell you is highly classified information. It goes no further."

I thought about that. "I can't promise that if it bears on the case."

It was Dill's turn to think. "It doesn't have any direct bearing, but I'll trust your discretion. Please don't make me regret it." He paused. "The Cadre is what the consortium I've been telling you about calls itself. Like the Mafia, they have no hesitation about using violence, and one of the things we do is keep track of their enforcers. When we get a chance, we bring them in or take them out trying. We stay within the law as much as we can."

He paused again. "One of the things we find useful is to keep profiles of the enforcers. We pay particular attention to their method of operation, just like the police do with common criminals. Unfortunately, we often don't have a name to go with the profile, and one of my jobs is to identify those people. One of those people we haven't been able to identify fits what I know of Edward Posey. So to answer your question, I think that Edward Posey bailed out of the

Special Forces in Vietnam and set himself up as a professional killer. I think he operates out of Southeast Asia, but he shows up all over the world. I have no evidence, but that's what I think."

"That would fit," I told him. "My first impression was that it looked like a professional setup." I described the shooter's nest and the details of the case as they stood. I also told him about Luther Adams.

When I was done, Dill nodded. "That sounds like Posey, particularly with the way Adams was killed. He's always very careful to take out any witnesses."

Several things came together suddenly, and I felt a chill go down my back. If I was right, Robert McNutt had seen Edward Posey on two occasions. I told Dill my thoughts, and his response was immediate. "We need to get that child under guard. Tonight." He pulled to the side of the road and whipped out a cell phone like Kruger's. When the other end picked up, he spoke to whoever answered in hushed, urgent terms.

When he was done, Dill turned the car around and sped back toward Oak Grove. "A team is on the way from Washington," he told me. "They'll be in sometime tomorrow morning."

"What about tonight?" I asked. "I can't call in protection without telling DiRado something."

"Tonight will be up to James Mason and me," Dill said grimly. "I almost hope Posey shows up. I've been after him a long time." He made another call, then relaxed a bit. "James is in place. He has Robert in sight. He's sticking close by him."

"He's not armed," I said. Dill gave me a strange look and I told him about our promise to the pastor.

"What the pastor didn't know won't hurt him," Dill answered with a chilly smile. "We are always armed, Jazz. We have to be. The Cadre knows who we are. I'm pretty high on their list."

"I'm available, too," I told him. "My gun's in the car."

Dill took a moment answering. "I appreciate your offer, Jazz. However, I think this may be outside your set of skills. James and I are trained to do this kind of thing. You might put someone else in danger."

"You could put me inside the house with the McNutts," I said. "A shotgun covers a lot of ground."

"That would mean alerting them to what's going on," Dill said. "I'm not sure that's a good idea. We don't know for sure Posey will try anything."

"You're sure enough to call in a team," I said. "They need to know Robert is in danger."

Dill shook his head. "What if they panic and try to take Robert away from here? That could put him in even greater danger. Here we can protect him."

We went back and fourth about it, but I eventually gave way. I didn't like it, but there was not much choice. Dill had taken charge, and I was just as glad he had. From what he told me, I had to admit that Edward Posey was out of my league. Dill did agree to my telling Dee what was happening. When I asked about Kruger, he asked me to wait until the next morning if I could. "The last thing we need is the Bureau involved," Dill added. "With the connections the Cadre has, they'll know every move we're making."

"This isn't their affair," I reminded Dill. "Assuming Posey is our shooter, this is a personal thing with him."

"Yes, but I think we have to assume he's in touch with them," Dill replied "He's one of their best contractors, and it's in their interest to at least try to warn him off if they're aware of something. I hope he makes his move tonight. If he does, we'll have him."

"We don't have any evidence against him," I said.

"Not in the murder, no, but we have lots of other things on him," Dill said. "There's desertion for openers, assuming we bring him to trial." He saw the look of shock on my face and added, "No, we're not going to take him out and shoot him, Jazz. We don't do things that way. But we can hold him a long time. I'm sure he has a lot of information we could use." I must have still looked doubtful because he added, "No, we don't use thumb screws, either. We break them down, but we don't use physical torture." The haunted look in his eyes told me thumb screws might be kinder than some of the things they did, but I reminded myself this was not my business.

As I drove back to Nashville that evening, I was plagued with questions. I was ninety-nine percent sure Posey was our killer, but some things still didn't fit. *Why did he wait so long to kill Smiley? Did Luther Adams see him do it? Then why did Luther tell us, "Luther done it!" Did he mistake Edward for Slide? Was Posey the man in the vest scouting out the terrain? What about the other evidence…the wax on the porch and the powder smudge on the outhouse? Did they have anything to do with the case? What about the bullet Weaver retrieved from the store front? Where did the bullets that killed Smiley go?*

I told myself some of those were questions that might never be answered and to concentrate on the ones that might. *Where did the bullets go?* That went to the top of my list, and I decided to check it out the next day. That would be a good excuse to go back to Oak Grove, and it would provide an opportunity to keep Robert close to me. I wondered if there were a casual way I could get him into a bulletproof vest, then decided I was being too jumpy. The best protection Robert could have was Willie Dill and a man he trained.

I called Dee when I got in. I greeted his sister when she answered the phone and asked if he was available. She laughed and told me he would have to call me back. "You caught him in the shower," she told me, but from the way she said it, I knew he was otherwise occupied.

"You caught me in the confessional," Dee told me when he called back.

I asked how he was, and he told me he was going crazy sitting at a desk all day. With nothing else to do, he started searching the Internet for references to anything he could think of related to the case. "Do you know how many hits I got on Smiley Jones?" he asked.

"You're getting hits on both words," I told him. "Try limiting your search to sites with both words together."

"To hell with it," he growled. "I'm just keeping myself busy. What's up?"

I told him Dill's theory about Posey, leaving out what he told me about the Cadre and Agency operations or about James Mason. I also told him my concern for Robert McNutt and about the measures Dill was taking. "Sounds like they have it in hand," he told me. "I'd feel better if it wasn't just Dill out there by himself tonight."

"They had another agent in the area," I told him. "Dill was able to get him to help tonight."

"Good," Dee replied. "What are you holding back, Jazz?"

"I can't tell you," I said. "Dill gave me some background I can't pass along. It doesn't have anything to do with the case. I can tell you this. We seem to have stumbled into a major national security minefield. Ed Posey seems to be right in the middle of it. We need to be very discrete."

I could tell Dee didn't like it, but he didn't push. "That explains our elusive Captain Smith," he said. "I hope it doesn't mean letting Posey off the hook."

"I think he might rather be in our hands than Dill's," I told him. "I really can't say more than that."I decided to change the subject. "Are there any lab results back yet?"

"Yeah, I sent them with Kruger," he told me. "He stopped by here with the cigarette butts and the lottery ticket. One result stood out. The DNA from the blood from the privy was from a black male who is a close blood relative to Jones. I asked Kasey how close, and he told me son or grandson."

"So Posey was there!" I said. I felt myself getting excited. I told him about the man I saw in the foyer at the funeral. "So he's around. What was he doing in the outhouse?"

Dee laughed. "Besides the obvious? Maybe he thought about using it as a shooting stand."

"And gave it up because it involved too much unpredictable traffic," I said, finishing the thought. "But he must have tried a shot from there when nobody was around. That must be the bullet from the store front."

"That bullet is interesting," Dee told me. "You'll see it in the report, but it was fired from a weapon I never heard of before. Weaver tells me it comes with an integral two-power scope, and I would guess Posey had it fitted with a silencer."

"So he must have been using a subsonic load," I said. "At least, he must have with his trial shot. That would explain why it didn't penetrate deeper into the store front."

"I would guess he went back to hot loads for the kill," Dee answered. "The bullets would have lodged in the body if he didn't."

"He's a clever asshole, isn't he? He picked his spot and was shooting so the bullets wouldn't be found. He didn't want us to know what kind of weapon he used. I bet it's his signature, using this particular type of weapon."

"Only, this time he didn't want it identified," Dee murmured. "I wonder why. Any ideas?"

"Too many to be useful," I told him and he laughed. "The further we go, the less sense this thing makes. Why did he wait so long? I can understand his wanting to ruin Smiley's party, but why didn't Posey take him out years ago? Smiley had been living in Oak Grove a long time."

"It could have been the article," Dee suggested. "That could have set him off, seeing Smiley treated like a saint."

I thought about the article. "You know, he may not have wanted the connection known," I suggested. "He may not have wanted credit for this kill."

"Are you suggesting doing a personal hit might ruin his professional reputation?" Dee asked. "All we have is speculation, even with the DNA and the bullet. No prosecutor I know would touch it."

"No, I'm not thinking about evidence. Or even about his reputation. It's more like being tied to this case might give the people he works for an angle to get at him," I said. "The way I understand these things to work, there's never any personal contact with the clients. There's a broker who acts as a cut-out, and payment is made to a numbered account. Being identified by weapon with a particular killing not contracted out would give the broker a potential line to personal information about Posey himself. His best protection is staying anonymous."

"Sounds pretty thin," Dee observed. "On the other hand, we don't have anything better. Say it is Posey. How are we going to pin it on him?"

I told him my ideas about finding the bullet, and he agreed it was the most promising line to follow at the moment. He also reminded me to be very careful. "These guys are way out of our class, Jazz. I hate to admit it, but they are. Dill is one of the very best, so let him take point since he's willing. Let his team take Posey if they can. We can work out who gets first shot at Posey after he's behind bars. Who knows? Posey might get himself killed and save the state a lot of money for a murder trial."

I told him about Dill's suggestion of federal detention. "Then what more do you need, man?" he asked. "That's win-win as far as I'm concerned. They can leave this case open forever as far as I'm concerned."

"I still think we need to gather evidence," I told him. This was not like Dee to give up so easily.

"Of course, we do," he replied. "We need to have it in case they ever give him back to us. I'm just saying I won't be sorry if they don't. I'm looking forward to being out of here, and I'd rather not have to testify."

We talked a while longer. When we were done, I looked for Kruger, but he wasn't in his room. Changing into my sweats and walking shoes, I set out to get some exercise and spotted his car at the drive-in. He was sitting by himself with a milkshake and a burger, so I joined him. Seeing the burger reminded me I hadn't eaten supper, so I ordered the works: a chicken-fried chicken plate with fries and cole slaw. To top it off, I ordered a chocolate shake.

"You're going to have to walk extra miles to work that off," Kruger smiled. He was more relaxed than I've ever seen him.

"That must have been some date," I replied, and he smiled even more. "Are you ready for an update?"

"Only if you must," he answered, but I could see I had his attention.

I looked around the dining room. There was no one else there. Keeping my voice low, I told him about the funeral and about seeing someone I thought was Posey in the foyer. "I can't be sure, but I think it was him."

He nodded. "That makes sense. The DNA report fits, too. The question is how we build a case."

"I think the first thing is to find the bullets that killed Jones. I asked Ben Weaver to see if he could get DNA from the can. That would place Posey in the blacksmith shop."

Kruger nodded. "With that particular type of rifle, finding the bullets would really help. Of course, finding the rifle in his possession would be better." He frowned. "That kind of rifle is pretty unusual for a casual sportsman to own."

I thought about what he said for a moment, then told Kruger I had access to information that shed light on this, but that I couldn't reveal my source. He frowned, but nodded, and I told him the theory about Posey being a professional international assassin.

"That's interesting," he replied. "When I ran the details through our data base on Monday, I came up with a solid hit. There have been several killings by an unknown assassin that carry the same method. The signature is three shots from a .223 at intermediate range, and the bullets that were found all came from the same kind of weapon as the bullet Weaver found." He gave me an odd look. "Your source must either have access to our data base or access to information we don't have. My guess would be you have been talking to someone with the CIA."

I said nothing. I hated lying with my silence, but there was nothing I could do about it. Kruger looked at me and continued. "Since this unknown killer is also responsible for the deaths of several witnesses, I would guess that Adams must have seen something. Assuming we're talking about the same man. What I find hard to believe is that our international assassin comes from a place like Oak Grove, Arkansas." He waved off my objection. "I know, they have to come from somewhere." Then his eyes narrowed. "Did it occur to you that Robert may be in danger? Assuming it's the same killer."

I told him that it had, and protection was in place. "Nothing against John Tanner, but I don't think rural deputies would stand a chance against this guy," Kruger replied. He took out his phone. "I better call in some of our people."

I stopped him before he could dial. "It's being covered," I told him. There was nothing else to do, so I told him a national team was on the way.

"Who are these people?" Kruger demanded. "They sure as hell don't have jurisdiction!"

I gave him the name of McKee's agency. "Jesus!" he exclaimed. "You don't mess around, do you? Those guys are as good as the Mossad. What were they doing in Oak Grove?" He put his phone back in his pocket.

"I don't know," I told him truthfully. "They may have picked up on the details of the shooting just like you did. We've been running things through the national data base. They hinted there was another operation they were running around here."

"Do you remember that white supremacist camp that was wiped out by a rival group in Wyoming a couple of years ago?" I nodded. "That was their work. They didn't do the killing, but they set it up. It was a massacre. Then they took out the group that won."

"How do you know so much about them?" I asked. "I never heard of them before." Too late I realized I had slipped and I knew Kruger caught it.

Kruger gave me a sardonic smile. "I see. I won't ask before when. Well, then, while we're sharing secrets, I crossed paths with one of their agents a few months ago. I made it a point to find out everything I could. They're good. Did they recruit you?"

I didn't even try to hide my surprise. Kruger laughed. "They did me. I don't know how they did it, but they found I was nosing around and came to me. I think McKee could sell ice to Eskimos. Did you meet Dill?"

I answered carefully. "Don't be surprised if you run into him tomorrow." It was my turn to be the inquisitor. "You turned them down?"

Kruger shook his head. "Not really. There was some advanced training coming up at the Bureau I wanted. So I passed for the moment, but I left the door open. The last couple of weeks I've been thinking about giving them a call."

I outlined what I wanted to do the next day, searching for the bullets, and asked Kruger if he wanted to join me. "Does a dog have fleas?" he replied in his best imitation of rural Arkansan. I agreed it did, and we set a time for getting together the next morning. When I took off to finish my walk, Kruger was back with his own thoughts and smiling the way he had when I came in. I laughed to myself. That must've been some date.

November came in with a beautiful morning the following day. I was up early and walking by sunrise, wondering how I had managed to miss Halloween the day before. There were the usual decorations in the stores and on some of the houses in Nashville, but I was out too too late to run into any ghosties, ghoulies, or long-legged beasties, and I slept through the things that go bump in the night. I did notice a number of egg shells scattered here and there, but I was thinking about the case and didn't put it together. So much for the great sleuth. Nellie tells me I do that all the time.

I was feeling pretty good that morning. There's nothing like zeroing in on a suspect to change the whole tone of an investigation. At this point, it was just a matter of gathering evidence, and we knew where to look. Once we had that, my part of the case was over. Someone else could do the dirty work of bringing our suspect in and I could get back to driving Nellie crazy hanging around the house and getting underfoot.

Kruger and I had an early breakfast. He was still mellow from his visit to Little Rock, and I was looking forward to getting home soon. John Tanner came in and joined us, and when Louise wasn't hanging around, I told him who we had for a suspect. He was surprised to hear Posey was still alive and agreed to let us have James Mason for a couple of more days.

When we got to Oak Grove, I parked in the church lot and Kruger and I walked over to the blacksmith shop. No one seemed to be around, but when we went to the back of the building, Willie Dill appeared out of nowhere, dressed in full camouflage. He was carrying a shotgun and had an automatic pistol holstered at his waist. He greeted us both.

"It was a quiet night," he told us. "There was no sign of our suspect."

"When does your team arrive?" I asked.

"They got here two hours ago," Dill answered. "They're out scouting to see what they can find."

I told him what I had in mind for retrieving the bullets. "Robert is going to be out before long. Why don't I keep him with me this morning? I'll stay where there's plenty of cover."

"He's out supervising our team," Dill said. At my look of alarm, he told me not to worry. "He's with two of the very best."

"What about James Mason?" I asked. Dill told me Mason was taking a nap in Luther Adam's place. He was headed that way soon himself.

Kruger headed for the community center, and I went into the blacksmith shop. I spread out a sheet of white canvas in front of the knot hole and took out a small tripod and attached a laser pointer to the top. I moved back far enough so that only the tip of my imaginary rifle protruded through the knot hole. From where I lay, I could see Kruger standing toward the end of the porch, and I spoke to him through the small communicators we brought along. I asked him to move about two feet to his right, and when he was in place, I told him to shield his eyes. Then I set the tripod so the laser focused directly on the middle of his throat.

When I asked Kruger to move aside, I saw that the laser pointed to almost the dead center high in a large tree several yards behind the community center. I found myself getting excited. We had a chance to find the bullets. I radioed Kruger and gave him the news.

As I was getting up, I almost bumped into a thin man who was squatting right beside me, watching every move I made. "Good morning, Doctor," he said, enjoying my surprise. "I'm Alex Redbone. Sam McKee sends his regards. I'm here with Willie Dill."

"I didn't hear you come in!" I told him as I scrambled to my feet. There didn't seem to be any threat, so I took my hand off the butt of my automatic where it had dropped automatically.

"No, I didn't either," he assured me, nodding solemnly, showing me his empty hands. "It's an old Indian trick my uncle taught me." His face might be solemn but his eyes were filled with humor. "Then I taught it to Martha." He pointed. I turned to see a young woman standing directly behind where I lay. Right behind her I could see Robert. He was grinning from ear to ear. "Let me introduce Martha Johnston."

Martha Johnston was dark and petite and looked much younger than her years. I would later learn she had three children, one of them a man grown. I would also learn she was one of the best shots in the nation. At the moment, I was struck by the intense vitality that seemed to surround her like a magnetic field. It was this bright vitality that made her beautiful, stunning in that terrible and wonderful way of guardian angels. Only a fool would mess with Martha, and then, only once.

The angel smiled, transforming herself into a self-conscious young girl. "I hope we didn't give you too much of a shock, Doctor Phillips. Alex is incorrigible."

"Please," I told them. "Call me Jazz. Doctor Phillips sounds like a brand of prosthetic equipment."

"You're saying you can be truss-ted," Redbone observed, and Martha rolled her eyes. Robert looked puzzled.

"As I said, Alex is incorrigible," Martha told me. "I hope you have a high tolerance for puns."

"A pun is its own reword," I assured her, shamelessly stealing a line from Kruger, though I expect it was not original with him. "What did you find?"

Redbone was immediately all business. "Someone was here last night," he said. "We found one clear track back of the church and another not so good one behind the old man's shack. They were about size ten medium running shoes, and I would guess it was someone about five nine and a hundred and fifty pounds. It looked like he was trying to hide his tracks by brushing them out, but he missed those two."

"Do you think he spotted Dill or Mason?" I asked.

"I don't think so. He didn't come anywhere near where they were hidden. I think he was doing reconnaissance, maybe for an attack tonight." He frowned. "We followed his tracks back to the road. There's a clearing he parked in a half mile south of here, and he headed south when he drove out. The tracks looked like passenger car tires. Assuming it our man, we may have gotten lucky."

Redbone took a plastic bag out of his pocket. The contents looked like wet coffee grounds. "These guys never learn," he said. "Dipping is bad enough, but he let down when he got in the truck. This was fresh when we got there, still slightly warm. He must have spit it out a half hour before we got there."

I took the bag of snuff. "Good work. We can pull his DNA up from this and know for sure. I suppose you covered your tracks?"

Redbone nodded. "Unlike him, we were working in the light. I don't think anyone can tell we were on his track. Assuming he parks there again, he won't know we were there." Then he looked thoughtful. "Unless he's very subtle and was watching us all the time. The spit could be a challenge."

I thought about this. "That could be good news and bad news, too. He may be breaking down, and if so, we stand a better chance of catching him. On the other hand, that would make him even more dangerous."

Redbone nodded. "We better talk to Robert's parents. I think we need to put someone inside tonight." Robert was shaking his head, but Redbone insisted. "No, Robert. This man is out to kill you because you saw him, just like he did with Luther Adams. I think Willie needs to introduce Martha to your folks."

Martha gave him a sharp look, but Redbone did not respond directly to her. He spoke to Robert. "Martha is the best personal guard we have, and I think your parents might be more comfortable with a woman in the house than with a strange man."

Kruger called on the radio to ask where I was. I told him I would join him in a couple of minutes. To tell the truth, I was very happy to delegate the work of talking to the McNutts to Willie Dill. "Why doesn't Robert help me while you're talking to them?" I asked.

I checked the laser again before we left the blacksmith shop. It was holding steady, and Robert and I walked around the store and across to the community center. I was careful to keep myself between him and the woods, and we crossed the road without incident. I called Kruger to meet me at the back and told him how I wanted to do the search.

Redbone joined us a moment later and waited in the woods with Robert while Kruger and I spotted our tree. When we joined them, I saw Redbone had changed sweatshirts with Robert, and the youngster was wearing a dark cap. He saw my look and nodded. The two of them were about the same size, and Alex was wearing body armor.

The tree the laser pointed to was a large pine, and the first limbs were at least fifteen feet above us. I asked Robert if his dad had a ladder when he grinned and pointed behind me. I turned around to see Alex Redbone grab the first limb and haul himself over it. A couple of minutes later, I heard him tell us he had spotted the laser.

Two minutes later, he was on the ground pointing to another tree deeper into the woods. "I found a mark where the bullet grazed a branch," he told us. "It may have hit that one." Ten minutes later, he was standing on the ground again, handing me a plastic bag containing a small bullet. It was bright and unmarked except for the tiny grooves left by the rifle barrel. More to the point, I could see it was a .223.

Kruger shook his head. "How in the world did you do that?" he asked.

"My grandfather was half squirrel," Alex told him solemnly.

"I believe it," I told him. "How did you know where to look?"

Redbone shrugged. "I don't know. I just did." Then he grinned. Reaching in his pocket, he brought out another bullet, one just like the first. "It's an old Indian trick!" Kruger couldn't figure out why the rest of us were laughing.

We went back to the community center and stood in the deep shade cast by a large gum tree behind it, talking about what to do next. Then I heard a soft pop and Redbone fell to the ground. I threw myself at Robert, knocking him down and pinning him to the ground beneath me. My automatic was in my hand, and I raised it straight up, firing three quick shots. I saw Kruger crouched behind the gum tree, his pistol pointing toward the woods.

For a moment there was silence. Then gunshots broke out on the other side of the woods, near the road. My ears were still ringing from my own shots, but I could hear someone crashing through the woods, and at least one other person in pursuit. Grabbing Robert by the shirt, I hauled him into the community center. "Are you hit?" I asked, looking over him anxiously.

"No," he said. His face had lost all color. "Is he dead?"

I turned to look for Redbone, but he was coming through the door holding his side. "No such luck," he groaned, falling into a chair. He was having trouble breathing.

"Watch the front door," I told Robert. I helped Redbone to the floor and stripped off his jacket and shirt. His body armor was badly torn, and I could see blood seeping through. When I peeled back the armor, there was a shallow gash in his side, and I could see a massive bruise forming. I told him what I saw.

"It feels like I have broken ribs," he told me. "The bastard must've been using hunting bullets. I was lucky."

I glanced at his wound again and saw something else. "Hold still," I said. Taking out a pair of tweezers, I reached into the wound and pulled out a small metal mushroom. I held it up so he could see it.

"Hey, I found another bullet," Redbone quipped, managing a faint smile. He poked his little finger through a hole in the jacket he had been wearing. "I'm sorry, Robert. I seem to have ruined your jacket."

"Cool!" said Robert, taking the jacket and looking at the hole.

"Robert," I said to him sternly. "Whoever did this was trying to kill you."

"I know," he said, shrugging off my concern. "He missed."

I looked at Redbone, who shrugged. "I think your dad may look at it a bit differently."

"You not gonna tell him!" Robert protested.

"I have to, Robert," I said. "He's your dad. He needs to know so he can protect you."

Robert was saved from any reply by the front door opening. I had my gun up and leveled before I saw it was Robert senior. "What in the hell is going on?" he demanded.

"The man who killed Luther Adams just took a shot at Robert," I told him. "Alex here took the bullet. He was wearing Robert's jacket."

McNutt looked at Redbone's wound and at the jacket. Robert had his little finger through the hole. "Why did he do that?" McNutt demanded.

"We think Robert may have seen Smiley Jones' killer," I told him. "So did Luther Adams."

"No, why was he wearing my son's jacket?" McNutt corrected.

"We thought there was an outside chance this might happen," I replied. "I thought it was a good idea while we were outside."

"It turns out we were right," Redbone added.

For a moment I thought McNutt would hit me. "You get back to the house, son," he told Robert in a quiet, angry voice. "I need to talk to these men."

"Wait!" I said. "It's not safe for him to go outside just yet. The killer may still be out there." Redbone nodded.

"Why wasn't I told about this?" McNutt demanded.

"That's my fault," came a voice from the doorway. It was Willie Dill. "We didn't know there was a definite threat." Martha Johnston came in the door right after him. She was carrying a Uzi.

"Who the hell are you!" McNutt snarled.

Dill did an impressive federal flip. The case was FBI, and the badge was gold. "My name is Willie Dill. We are federal agents. This is Agent Johnston, and this is Agent Redbone."

McNutt took the identification folder and looked at it carefully. "All right. Let's assume who you say you are. Who's trying to shoot my son?"

"We don't know for sure," Dill told him. "We think it's this man— Edward Posey." He showed McNutt a photo.

"He looks like Smiley Jones," McNutt said.

"It's his son," Dill told him.

216

"His son?" McNutt said. "His son killed him?"

"It's a long story," Dill said. "Dr. Phillips can fill you in. Right now I'm concerned about the safety of *your* son. This Posey is bad news."

"I'd like to get my hands on him," Robert McNutt said softly. "Take a shot at a child of mine!"

"We need to talk about protective custody," Dill responded. "How long has it been since you had a family vacation?"

Robert McNutt looked at Dill like he had gone crazy. "We can't be taking a vacation," he said. "We've got a store to run. Robert has school."

"Robert can't go to school until we catch Posey," Dill insisted. "I don't want to get pushy, buy he's a material witness. We can put him in protective custody if you don't cooperate. I don't want him killed like he nearly was today."

McNutt didn't like it, but he saw the sense of what Dill was saying. "You take Robert and his mama," he said. "I'll stay here and run the store. She can make sure he keeps up his lessons."

"You take his mama where?" a new voice sounded from the front door. It was Robert's mother. "What's going on here?"

It took a few minutes to sort out, but when Dora McNutt found out her son was in danger, she insisted on closing the store. "You're crazy, Robert McNutt!" she told her husband. "The man's offering us an expense-paid family vacation, and you're not taking it? What's the matter with you? We haven't had a family vacation since we got here! Where will we be going?" she asked Dill.

"I had a family ranch in Wyoming in mind," Dill told her. "We use it as a safe place sometimes. Martha's husband runs the ranch, and it's quite nice this time of year. We could send you somewhere else, too, I suppose, but it wouldn't be nearly as comfortable."

"We'll be ready in an hour," Dora replied. This precipitated an argument with her husband, but she cut it off. "We're the only store in town, and it won't hurt business a bit. Clara can run the place until we get back, and I don't care if she steals us blind."

McNutt tried to put up a good fight, but two hours later the three of them were in the car and headed to Little Rock with Redbone and

Martha Johnston. I hated to see Robert go, but he was excited. Even Robert senior was showing some excitement by the time they left. He smiled when he hung a "gone fishing" sign in the store window.

When they were gone, Dill suggested we head into Nashville for a belated lunch. "I'm too pumped to sleep," he told me. "Why don't you drive if you don't mind?" I agreed, and Dill was out like a light before we were three miles down the road. I took my time getting to Nashville.

That afternoon I headed for Little Rock. I phoned Weaver to let him know I was bringing him some fresh bullets, and he told me he would stay late at the lab to run ballistics. He hoped to have the DNA from the cigarette butts ready, as well as fingerprint results from the lottery ticket.

Walking back into my old office was a strange experience. This was the first time I had actually been there since retiring, although I had visited the lab several times. There had been other meetings in the building, but I had never gone to the area where Dee had his office. The staff were gone for the day when I got there, which made it easier in some ways, but having to wait in the foyer for an escort was a new experience. Nor did knowing why this was necessary change much in the way I felt.

I was glad when Dee showed up to escort me to the office area himself. He was apologetic about it. "It won't be long until I'll have to have an escort, too," he laughed. "Only, I don't think I'll be coming back."

"Any idea what you're going to do?" I asked when we were in the elevator.

"The first thing is trying to get my life back," he answered. "I don't know if my wife and I will make it, but I've got to try." That was strange, the way Dee referred to her as his wife and not by her given name. It sounded to me like there was a lot of distance between them already. "I'm not sure what she wants to do," he added. "She seems to be doing better now that we're apart."

When the elevator stopped I was surprised to see we were on the lab floor. "I thought we would stop by here," Dee explained. "Weaver called and asked me to bring you here first. He wants to fill us in together."

Weaver was waiting for us in the lab conference room. He was as excited as a young pup on its first hunt and was holding a FedEx envelope. When he saw us, he opened the envelope and set the papers in it on the table. Without pause for a greeting, he launched into his presentation. "This came this morning from the Department of Defense," he said, handing us a letter encased in a clear plastic sheet protector. "No one from this office has touched these documents without gloves, and I was able to raise some good prints. The original paper looks like standard government bond."

Weaver handed us photocopies of the letter. It was on what looked like a Department of Defense letterhead and at the end was a scrawl that could have been made by a chicken scratching for food. The letter was addressed directly to Weaver as head of the CID, which was odd, and it was short and to the point:

Enclosed you will find a DNA profile and fingerprint chart for 1st Sgt. Wilbur Edward Posey, deceased, United States Army. The profile was taken from blood on dog tags removed from Sgt. Posey's body by Graves Registration in 1972. His remains are not available for examination. The date of his death and the manner of his death is classified. We affirm he died in service to his country. No further information is available. Our condolences to his family.

"Is it just me, or is that exceptionally cold?" I asked.

Both men nodded. "Even by Department of Defense standards," Dee said. "Did you catch the name above the signature?"

I nodded. "It appears our Captain Smith's first name is John. He either doesn't have a middle initial or didn't bother with it."

"His fingerprints are classified, too," Weaver told us. "I ran them as soon as I brought them up from the letter. There was only one set of prints, and we got a very fast bounce. The one thing that is for real is the FedEx account. This was sent from the Pentagon." He stopped and let us absorb the news.

"Why did he even bother leaving fingerprints," Dee said. "Why not just send it without them? He could have worn gloves."

"To check us out," I replied. Seeing the question in Dee's eyes, I added. "I doubt the fingerprints on the letter are even his. However, he knows whose they are and just the fact that we ran them will give him a heads-up."

"Shit!" exclaimed Weaver. "I screwed up, didn't I?"

"Not at all," I told him. "I would have done the same. Captain Smith was giving us the finger."

"Why send anything at all?" Dee asked.

"To take the heat off the Pentagon is my guess," I answered. "Or to take the heat off Posey if he's still alive and working for them. It could be classic misdirection, telling us he's dead when he's not."

Dee shook his head. "On the other hand, this may be for real. At least, part of it may. They may actually believe Posey is dead. They may not know he deserted and went into business for himself."

"Or they may know he's alive and may be using him as an outside contractor," I added. "There's no way of knowing, but Posey would be very deniable if an operation went south. Or maybe he switched over to CIA."

"Damn," Weaver murmured. "Wheels within wheels within wheels!"

"That's the whole way this case has developed," I said. "What I can't figure out is whether there is a good reason for this, or if Smith is jerking us around just because he can. I think we have to assume there's a good reason."

"Yeah," Dee nodded. "Those bastards don't do anything without a reason. It might be a twisted one, but there is some kind of logic involved."

"Just like a psychopath," I said. "Accept their basic assumptions, and the crimes they commit make perfect sense. What's twisted is how they see things."

"You want to know a really strange thing?" Weaver asked grinning. "I compared the DNA profile they sent with the blood from the outhouse door by the community center. It's a perfect match. So is the DNA we were able to take off the pop can."

"So it's Posey, then," Dee said, nodding. "We've got our shooter, assuming it was his blood on the dog tags."

I laughed. "Rumors of his death were exaggerated, just like happened to Mark Twain. I still wonder what's driving this thing. Why are they going to so much trouble covering for Posey? Or are they? You know, I really think they believe he's dead."

"I almost hate to mention it, but there is another possibility," Weaver said. "The blood could be from a twin."

I shook my head. "I checked the county birth records. Only one Posey child was registered with that date of birth."

"Yeah, but didn't you tell me the grandfather registered Edward's birth a couple of years after he was born?" Dee asked. "Maybe there were two kids born and he didn't register one of them. Maybe we need to check the state records, too."

"Why wouldn't he?" I asked, but I knew the answer. Like everything else, it was a matter of perspective. If we knew what was in the grandfather's mind, it would make perfect sense. "I shook my head. What else do you have?" I asked Weaver. "What about the cigarette butts?"

"We got a good DNA sample from them," he told me. "There is only about an eighty percent match between that and Posey. So they are closely related, but not the same person."

"Let me get the picture," I interjected. "We have the same percentage match between Smiley and Edward as we do between Smiley and Slide, right?" Weaver nodded. "So Smiley could be the father of them both?"

"Very likely," Weaver affirmed. "The markers are perfect for that."

"You think Slide knows?" Dee asked me.

I shook my head. "I don't think so. I think he would have told me, but I may be wrong. What about these bullets?" I asked Weaver. How soon can you get me a comparison on those?"

"Right away," he said. "Give me three minutes. It looks like there's still enough left of this mushroomed one to compare, but the blood work will take a couple of days if you want DNA on that."

I told him that wasn't necessary. Then I remembered the gob of snuff that Redbone recovered and asked him to run DNA on that. Weaver dropped it off for the night shift to run, and Dee and I followed him to his microscope station. He took the bullet taken from the tree and placed it in the clip along with the one taken from the store front. A moment later he said, "Bingo! It's a different bullet maker but the same gun. Let's see about the one that's mushroomed." This time the comparison took longer, but when he was done, Weaver nodded. "I would be willing to testify they're from the same weapon. There's a lot less to compare, but I'm ninety-eight percent certain it's the same gun." He began to give us the details, but we assured him his word was enough.

"What about the lottery ticket?" I asked.

"It was sold at a convenience store north of Texarkana, and there are two solid sets of prints. One belongs to Slide Jones and the other to another male. I also found two partials, front and back, on one of the corners of the ticket. They were from someone else. I would guess a female or a child from the size. It would help if you had a suspect for the third set."

I told him we did and that I would get him something to compare right away, but when I called Texarkana, there was no one on duty who could help me. "It's all these budget cutbacks," the voice at the other end told me. "We're awful short handed these days. Why don't you call back in the morning?"

I gave Weaver the particulars on Louella, and he told me he would follow up the next day. While we were talking, the phone rang. Weaver answered it, but the call was for Dee. When he took it, he listened a while before asking a couple of questions. Then he thanked whoever was on the other end for calling.

"That was the Highway Patrol," he told us. "They just found someone in a pickup crashed between Nashville and Hope. It was a dead Negro male about forty-five-years old. There is no identification, but he was dressed in camouflage and was carrying .223 ammunition. No weapon has been found yet, but they're still looking. The cause of the wreck was apparently a skid that went out of control. It's a deer crossing area."

"Could someone have found the wreck and taken the rifle?" I asked.

"It could have happened, but I doubt it. The truck was at the bottom of a deep ravine. The trooper noticed skid marks on the road and investigated. He had to climb down the side of the ravine a good way before he could see the truck."

"Where are they taking the body?" I asked.

"They're still trying to get it out," Dee told me. "The wrecker isn't even there yet."

"Let's go!" I said. "Call back and tell them to keep the body and the truck where they are until we get there. Tell them to treat it like a crime scene."

I turned to ask Weaver to come with us, but he was on another line telling his crew to meet us at the site. By the time Dee was off the phone, Weaver was holding two large duffel bags and asking me to carry another. "I'll ride with you guys," he said. "That will save some time."

I called Kruger to let him know what was going on and asked him to get in touch with Dill. When we arrived at the crash site a couple of hours later, both of them were there. "It's Posey, all right," Dill told us. "There was a flash fire but it didn't burn everything. His face was hardly touched."

Weaver headed down the slope right away. His team had arrived twenty minutes before us and was already at work. Not that there was a lot to do. The fire had destroyed whatever evidence had been in the cab of the truck. All that was left was the remains of an automatic pistol stuffed behind the seat and some .223 rifle ammunition. There was no rifle.

The light was beginning to fade fast, so Dill and Kruger organized a search for the rifle while Weaver talked to Dee and me. "I've never seen one quite like this," Weaver told us. "The fire that burned the cab didn't come from the engine or fuel tank. It came from what we used to call a Molotov cocktail—a bottle filled with gasoline and corked with a rag. It looks like our dead man was trying to light the thing with one hand while driving with the other. Why, I don't know, unless he planned to give someone a nasty surprise. What I can't figure out is why both hands are so badly burned."

"Maybe he tried to ditch it," Dee suggested.

"Yes, but that wouldn't explain why both hands are so badly burned," Ben mused. "Unless, of course, that was what made him veer off the road and he was using both hands trying to control the truck." He shook his head. "We'll need to get the truck to our garage in Little Rock and go over it more carefully. We've done about all we can do here."

I asked him to run DNA and dental records on the corpse right away. He agreed and was about to say something else when we were interrupted by a shout. It was Kruger. He'd found the rifle and was waving for one of the CSI technicians to come and take pictures.

A few minutes later, we were looking at it. At first, I thought Kruger was mistaken. Except for the obvious workmanship, the weapon looked like a toy or something out of a science fiction catalogue. It was very light and the composite stock had a gray matte finish. There were no obvious sights, but there was an integral scope in what looked like a carrying handle, and the whole shape of the stock was smooth and streamlined. Nor was it damaged from being thrown from the truck. As I said, it looked like an expensive version of a prop from an old Buck Rogers movie.

"Nice," said Weaver, reverently. "I haven't seen one of these except in a catalogue, thirty years ago. There weren't that many of them made."

"So that's the murder weapon?" Dee asked. His tone said he was having as hard a time as I was believing this was a real weapon.

Weaver nodded. "Unless there are two of these in southern Arkansas, it is. I'll know for sure when I get it back to the lab, but I'm almost certain. From all I read, it's a deadly little beast." He hefted it. "It feels like a toy."

"Well, I guess that about wraps it up, then," Dee observed. "We have the killer and we have the murder weapon. Assuming lab results confirm it."

Weaver shook his head. He looked troubled. "Not if the bullet Jazz brought me this morning is a match," he said. "Casey will be able to pinpoint the time of death much better than I can at the moment, but the initial evidence seems to point to something between eighteen and twenty-four hours. Assuming the new bullet is a match, then someone fired the shot this morning and then ditched the gun here later." He shrugged and glanced at his watch. "I could be wrong, of course, but I think this guy has been dead longer than seven or eight hours."

"So our killer is still out there?" Dill responded. Weaver nodded. "With Posey dead, that leaves us with Slide as the best candidate," Dee went on. "That doesn't feel quite right."

"I can't see Slide doing the attack this morning, either" I replied. "He doesn't strike me as being in good enough shape to run off through the woods like our sniper did." I looked at Dill. "Whoever it was could run fast enough to get away from you and Mason."

Dill nodded. "He had between fifteen and twenty-five seconds head start, at most. Mason took off after him right away, and I wasn't far behind. Neither of us caught more than a glimpse."

"It looks like we're back to square one," I said. "Why don't Kruger and I go to Texarkana and check out the lottery ticket? We're not that far away and the same clerk may be on duty."

"Why don't I come with you?" Dee asked. I knew he was hurt at not being included, but nothing showed.

"Of course, Dee," I told him. "You're supposed to be on light duty. I don't want to get you in a jam with your boss."

"Frag him and feed him to the fish," Dee responded. "I'll get some rest in the back seat if I get tired."

"Well, I'll be at the motel," Dill said. "You ladies can tell me all about it at tea tomorrow morning. I'm going to get some sleep."

———

When we got to the convenience store, we were in luck. The clerk on duty recognized Slide's picture and remembered his coming in. "He bought two tickets that night," he said. "One of them was the big lottery, but he got a dollar scratch ticket, too. I remember because he won fifty dollars. You don't see many of those."

"Do you remember what time this was?" Kruger asked.

The clerk shook his head. "No, but it's printed on the lottery ticket. Take a look at that." He grinned. "It's a lot more accurate than my watch."

That was a long drive for a short answer, even though it was useful. Just to be thorough, I pulled out a dollar and asked the clerk for a random numbered lottery ticket. When it was printed out, I picked it up carefully, being sure to touch only one corner. Sure enough, the time and date were printed at the same time my numbers were.

Once we were outside, I put it in a plastic evidence bag and handed it to Dee. "There's something else for Weaver to play with. The prints should match those on the other ticket. All I touched was the lower right hand corner."

It was getting late, but none of us had eaten, so we headed for one of the places Kruger and I had been before. That was closed, but a Chinese place down the street was still open, and we stopped. The food was singularly uninspired but not really bad, and we got a laugh out of Kruger's fortune cookie. It read, "Hunger will strike you again in one hour."

We talked about the case a bit, but gave it up after a while. We were going over the same ground we covered before, and I think all of us were tired and disappointed. Kruger excused himself to report in to Lonnie, and while he was gone, Dee and I talked over what the next step might be. It looked like we were at a dead end unless something new popped up.

I pulled out my notebook and glanced through it for any leads we had not followed. I came across the names of Posey's honorary aunt and uncle who I had never gone by to see. I told Dee I might go by to let them know Edward had been killed in a car crash. He agreed, indifferent.

"I guess someone needs to tell Pastor Jones, too," I added. "I think it would be better done in person."

Again, he agreed. "You could save me a trip, if you don't mind," he said. "You're a lot closer to him than I am, anyway. Maybe he'll tell you something to get this case off dead center." He sighed. "Not that I care that much, anyway. We have enough to clear the damned thing right now. Maybe that's what we need to do. Clear the sucker and get on with our lives."

This was completely out of character for Dee. It told me how tired he must be, not tired in body, but in spirit. Neither of us would have stood for clearing the case the way things were in the old days, but that was then. The passion clearly wasn't there any more for Dee, and I found it strange to find the same was true for me. I was tired of the world of ballistics and blood splatter and fabric samples and lying witnesses, not to mention political glory-hounds who make our work even harder. I found myself anticipating doing some work for McKee. I realized I was more than ready to move on to something new.

"It's tempting," I said after a long silence. "Can you live with that?"

"I don't know," Dee replied, grinning. "I could give it a damned good try." He looked at me. "You realize that you and I are about the only ones who really give a shit. Kruger may, but he's not his own man."

Kruger came back to the table just then and sat down. "You're right about that," he told us. He had overheard Dee's last remark. "Lonnie is pulling me off the case. As far as he is concerned, Posey is our shooter, and since he's dead, no further investigation is necessary. I have to be in Little Rock the first thing tomorrow morning to make my final report."

"How does he explain the shot that hit Redbone?" I asked.

Kruger chose his words carefully. "Lonnie is taking the position that they're two unrelated incidents. That's the official view now."

"Two unrelated incidents? Where the bullets match?" I asked. "Weaver's initial examination says they do."

Kruger looked uncomfortable. "I don't know," he told us. "My guess it that it would take more than that to justify further Bureau involvement. There'll be a press release later today."

Dee laughed and made a pumping motion with his right arm. "Kerfloosh!" he said. "There it goes. Right down the Bureau-kratik tubes." He grinned. "We like you, Kruger, but it'll be a relief to get the Bureau out of our hair."

I thought about that. With Posey dead, Dill would probably be headed back to Washington, too. James Mason would go back to being a deputy sheriff while keeping tabs on the Klan, and I would be pretty much on my own. Maybe it was time for me to write up my report and turn in my bill. I said as much to Dee, and he nodded, flagging the waitress for the check.

The drive back to Nashville that night was very quiet. None of us felt good about the way this case was ending, but there wasn't much we could do about it. It sometimes turns out that way, and a cop needs to move on to other things. Those who don't go crazy.

Since Dee needed to get back to Little Rock anyway, Kruger offered to give him a ride there that night. We said our goodbyes, and I took a shower then fell into bed and slept soundly for several hours. When I awoke, it was out of a dead sleep, and I was aware something had come together in my mind. Yet, I couldn't remember what it was or even if it had anything to do with the case.

Nor did a long morning walk help me remember, and I finally set it aside. I tried to call Willie Dill, but he wasn't in his room. Nor had he left word where to reach him. So I had a cup of coffee and a light breakfast by myself and took off for Oak Grove.

Albert Jones was sad to hear the news about Edward Posey. He offered to claim the body and take care of funeral expenses, and I gave him the number he needed to call. Then we talked a while about other things, and Emma insisted I stay for lunch. It was a wonderful visit, and I wished Nellie was there to share it. I thought she and Emma would find a lot in common.

When I knocked at Percy and Beulah Adams' door, I heard someone get up and move around, but it took a minute for them to get to the door. It was Percy—Edward Posey's honorary uncle—and he didn't look pleased to see me. I told him I only needed a few minutes, and he reluctantly let me in. He led me into the kitchen where Beulah was sitting at the table. Percy pointed to a chair opposite his own and asked me if I would like some coffee.

I declined, then told them about the accident. I told them we were pretty certain it was Edward who was killed, but we would know for sure very quickly. I avoided getting into details, mostly to spare their feelings.

When I was done, the old people sat quietly for a while. Then Beulah took a deep breath and sighed. "Well," she said quietly, almost as if to herself, "they both be with the Lord now."

Percy shot his wife a warning look, but it was too late. Beulah looked at me with wide eyes, as if I had pried a deep secret out of her while she wasn't looking. Yet, I couldn't let it go. "Both?" I asked Beulah. "Who else besides Edward?"

"She talking about the boy and his mother," Percy said, trying to gloss it over, but Beulah shook her head.

"Edward and Daniel," she told me, ignoring her husband.

"Daniel Posey?" I asked and she nodded.

"No need bringing him up, woman," Percy said, trying to cut in, but we both ignored him.

"Who was Daniel?" I prodded gently.

"Daniel be he brother," Beulah said. "He born the same time."

Gradually, the story came out of Beulah. Edward's mother had not given birth to one child, but two. They were twin boys—identical twins—and one of them had been sent to be raised by relatives near Magnolia. The family was just too poor to raise them both, and one child born out of wedlock was shame enough. Nor had the grandfather allowed the boys to meet one another again. Daniel was given the surname of the family who raised him and was never told that he had a twin brother. Nor was he told that the woman who raised him was not his birth mother.

Edward was never told about his brother, either. No one in the family ever spoke of Daniel, and it was only by accident that Edward overheard his mother arguing with his grandmother one day while he was in his teens. When Edward asked them what that was about, he was told he misunderstood what they said. Yet, he knew, and several months before Smiley's death, he had come to Percy and Beulah insisting they tell him everything they knew.

"He was at the funeral," Beulah told me. "Him and Edward both. I seen them talking by the door."

I sat there for a moment, thinking. "Why did you say they were both with the Lord, Beulah?" I asked.

The old woman was very confused. "What you mean? They both be dead. They be killed in that wreck."

"There was only one man killed in the accident," I told her. "We thought it was Edward, but it might have been Daniel."

"Well, praise the Lord!" she declared. "That child still alive!"

I talked with them a while longer, but there was nothing more they could tell me. So I took off for Nashville, hoping to find Dill and let Dee know what was going on. When I got to a phone and asked for Dee at the office, it was Weaver who came on the line. "Hello, Jazz. Dee asked me to take it if you called in. He had to go to the hospital."

"What's wrong?" I asked. "He was all right last night."

"His wife was in a bad car accident last night," Weaver told me. "She's all right now, except for some bruised ribs. She got broadsided by a drunk driver."

I filled Weaver in on what I learned in Oak Grove. I asked him to check the state birth records for a week either side of March 15, 1948, for black males and to get the report to me right away. I told him I was looking for a first or middle of Daniel, but didn't know the last name. Percy and Beulah Adams had refused to tell me. "Pay particular attention to any children born at home and registered a couple of years later. The grandfather's name is Posey, but someone else may have registered them."

"Yes, sir!" Weaver laughed. "It's just like old times."

I tried to apologize, but Weaver laughed it off. "Hey, we miss you around here, fella. Not just us old timers, either."

"Tell the crew I miss them, too," I replied. I couldn't think of anything else to say. I asked for the name of the hospital and room number.

"By the way, I have a hit on the DNA for you."

"That was quick. You just got it yesterday. Were you up all night?"

"No," Weaver laughed. "I left it for the night shift," he reminded me. The DNA from the spit-wad you picked up was a good match for the outhouse blood and what we got from the can. It's the same guy."

"Now it looks like it's one of two guys," I said. "Can you imagine what even a half-assed defense lawyer could do with that?"

"I don't suppose we could hang them both," Weaver said. "With the hands burned off the guy in the truck, it could be either Posey or his brother."

He was right. Fingerprints are different even for identical twins, but DNA is identical. "So how do we identify Daniel, if that's who it is?" I asked. "Dental records?

"Yeah, it'll definitely be low technology," Weaver agreed. "Maybe we'll find tatoos or significant scars or even a birth mark." He laughed again. "I just had a terrible thought. What if they were triplets, like those guys in that old movie? You know, the one with the voodoo killers. How would you ever figure out who was who without finger prints?"

"If it's triplets, I'm moving to Mexico," I laughed. "How about the prints from that lottery ticket I sent with Dee? Did you get anything on those?"

"I knew there was something else," Weaver told me. "The second set on the ticket he gave me was identical to the unknown set on the first ticket."

"So Slide and the clerk were telling the truth," I said.

"Unless they were in cahoots," Weaver answered.

"There is that," I said. Then two thoughts hit me. "Damn! What if they were? What if the clerk was Slide's accomplice? Maybe he's the one who took a shot at Robert yesterday."

"How would he tie in?" Weaver asked.

"I don't know," I told him. "Forget it. It was just a wild hare. I'm grasping for straws."

"At least you've got hair," Weaver quipped. "I could use a few wild ones—or any other kind, for that matter." I could imagine him running a hand over his bald head.

"All right, here's another thought. What if Edward took Daniel's place? What if he arranged the accident intending to leave this world as Edward and begin a new life as Daniel?"

"He wouldn't have taken the shot at Redbone then," Weaver said. "That messed up his timing."

"Yes, but he didn't know it would. The only reason that truck was found when it was is because the Highway Patrol spotted skid marks so quickly. It was bad luck, pure and simple."

"So he took the shot and ditched the gun on his way by," Weaver said. "It could work."

"It damned near did work. Posey couldn't know that Crime Scene would be called in, and certainly not so quickly. The whole thing could have been written up as a truck wreck. The trooper only called us because Dee put out an alert."

"Makes you wonder who's in charge of the luck division, doesn't it? All right. Say you're right. What now?"

"We check out Daniel without tipping Edward to what we're doing?" I said. "I need to talk to Dee to set that up."

There was an uncomfortable silence on the other end of the line. "What is it, Ben?" I asked.

"I don't want to be talking out of school," Weaver replied. "I wouldn't tell anyone else but you, but you're still Dee's best friend, aren't you?"

"Yes, as far as I know. I'm your friend, too, Ben."

"Well, between us friends, Dee hasn't been himself for the last year or so. I don't think he's drinking, but it's like the fire went out inside him."

"It's called burn-out," I answered. "That's why I quit, Ben. I used to love the job, but I was having to drive myself to do it."

Weaver sighed. "I remember, but you quit before anyone much noticed. I don't think there's anyone who hasn't noticed with Dee."

"How has he been the last couple of days?" I asked.

Weaver thought for a moment. "He's been almost like his old self, now I think about it," he replied. "Even with the accident. He's...focused. Now he's set to retire, he's doing fine."

"Keep that in mind when your time comes," I told him. "Dee is the one who told me how I was getting."

"Dear God!" Weaver murmured. "None of us had the balls to tell him! We did him a great disservice."

"Don't beat yourself up too much," I laughed. "Dee might have regretted it afterward, but he might have killed the messenger."

"There is that," Weaver replied. "What are you going to do now?"

I thought about it a moment. "I think I may head down toward Magnolia and check the county records there. I may nose around a bit in Texarkana first. I need to check out that convenience store clerk."

"Sounds like a good plan," Weaver replied. "Who's going to back you up?"

I thought about that for a moment. "I'll work with Dill if he is still around. I think Tanner might let me have Mason for a bit longer, too."

"All right, then," Weaver said. "Just don't try to go in alone. This guy is pretty nasty."

"And I'm not as young as I once was?" I asked. There was silence from the other end. "You're right, Ben. I'll get some help."

"I believe it was my former boss who told me that was a cardinal rule for any investigation," he answered dryly. "I think his exact words were that a cop who goes in alone has a fool for a partner. I'll get on those birth records STAT."

When I hung up, I tried to get in touch with Dill again, but the desk clerk at the motel told me he had checked out. "He did leave you a message," she said, handing me a sealed envelope. When I opened it, there was a brief note telling me he had to leave to meet another commitment and asking me to call his central office if I needed to get in touch with him. He added that he hoped to meet again when we had more time to swap yarns. The note was signed with a scrawl I had a hard time deciphering except for the initials.

I had better luck with James Mason. Sheriff Tanner agreed to let him stay on as my partner for a few more days, but I could tell he was reluctant. I knew he wanted the case closed, and I couldn't blame him. When I told him what I thought about Edward Posey killing Daniel and switching identities, he was a bit skeptical. "Let's see what turn up," he said. "You take James Mason next three days. After that, you on your own. I can't spare him. This case done took too much time. Damn vandals raising hell all over and folk getting hot about it."

I thanked John Tanner and gave Mason a call. He was due to go on shift at three that afternoon, but agreed to come in right away when I outlined what I had in mind. I asked him to wear a sport coat and tie since we were going out of the county, and I asked him to pack an overnight bag. Civil servants tend to be more helpful when investigators dress the part, and we needed every advantage we could get. All we had to work with was a first name, a photo of Edward Posey, and only a general idea of where to look.

When we got to Magnolia, the first thing we did was to let the local police know we were around. The chief wasn't someone I knew, but my name was familiar to him, and he was very cooperative. He posted a five by seven print of Posey's picture on the duty board and passed a copy around to officers on shift. No one recognized the picture, but one of the officers thought it looked familiar. She was not sure just when she had seen the fellow, but it had been some time before. She took one of my cards and promised to call right away if she happened to remember.

Our visit to the sheriff's office was less productive. I knew the sheriff from a long time back, and it was not a pleasant memory. We had been called in to investigate the way his department handled prisoners when I was new to the CID, and the man was dirty. We could never find any proof of wrongdoing, and no one dared testify. The man had been in office thirty years or more and knew where all the bodies were buried. He ran his county like a feudal fief and even the district judge was afraid of him.

"Never saw the man," the sheriff said, tossing the photo of Posey back at us without even looking at it. "Of course, so many of them is so interbred I cain't tell them apart, anway. He ain't one of ours."

"How can you know if you don't even look?" James Mason asked in a quiet, deadly voice. The sheriff didn't even glance in his direction.

"It wouldn't hurt for us to talk to some of your officers," I replied. "One of them might have seen him passing through."

"Particularly since he was traveling with a white woman," James Mason added innocently. A deep flush blossomed at the sheriff's neck and spread to his face but he refused to rise to the bait.

"I'll ask them myself," the sheriff said. From his tone, I knew I better not hold my breath until it happened. "I'll let you know."

"Thank you, Sheriff," I told him. "I appreciate it. Just so you're aware of it, we'll be asking around, too."

The man didn't respond, even with a nod. He looked down at his desk and started going through a stack of mail, not even looking up when Mason and I left the office. "I'm sorry about that," Mason apologized when we got down the hall. "I hope I didn't make things worse."

"I thought it was just fine," I told him. "The asshole never acknowledged you at all, even when I introduced you."

"I bet he wears a sheet," Mason replied. "I'll find out."

"Be careful in his county," I warned him. "He's pretty much king here."

"We'll see about that," James Mason said, and I was glad I wasn't in the sheriff's shoes. He grinned. "I suspect the IRS just might audit his accounts. I bet the bastard has a trove buried in some bank." He grinned. "And while he's distracted with that..." He left the thought hanging.

"I hope I don't ever seriously piss you off," I told him.

The next two days were nothing but frustration. Word had gone out from the sheriff's department and people would barely talk to us. Most of them just shook their heads and turned away, but one man was honest enough to tell us the truth. "I don't want no trouble with old Earl," he said, clearly frightened. "I got to live around here. I'd like to help you, but I don't know nothing."

Then our luck changed on the morning of the third day. We were back in Magnolia checking in at the police department when one of the custodians came up to us and asked, "You the gentlemens looking for Dan Tatum?" he asked.

I fished out a picture of Posey and showed it to him. He nodded. "That's him. I never seed him all dress up before, but that's him."

Ten minutes later, we not only had a name, but a family history and a visit to the county records confirmed this. Daniel Lee Tatum was registered as born on March 15, 1948, at home to one Dora Lee Tatum. What was odd is that the birth was registered by his grandfather Posey, the same one who first registered Edward, but the name of the father of Dora Lee's child was listed as unknown.

The custodian gave us directions to where the family lived, and Mason and I headed there after our visit to the courthouse. Since the family place was in Hempstead county, I thought we might find more cooperation and we did. When I stopped for directions at a rural station, the owner turned out to be one of Daniel's cousins, and he was quite helpful.

"He ain't in trouble, is he?" the cousin asked us. I told him Daniel was not and that we just needed some information from him. "He one of the best," his cousin assured us. "Ain't nothing he won't do for you." He went on to give us two examples of Daniel's shining character in great detail. "And sing?" he added before we could break away. "That man voice like a angel."

That got my attention and I could see this was true with Mason, too. "Did he sing in the choir?" I asked.

"Did him sing in the choir? That child am the choir, ever since him a titty baby." He shook his head sadly. "Then that accident took he voice."

It turned out that the accident almost took Daniel's life when he was just out of his teens. A piece of equipment at the furniture factory where he worked had kicked back a board, striking him in the throat and almost shattering his larynx. Daniel survived but was left with a terrible scar on his throat and only a harsh rasp for a voice.

When I asked if he had seen Daniel recently, the cousin told me it had been a couple of months. "It strange," he said. "He come by all the time, once, twice a week. Then he tell me he going t'work up round Hope. I ain't seen him since."

Neither had any of the other relatives we talked to that afternoon. One of them did mention Daniel told her something about finding family "up north" where he was headed, but she didn't have specifics. No one thought anything of it since they all knew there were cousins around Nashville. Yet, none of them could remember meeting any of those cousins, and everyone I talked to was quite surprised to learn they were kin to Smiley Jones. All of them had heard of him and knew his music, but none were aware they were family.

I found a pay phone and called the CID crime lab in Little Rock, hoping to catch Weaver and mention the scar. Who I got was Casey himself who had just finished the autopsy on the body found in the truck. When I asked him about a possible scar on the victim's throat, he told me the larynx looked like it had been almost crushed years before. I gave him Daniel's name and told him where to look for possible dental records.

James Mason nodded when I was done. He had been listening to my end of the conversation. "So Posey is still alive," he said. "We better let Willie know." He used the same phone to call the Agency, but I noticed he slipped a small black device over the mouthpiece. It looked like a cradle for the handset, but was thin and narrow. "Scrambler," he told me, seeing my look. "Makes any line secure."

When he was done talking, Mason handed the phone to me. "Sam wants to talk to you," he said.

"Hello, Jazz," McKee greeted me. "Sounds like you and James are kicking ass and taking names down there." I laughed and he went on. "Listen, I want to ask you a big favor. Edward Posey is really bad news, and I think he's gone to ground. I don't think there's much more you can do. The favor I'd like to ask is for you to back off now and let us take care of him."

What McKee was asking made good sense, and I was surprised to find myself digging in my heels. "I don't know," I replied. "Let me think about it."

"Do you understand where I'm coming from?" McKee asked. "This guy is one of the best, and I don't want him coming after you. I promise we'll get him. It may take a while, but we'll find him and we'll bring him in."

"Dead or alive?" I asked, wanting to call the words back as soon as I uttered them. There was dead silence from the other end. "Sorry," I hurried on. "You didn't deserve that."

"Sounds like it's getting personal," McKee observed.

I was surprised to find just how right he was. "Yeah," I replied. "I guess it is. I think it happened when he took a shot at Robert."

McKee was wise enough to wait. "You're right," I said. "You have the resources and I don't. I'll square it with DiRado. The Bureau shouldn't be a problem."

"I gathered as much," McKee answered dryly. "I read their press release yesterday. The good news is they can't jump back in now without stepping on their dicks."

"Assuming they're long enough," I quipped and McKee laughed. "Let me talk to Dee, and I'll head back to Ft. Smith tomorrow."

I handed the handset back to Mason. He talked with McKee for a moment before hanging up. He shook his head. "Damn. Just when it was getting fun. I guess we head for Nashville now."

I dug out my tape recorder and asked Mason to drive, dictating my report to the CID on our way home. It didn't take that long and when I was done, Mason asked who would transcribe it for me. I told him my laptop was loaded with a good voice recognition program that would prepare a word processing document for me to edit. He asked what software I used, and when I answered, he told me about several improvements McKee's brother had made tweaking that specific program. This led us to other things, and I was surprised how quickly we arrived in Nashville.

"Thanks, Jazz," Mason said, offering me a hand as he got out of the car. "I've really enjoyed working with you. I learned a lot."

"The pleasure was mine," I told him. "Maybe we'll run across each other if I do some work for McKee."

I called the CID office hoping to catch Dee there, but it was Weaver who took my call. He told me Dee's wife was doing better, but Dee was spending most of his days at the hospital. "There is one thing I need to tell you before I forget," Weaver said. "You know the DNA profile the Pentagon sent us? They sent us two profiles, not one."

"What?" I was confused. "You mean they sent us two copies?"

"No, they sent us two completely different profiles. I thought it was two copies of the same profile when I first glanced at them, but it wasn't. When we compared the second profile to what we got from the can and the snuff, it wasn't even close. About the only common factor was that it was from a male. I would guess generic European for the source, but not African."

I thought about this for a moment. "Why did they send us two profiles? Any ideas about that?" I asked.

"Yeah, I thought about it on the way to work this morning. It was an easy enough mistake. When they did the lab work, the technicians probably filed the results without a narrative report. Anyone who works with the things would spot the difference right away, just like I did when I did more than glance at them. Unless the guy who put them in the package was familiar with DNA profiles, he could think they were all part of one profile since he found them in the same folder."

"Or maybe they're playing with our heads," I said.

"There is that," Weaver admitted. "I can't see why, but then, this whole thing is crazy. I guess they'd have their reasons."

"Any thoughts why there might be two men's blood on the same tags?" I asked. I had several ideas about that, but I wanted to hear what Weaver had to say.

"The only thing I can figure is that Posey was next to someone who got hit and caught some blood splatter. Either that, or someone switched dog tags."

"I like that last one," I told him. "That sounds like our man. It's exactly the same thing he did with the truck crash. He used a dead man to give himself a new identity and a new life."

"There's always the possibility you mentioned before," Weaver said. "This may be Captain Smith's way of throwing us off track by making sure we can't preserve a chain of evidence."

"Who knows?" I answered, suddenly feeling very old. "The clearer it becomes who did it, the more clouded the reasons why. I don't think we'll ever know the whole story behind Edward Posey, and I don't know if I really care. I don't see much more I can do. Tell Dee I'm headed that way tomorrow to see him and to turn in my report. I think it's time to go fishing."

The next call I made was to Nellie. I told her I was headed home by way of Little Rock and that made her happy. The road from Nashville to Hot Springs is much safer than the roads through the mountains, and twenty-five miles out of Hot Springs I could pick up the interstate. It's not as pretty a drive, but it is nice, and it's far more relaxing.

———

There's not much more to tell. I headed home and got in some late fall fishing before it got too cold. The fish weren't biting that well, but I didn't mind. The name of the game for me is fishing, not catching, and I didn't miss cleaning my catch. Then it was time to do some serious duck hunting, and I punctured the sky with a couple of boxes of shells without hitting a single bird. That was fine with me, too, though I don't think I missed on purpose. Or maybe I did. I find cleaning ducks worse than cleaning fish, and I had a good time just getting out early enough to get chilled to the bone, then coming in for a cup of strong, hot coffee and a big waffle breakfast. Being a duck hunter is *prima facie* evidence of utter insanity.

There were also a couple of trips Nellie took with me to Washington to do consulting with McKee, and we had a wonderful time being tourists. McKee is a marvelous host and I found the project he had in mind for me challenging. The best part was that I could work at home in Ft. Smith most of the time. So, for the most part, life that fall and winter was spectacularly normal.

Even so, two separate incidents occurred over those next months that were tied to the case. The first was a call from Weaver not too long before Christmas. After we talked fishing and hunting for a while, he asked me an odd question. He wanted to know if I had included the lottery ticket I bought to get the store clerk's prints in my expense statement. I told him I had not and I told him why. State auditors tend to have very little imagination and even less of a sense of humor. They seem to assume people will cheat and are ready to assume the worst. I know there's a reason they're that way, and I didn't include the lottery ticket because the last thing any of us needed was for some low-level clerk to challenge the expense and stir up a fuss. When it comes to politicians and auditors, I assume the worst, and I could easily imagine the political capital Pea Vine and his cohorts might make of this.

I said as much to Weaver. "Good," he said. "Then that means the ticket is your property, not the state's."

"I guess you're right, but it's not worth the paper it's written on now."

Weaver laughed. "You might want to check that out, Jazz. You didn't hit all the right numbers, but you hit five out of six. You damned near had fifty million dollars."

"Damned near is only good playing horshoes or hand grenadcs," I replied.

Weaver laughed again and I asked what was so funny. "You are," he said. "You don't realize you just won a hundred and eighty thousand dollars."

That's how Nellie and I ended up spending half the winter exploring the rain forests and mountains of New Zealand. We talked about it for years, but had never felt we could afford the trip. So that's what we did for six weeks right after Christmas. It was wonderful and when it came time to come home, we were both sad to leave.

———

The other incident was not wonderful at all. It happened just before Easter and I never saw it coming. I tell myself now I should have known, but how could I? There's no predicting insanity.

I was driving home from an errand one afternoon when I saw an old man pushing his bicycle. It was obvious he was homeless. He had a beat up suitcase strapped to a home made rack behind his seat and wrapped in a plastic garbage sack to keep out the rain. There was a basket in front, too, with what looked like a bedroll wrapped in clear plastic strapped on top. Yet, what was most unusual was the long horn case tied to the frame of the bike. It looked awkward, out of place, and the old fellow had to straddle it to pedal. I wondered why he had not hocked the horn a long time ago for whatever he could get.

It was a wet day and I was in the pickup. So I stopped by the old man and offered him a ride. He shook his head and waved me away, muttering under his breath and not even looking up. When I asked if he was sure about that, he didn't act as if he even heard me.

I drove on, wanting to help and knowing there was little I could do. Many of the street people these days are mentally ill, remnants from the Reagan era when we closed our mental hospitals and turned the patients out onto the street. There's little we've done in our nation's history which was more cruel or more barbaric. Those folks, unable to defend themselves from urban predators or even from their own insane impulses, became immediate targets of violence and degradation. Many of them died soon after being released. Those who did not were condemned to a life of constant fear from human predators.

When I got home, Nellie was not yet back from the hospital. She volunteers there, and sometimes she needs to stay longer than she planned. So I didn't lock up the way I normally do after coming in. Ft. Smith may not be a large city, but it does share some of the same problems metropolitan areas experience. When I was with the CID, we used to preach simple home security as the best protection from casual crime, and I try to practice what I preach. So we lock the doors and windows when we leave and when we're home alone.

I was working at my laptop in the den when something made me look up. When I did, I found myself staring into the dark mouth of the biggest automatic pistol I've ever seen. The cop part of my brain registered the fact it was a .44 auto, the most powerful production handgun in the world. Who was holding it as steady as a rock was the old man on the bicycle I'd offered a ride to.

I don't know why I wasn't startled. A part of me must have expected this confrontation. Or maybe something registered when I passed the old man on the street. Whatever it was, I found myself strangely calm.

"Dr. Phillips, I presume." The mocking voice was strong and clear, and I could see the man was not nearly as old as I thought. His hair was gray around the temples, but his skin was as unwrinkled as a man half his age. The hand that held the heavy pistol was firm and steady.

"Hello, Edward," I heard my voice saying. "Excuse me. Let me save my work." I pushed a couple of keys on the laptop and placed my hands on the table where he could see them.

That was clearly not the response he expected. He looked around quickly, then crossed to the window and pulled the shade. Never once did the barrel of the pistol move from its point of aim in the middle of my chest.

"Move over to the recliner," he told me, watching every move I made until I was there. "Lay it back," he said.

When I did, he nodded and pulled up a chair facing me but too far away for me to made a move. Smiling, he took out a smaller pistol fitted with a silencer and stuck the heavy magnum under his jacket. "Now then, Doctor," he said. "You and I need to have a talk about what you know and what you don't."

There was no point in balking. I knew how he would respond if I did. The first shot would be to one of my ankles, and he would move to other joints until I told him what he wanted to know. So I summarized what I knew about him very quickly, covering the high points.

"All right," he said. "Now give me details."

I did so quickly, talking about the men's choir and everything I had been told. His eyes darkened when I mentioned learning that Smiley stole his music, but other than that, he did not respond. Then, when I mentioned the Pentagon's sending us the wrong DNA, he smiled.

"That's how you got out of Asia, isn't it?" I asked. "You switched dog tags with someone and took off."

Posey nodded, almost impatient, and asked me a number of questions. I answered them as carefully and truthfully as I could. When we were done, he sat there looking at me. I knew he was deciding how best to kill me.

I heard the door of my study swing open. Posey swung to his right to bring the pistol to bear but his hand dissolved in a red mist as a deafening explosion filled the room. He tried desperately to pull the big magnum from under his jacket with his left hand, but a second explosion took his arm off at the elbow. Most men would have died from shock, but Posey jumped up and made a run for the window. Just as he was about to throw himself through it, a third explosion slammed into his right knee and he went down.

I glanced to my right. Nellie stood in there in the door of my study, calmly pushing more shells into my twelve gauge riot gun. "What's your name?" she asked Posey calmly, and when he didn't answer, she pointed the shotgun directly at his crotch. Posey screamed his name in terror.

I was on my feet by then. Nellie handed me the shotgun and calmly began to tie a tourniquets around Posey's right wrist and left arm. The hands were both missing. "Nothing personal, Edward," I heard her saying. "You just don't mess with my man." Then, when she was done, she excused herself and walked into the bathroom next to my study. Even through the insulated door, I could hear her retching.

———

That's where it ended. There were other details, like when Edward Posey tried to sue Nellie for making him a cripple. When Dee pointed out to Nellie she wouldn't have that problem if she had shot to kill, she smiled and said that this way was a far worse punishment. He could repent at leisure.

McKee heard about the lawsuit and took care of it quickly, sending Dill to point out to Posey exactly why he needed our good will. Without hands and the use of one of his legs, Edward wouldn't last three months incarcerated with the general prison census. Posey was defiant until Dill suggested we could plant the rumor that Posey was a child molester and a snitch. Not wanting to die from the gang rape Dill predicted would result, Posey crumbled.

Yet, there was a lighter side to the way things turned out. Steve DiRado bought a small resort near Mountain Home, and after some intense work with a counselor, was able to persuade his wife to join him there. There are still rough patches between them, but the last time I talked to Dee, he looked happier than I have seen him in years. His wife, Karin, is able to walk again, and she told Nellie they play a lot these days.

I also ran into Dick Kruger one day when I was in Washington. He was working for the Agency by then and was very taken with his companion. Over lunch, Kruger's beloved confided that they met in Little Rock where McKee had sent her to help persuade Kruger to leave the FBI and join the Agency. Cassie herself had been with the Bureau for a couple of years and knew the issues he faced. What McKee didn't anticipate when he sent her south was that the interview might turn romantic. As Cassie told me, much to Kruger's discomfort, it was lust at first sight.

About the Author

Joel B. Reed is the author of nine novels, six nonfiction books, and two works of poetry. Four of his earlier titles are in print and available through White Turtle Books (whiteturtlebooks.com) and at Amazon. *Murder In The Choir* is the first in a series of mystery stories featuring Jazz Phillips, former head of the Arkansas CID. *Murder by the Board*, the second title in the series, is scheduled for publication April 1, 2006.

A former resident of Hope, Arkansas, where he wrote his first novel, *Angels Fight Dirty*, Reed grew up in the Big Bend area of Texas. He now makes his home with his wife and two furry 'kids' overlooking the big bend of the Minnesota River.